BLACK BUTTERFLY

TIFFANY PATTERSON

TMP PUBLISHING LLC

CHAPTER 1

"What brought you to burlesque?"

Jazmine bit her lip and ran her thumb across the tiny scar on top of the knuckle on her left pointer finger. Feeling the almost imperceptible abrasion reminded her of how far she had come in healing. It reminded her that she was a survivor. But, it also reminded her of the time in her life that ultimately brought her to burlesque. A time she rarely talked about with others.

Sitting under the spotlight of the camera in the dimly lit club with Shirley Bassey's *Diamonds Are Forever* playing in the background, Jazmine thought about how the song matched the personality of Mistress Coco, owner of The Black Kitty, and reason she sat in the spotlight of the camera now. Lifting her brown eyes to meet the documentarian's expectant gaze, Jazmine decided to give a simple answer to his question.

"I've always loved to dance and a few years back a friend took me to a show. I fell in love and decided to look up classes in my area. Now, here I am," she responded with a lift of her shoulders. It wasn't a complete lie, but wasn't the full truth.

"How nice. What's your favorite part of doing burlesque?" Sean continued.

This was an easy answer for Jazmine. "That's easy, the camaraderie. I've made some really great friends through performing. The Black Kitty has become like my second home because it feels like our own little family with the performers, Mistress Coco and even some of the regular audience members." Jazmine's full lips turned upwards in an effusive smile.

"Great, we have just a few more questions before, we'd like to stop to set up to record your performance later tonight."

"That's my favorite part of the day," Jazmine chuckled and winked teasingly.

For the next ten minutes, Jazmine answered Sean's questions about her participation in burlesque. She was relieved when he stayed away from questions about her past or her life before burlesque. When the interview was over, Jazmine headed backstage to don her costume for tonight's performance. Tonight she was introducing a new set. She would be performing to Michael Jackson's *Dirty Diana*. Jazmine strolled down the long hallway of the Black Kitty towards the dressing room, dressed casually in a pair of skinny jeans and a white v-neck. Over her shoulder was the strap of her bag that held her elaborate costume.

"Hey, girly how did the interview go?" Mistress Coco, owner of the Black Kitty asked as Jazmine passed her office.

Jazmine stopped, poking her head in Mistress Coco's office. She briefly admired the walls that were adorned with famous burlesque performers of yesterday and today, including pictures of the club's own performers, which included Jazmine. She loved that Mistress Coco took so much pride in showing off her "girls" as she referred to all her performers.

"It went well. Was only about twenty minutes. He's going to record my performance tonight. Gotta make sure I make it memorable," Jazmine joked.

"Oh girl, if you weren't memorable already there's no way you'd have lasted in my club so long. Just give 'em the show you always do."

That was Mistress Coco, always supportive of her girls. She was tough and expected the best, but she was quick to give praise when it was deserved. Jazmine admired the five-foot-three, light caramel-complected woman who, though in her sixties, could easily be mistaken for someone twenty years younger, even with her silver hair.

"Thanks, Mistress Coco. I'll remember that when I'm on stage," Jazmine responded.

"You better. Now shoo. Go get ready," Mistress Coco said, making a shooing motion with her hands.

"Okay, okay," Jazmine responded, laughing and heading to the dressing room. Once inside, Jazmine stripped down to her thong. She covered her dark, chocolate-colored nipples that were a few shades darker than her own chestnut complexion with a pair of black tassled pasties, adorned in colorful rhinestones, and covered them with a black lace bra. Moving down, she slid a pair of black fishnets up her long, toned legs before stepping into her three-tiered Victorian style black skirt, and paired it with a ruffled white button up shirt that she tucked in at the waist. After sliding on a pair of black four-inch stilettos, Jazmine examined her appearance in the full-length mirror. Once satisfied with her look, Jazmine placed a black masquerade mask over her eyes, latching it around her long Senegalese twists. She applied a generous amount of dark lipstick, but decided to forego any other type of makeup since she was wearing the mask.

Jazmine gave herself one last glance in the mirror, admiring the small curves of her hips and bust. Curves she'd been ashamed of years before, even though by most she would be considered thin. Thinking of that time in her life, her gaze slid down to her knee where she could barely make out the scar that was mostly covered by her fishnets. She fluffed her skirt and smiled, getting rid of thoughts of the past. Right now it was time to perform!

"ALRIGHT! Alright! Alright! Y'all having a good time tonight!?!" Mistress Coco's raspy voice boomed through the speakers around the club.

The audience clapped and cheered.

"Good!" she said in approval of their reaction. "Next to the stage, we have the illuminatingly illustrious...the tantalizingly sexy....and the raucous applause worthy...Jazmine Nooiiir!!!" Mistress Coco departed the stage as the audience cheered, leaving room for Jazmine to make her entrance.

The audience revved up as the opening chords began playing, and Jazmine stepped onto the stage. She moved slowly at first, crossing the stage, languidly letting her skirt drag across the hardwood.

Seconds later when Michael Jackson's voice began, Jazmine moved her hands to the top buttons of her shirt, and deftly undid the top two. She rotated her hips to the beat of the music, dipping her head and whipping her twists as the crescendo of the music built. Lifting her head back up, she spun around towards the other side of the stage.

The audience oohed and ahhed at her ability to spin and move so gracefully without getting dizzy. She stopped just at the edge of the stage, and the audience gasped, fearful she'd topple off the edge, but Jazmine simply smiled mischievously. She knew better. Years of training taught her to be aware of her positioning on any stage. Even when she couldn't see the edge, she knew where it was.

Jazmine finally undid the bottom buttons of her top, removing it and spinning it above her head while rotating her hips. She tossed the shirt to the side, moving back to the middle of the stage and placed her hands on the button of her skirt. The audience reacted approvingly with stomps and claps as she continued to tease them. She turned her back to the audience, wound her hips as she completely undid her skirt button, and slowly tugged it down her hips and thighs, finally letting it drop to the stage. She stood up, dressed now in only her black thongs and bra. She dropped to the stage floor on her knees, pumping her hips and whipping her twists to and fro. As her departing move, she undid the front clasp of her bra, stripping down to her pasties, giving the audience one final shimmy and letting the tassels of her pasties twirl before she departed the stage.

"Hell of a performance tonight, Stace," Jazmine looked up to see Devyn, also known as Black Pearl at the club, enter the dressing room about fifteen minutes after Jazmine's performance. Since becoming friends with Devyn and her best friend Mercedes outside the club, the women now often referred to each other by their actual names instead of their stage names.

"Thanks, Dev. You weren't looking too bad yourself," Stacey complimented as she pulled Devyn in for an embrace.

"Thank you. And before I forget, you're coming to the barbecue next weekend right?"

Stacey nodded. "Wouldn't miss it for the world. I can't wait to see Mercedes," Stacey said, referring to their friend who'd recently married and spent her entire summer in her new husband's native country of Brazil. Stacey had performed at the same club with Devyn and Mercedes for years, but only within the last year had they developed a deeper friendship outside of the club.

"Me either. Andre should be back from all his traveling this summer too, so the whole family will be back in Atlanta after a busy summer," Devyn said. Andre was Devyn's brother-in-law and former boss. Apparently, he'd had a busy summer traveling for work. Stacey met Andre at Mercedes' wedding.

"Oh, really. That's nice," was all she said, not able to think of anything else. She hoped Devyn hadn't picked up on the slight hitch of her voice at the mention of Andre Collins. She'd only met him once at Mercedes' wedding, but he'd left an impression. An image of a pair of cerulean eyes that, while holding a hint of laughter could also give the impression of reaching down to her very soul, passed through Stacey's mind.

For his part, Andre had been cordial, yet standoffish, though Stacey suspected he may have felt the pull as well. There were a few occasions when she had turned and found his gaze on her. But since he'd had a date—one that had clung to him like a second skin throughout the reception—Stacey figured he was taken, making him off limits.

"Alright, well great. I'm glad you're coming. Are you gonna stick around for the rest of the performances?" Devyn asked.

"Yup. You know I love seeing everyone do their thing." Stacey forced thoughts of Devyn's brother-in-law out of her mind. Despite trying to direct her attention to thinking of the remaining performances that night, she still couldn't fully ignore the slight giddiness she felt just thinking of seeing Andre Collins again.

CHAPTER 2

*M*aria sat up on her knees, putting her small, yet perky, alabaster breasts on full display.

"Are you sure you can't stay?" she purred, attempting to unbuckle Andre's Ralph Lauren belt and pull him back in bed.

Andre ran his gaze down the long, dark-haired vixen. She was beautiful, no doubt, but it was time to go.

"No can do, sweetheart. You know the rule. No over—"

"—night stays. Yeah, I remember," Maria pouted, plopping back down on her king-sized bed.

Andre was just barely able to restrain himself from rolling his eyes. He and Maria had had a thing off and on for a few years now. Whenever they weren't seeing anyone, and they were in each other's city or needed a date for an event, they hooked up. He'd been working hard for the past week and had found himself in need of some female company. Tonight, after his final meeting of the day, he'd called Maria and asked her out to dinner, which she happily agreed to. After dinner, they'd gone back to her place and indulged in a few rounds of adult activity.

Andre had fun, but that's all it was. He didn't do overnights with any woman, and Maria knew that. He looked down into those hazel eyes and pouty lips, which would make most men quiver, but Andre wasn't most men. He wouldn't be bogarted into a relationship with anyone.

"I was just thinking that maybe you could..." she trailed off.

Andre paused buttoning his shirt to look down at her skeptically. "Could what?" he asked lifting a dark eyebrow.

"You could spend the night. Have breakfast with me tomorrow morning. You know, like real couples do," she said hopefully, rising to kneel in front of him again and letting the five hundred thread count sheets fall from her body. She tried reaching for Andre but he stepped back, shaking his head.

"No, you know the agreement. I. don't. do. overnights," he said sternly. He slid his foot into his Steve Maddens and began heading to the door with barely a backwards glance. He felt his jaw tick as his frustration increased. Lately, Maria had been demanding more and more of him whenever they saw each other. It was the reason he'd avoided calling her until today although he'd been in Boston for the past week.

"Will I see you before you leave, at least?" she asked.

Her voice sounded too close to a whine for Andre's comfort. He turned and looked back at her still kneeling in the center of the bed, naked. He saw the hopeful look in her eye, but he was not swayed. She was a nice girl and all, and they'd had fun in and out of bed, but Andre remained undeterred.

"Maybe. I'll call you," he said before turning and walking out of her bedroom, down her spiral staircase, and out the door of her tenth floor luxury condo.

When he reached his hotel suite at the Boston Harbor Hotel, he kicked off his shoes and undressed to take a quick shower before settling in to review some work documents. He'd been in meetings all week with a mid-size finance company trying to negotiate the terms of an acquisition. As Chief Financial Officer of Excel Financial Corporation, the financial services company his father started going on more than thirty years ago, Andre often worked long hours and could be very type-A when it came to making sure all the I's were dotted, and all the T's were crossed in the paperwork. He'd been working on closing this deal for months now and he felt it was in his grasp. As he opened his laptop and settled in at the desk in his suite, he pulled up the financial reports he'd been pouring over for months. He wanted to get in one last look before bed, so he could go into the next day's meetings fresh and prepared.

Looking over the financial reports, all thoughts and annoyance with Maria's latest attempt to elevate their relationship status became an afterthought.

* * *

ANDRE STEPPED into the downtown office he was using for the week. Excel owned a satellite office in Boston due to the company's growing business dealings in the Northeast.

"Thanks, Margaret," he said as the older receptionist brought him his morning coffee. He'd made it into the office just before eight to review more documents and prepare for his meetings.

"You're welcome. I'll buzz you around nine. I know how you can lose track of time," she told him smiling.

"Hey Margaret, let's say you dump that husband of yours and run away with me to Atlanta so you can be my assistant," he said wiggling his eyebrows. He'd gone through three different assistants in the last few years ever since his now sister-in-law quit after marrying his brother, and giving birth to his nephews. Most days he was happy to have gained Devyn as a sister, but it'd been difficult finding an executive assistant who worked as well with him as she did.

Margaret giggled. "I don't think Richard would go for that. Or my kids."

"Bah," Andre waved her comment off. "You'll get to look at my handsome face every day. That will surely make up for any loss in family ties," he joked.

Margaret shook her head. "I can see how so many young women find themselves in trouble over the likes of you, Mr. Collins," she smiled.

He laughed. "What's life without a little bit of trouble? And you know to call me Andre."

"Okay, Andre. I'm going now. I'll buzz you in a half an hour," she said, turning to leave, a big grin still on her face.

Andre knew the effect he had on women, even women who were much older and married. At six-foot-two with piercing blue eyes, dark hair, muscled frame rom regular workouts, a year round tan from his mother's Mediterranean heritage and the short beard he'd recently grown out, he saw the double takes he often got from women. Luckily, this was a burden he was all too happy to carry. He enjoyed women's company just as much as they enjoyed his—that is, when they weren't looking to get involved beyond a casual affair.

Andre checked the time on his Cartier Roadster before returning his attention to the papers on his desk. One last look at his documents before going into the meeting. He knew these forms would be the key to finally settling the acquisition.

"Hey Nik, what's up?" Andre asked, answering his cell phone about twenty minutes later.

"Hey Dre, just checking in. How's it going in Boston?" Andre's older brother Nikola asked.

"All's fine on the western front. I have another meeting this morning with Jennings. This should be the last one before I get back to Atlanta," Andre said in reference to the meeting he'd been preparing for when Nikola called.

"Good, so that means you'll be back in town for the Labor Day barbecue, right? Mama's been nagging me about all the traveling you've been doing this summer."

"Well, since your slacker ass got married and had a family, someone has to make sure the family company doesn't go belly up," Andre joked.

"Haha, very funny. Just make sure you have your ass back here by this weekend for the barbecue. Speaking of which, are you bringing anyone?"

Andre paused, wondering where this question was coming from. Nikola knew Andre frequently dated, but he rarely inquired about his romantic life. He began to wonder if their mother, Iris, hadn't set Nikola up to ask the question.

"What's it to you?" he asked instead of responding to Nikola's question.

"Well, you are in Boston, and you've been seeing Maria off and on for a while now," Nikola let his statement hang in the air, waiting for Andre to jump in.

Andre snorted, "Whatever, bro. Since you and Raul got married, it's like you both are conspiring with mama to see me down the altar. Not. gonna. happen," Andre insisted.

Nikola sighed, "I seriously don't understand your insistence on never getting married. We both come from the same family. Grew up seeing a great marriage between mom and dad. When we were younger, you were the one who often talked of wanting the same type of family, but something changed in the last few years and I can't put my finger on it," Nikola stated in an oddly worried voice.

Andre knew his brother wasn't one to wear his heart on his sleeve unless his wife, Devyn, or their children were involved. Even though he heard the desire to continue this conversation in Nikola's voice, Andre was in no mood to go down the road of marriage discussions and his reluctance to take the plunge.

"Who knew you studied psychology at West Point? And here I thought your job was CEO of a financial services company, not Nikola Collins, resident counselor," Andre said with annoyance in his voice.

"Fuck you, Andre. I'm just stating an observation. Don't get your ass kicked," Nikola retorted.

Andre laughed, "Yeah right, we aren't kids anymore and you're getting up there in age, old man."

"Whatever, dickhead. Just make sure you get this deal done and have your ass back here by this weekend," Nikola warned.

"Whatever you say, big bro," Andre smugly answered. "Anything else?" he asked.

"Yeah, have a safe flight back," Nikola responded sincerely.

Andre smiled. Despite their sometimes sarcastic and wiseass

banter, both men had a deep affection for one another. Andre knew Nikola wanted nothing but the best for him and he, in return, felt the same for his older brother. They were a team in the family business and remained so because they knew that no matter what happened, they had each other's backs.

"Thanks, bro. Give Devyn and the kids a kiss for me. See you this weekend," Andre said referring to his niece and nephews before hanging up.

Andre stood from his chair, rolling his neck and shoulders to try to release the tension that suddenly built. He stared out of the window, looking down on the downtown area of Boston. He watched the hustle and bustle of the city as it came alive with commuters, professionals, and even school children dressed in uniforms. He had another day and half of meetings to get through before he could return home to Atlanta. It'd been a busy summer, and he was ready to be in the comfort of his own city to stay for a while. This wouldn't be his last meeting with Jennings as he was scheduled to come to Atlanta in a month's time to finalize the deal. Andre knew his last few days in Boston would be the turning point in this deal, however.

Just as he turned from the window, his office phone buzzed. It was Margaret. He knew she was calling to make sure he hadn't lost track of time.

Sighing, he shrugged off thoughts of his conversation with Nikola and answered the phone.

"Thanks, Margaret. I'll be out in just a moment." Hanging up the phone, he gathered his thoughts and straightened the files on his desk. He buttoned the dark silver jacket of his tailored Tom Ford suit, picked up the files, and strolled towards the door, his back completely erect and head high. He was ready to do business.

CHAPTER 3

 ndre entered the home in which he'd spent most of his childhood that was now home to Nikola, Devyn and their three children. The place looked much different than when his mother had lived in it. Devyn and Nik had replaced Iris' white and cream furnishings with a black and grey decor. Andre noticed the silver accented candles and fresh flowers throughout the living room and dining room areas as he strolled through the home to the back-yard. He could hear the laughter of children, probably his two nephews Jacques and Theodore, and the conversations of his friends and family as he got closer.

Stepping through the glass sliding doors that led to the spacious backyard, Andre saw a swarm of people mingling about. His stomach growled the moment he smelled the chicken and meat he knew was fresh off the grill. To the right, seated on the large, sea green patio sectional sofas was Nikola with Devyn by his side. She was holding their five month old daughter, Cassandra. Andre smiled, shaking his head. The couple had been married barely three years and already had three children.

Nik probably doesn't give her a moment's rest, he chuckled to himself. He watched as his mother came over to the couple, picking up

Cassandra and cooing to the baby. Just then, he noticed Devyn lean over and whisper something in Nikola's ear. Andre watched as Nikola's lips turned up in a mischievous smile.

Hm, maybe it's Devyn who doesn't give Nik a moment's rest. He smiled as he saw Nikola stand, helping his wife up and they strolled off.

"What are you smiling about?" he heard a familiar voice ask. Andre turned to see his mother approaching his side, still holding baby Cassandra. He smiled at his mother as he took in her still smooth, taut skin, blue eyes that she'd passed to both her sons, and the halo of long grey hair. She'd recently made the decision to stop dyeing her hair. Andre thought it gave her a regal appearance instead of the haggard look that he knew she'd once feared. Andre unconsciously gave his mother the smile he reserved only for her. He hadn't seen her much in the last few months.

"Hi mama," he beamed, reaching in for a hug and placing a kiss on her cheek. "Hey Sandy," he cooed to his young niece, using the nickname he'd given her.

The baby, with skin the color of cafe au lait and a mop of dark curly hair, smiled her toothless grin at Andre and giggled loudly when Andre tickled her chin.

"When did you get here?" Iris asked, shifting the baby to her other hip.

"Just arrived. I was looking around for you when I spotted Nik and Dev. They seemed to have disappeared now though," he said, chuckling.

Iris smiled knowingly. "Yes, it seems they have. I'm sorry Hwan couldn't make it to the barbecue. It's been awhile since I've seen him," Iris mentioned, talking about Andre's best friend. They'd known each other since their Stanford days.

"Yeah, he and Jerry are spending the week in Hawaii with Jerry's parents."

Jerry was Hwan's husband.

"Oh, isn't that nice. How lovely to have a family and loved ones to share the holidays and vacation with."

Andre lifted an eyebrow. He knew an Iris Collins rant on love

14

and marriage was coming. He could think of about a thousand things he'd rather do than sit through a lecture on the value of marriage and love by his mother. One of them being gouging his own eyes out.

"I'm just saying, look how happy Nik and Devyn are. And once Raul and Mercedes arrive, you will see how wonderfully happy they are. You know Hwan and Jerry have been together for years and are doing great. How wonderful that gay marriage has been legalized. You know…"

Andre tuned his mother out. He silently hoped Cassandra would start squirming or need a diaper change so his mother would have to focus on something else. As he gazed down at Cassandra's cherub cheeks and heavily lidded gaze as she laid her head down on his mother's shoulder, he knew he was in no such luck.

Maybe one of the twins will…

His thoughts were interrupted when he saw a figure emerge from the sliding glass doors. Andre's stance became fully erect as the odd sensation of butterflies in his stomach grew. His brows furrowed in dismay. He'd rarely reacted this way toward any woman since he'd hit puberty, and he'd been around hundreds of women. The only time recently he remembered having this reaction was at Mercedes and Raul's wedding when he first met *her.*

Her cinnamon colored skin had a natural, healthy glow. Her long legs and arms betrayed her barely five-foot six inch frame. When she moved, Andre thought it looked as if she floated rather than walked. She had an air of grace about her presence that was innate. She was dressed in a sleeveless black blouse and a white, flowing skirt that stopped a few inches below the knee in the front but flowed down to her feet in the back, and a pair of platform sandals. Her hair was different from the last time he'd seen her. She'd worn it in a straightened style for Mercedes' wedding. Now, it was long in some sort of twisted style that she'd put into a side braid hanging over her shoulder. Andre let his gaze follow the delicate curve of her shoulder, and when she turned he noticed a tattoo of a butterfly on the back of her right shoulder. He swallowed deeply, suddenly parched, as images of running his tongue along the outline of the wings of tattoo floated through this mind.

He knew her name was Stacey and that she was a friend of both Mercedes and Devyn's from their burlesque dancing. He'd only met her once and his body had the same reaction the first time he'd seen her. But, he had gone to the wedding with Maria, so out of respect for his date he'd opted to keep his distance. At least, that was what he'd told himself. He may have also been too taken aback by the magnitude of his response to her. Either way, he'd kept his distance, but he often found his eyes drawn to wherever she was. It was as if his brain had had a mental GPS tracker on her, his eyes always landing on wherever she was in the room. That had been nearly three months ago, and now here she was again, having the same effect on him.

The scowl on Andre's face grew deeper when he saw a man emerge from the door behind Stacey. He was about five-ten, medium build and a few shades darker than Stacey. When he put his hand on the small of her back, Andre's eyes narrowed and his fists flexed unconsciously.

Who's this fucker? He thought before he could stop himself.

Iris cleared her throat. "Are you listening to me, sweetie?" she asked innocently. Iris had watched Andre's entire body language change when Stacey entered the backyard. She'd seen the same reaction three months prior at Raul and Mercedes' wedding. She watched as Andre reluctantly turned his attention back to her with a glower on his face.

"I'm sorry, mama. What were you saying?" Andre asked as he steeled his face to cover the irritated look from only a few seconds before.

"Oh nothing, Andre. I think Raul and Mercedes just arrived. I'm going to go say hello. Why don't you go mingle...or something," she said in a sugary sweet tone before strolling off.

As soon as his mother departed, Andre turned to where he last saw Stacey standing, but she wasn't there. He scanned the rest of the backyard and saw Stacey and her companion by the pool talking with a few other women he believed performed at the Black Kitty with

Devyn and Mercedes. Andre's stomach muscles tightened when he watched as Stacey threw her head back laughing. His eyes glided down the column of her neck and he reflexively tightened his hands into fists. He was beginning to feel like a randy teenager, not a grown ass man who'd bedded plenty of women. Andre decided to go find his two nephews and greet Mercedes and Raul instead of gawking at the woman who had unknowingly held his rapt attention.

* * *

LORD, *he's gorgeous,* Stacey thought as she peeked over her shoulder at the tall, Greek god across the lawn. Thanks to his mother's ancestry, his beautifully bronzed skin was complemented by the sun and warm weather. His dark hair was in a short style that was gelled a little to keep it out of his face. And, that beard. Stacey wasn't readily attracted to men with beards, but the short beard he'd grown since the last time she saw him was winning her over.

"Do you want anything to drink, Stace?" the male voice of her date asked, pulling her from thoughts of Andre Collins.

Stacey immediately felt guilty for lusting after one man while she was here with another.

She shook her head. "No thank you, Damon. I'm fine," she smiled at him. She'd met Damon about a month ago. Her aunt had introduced them when she was in town for one of her business trips. This was their second date. She liked him well enough.

So, then why do I keep thinking about someone else? She wondered.

"Actually, I'm going to go to the ladies room," she said excusing herself from the group.

"Oh, I can come wi-"

"No, that's not necessary. You go get something to drink. I'll be right back."

She needed a minute to herself. Plus, she wanted to see if Mercedes had arrived yet. She hadn't seen her friend since her wedding and wanted to catch up.

"O-okay," Damon said, caught off guard by her abruptness.

17

She smiled at him and proceeded towards the glass doors. When she checked the downstairs bathroom and found it occupied, she decided to see if the upstairs bathroom was unoccupied. She'd been in Devyn and Nikola's home a few times before and knew her way around. As she ascended one side of the arch stairway, Stacey didn't know a pair of blue eyes had followed her up the stairs.

A few minutes later, Stacey looked herself over in the mirror, adjusted the braid that laid over her shoulder, and then reapplied her NYX butter gloss in the color strawberry parfait. It gave her lips a light pink tint that made her full lips stand out against her brown skin. She smoothed her skirt, washed her hands, and headed out the door to go look for Mercedes and Devyn.

Stacey stepped out of the bathroom and walked right into a brick wall. At least, that's what it felt like. She looked up to see a pair of laughing, but intense blue eyes looking down at her. Andre stood right in front of the bathroom door, his hands now locked around Stacey's arms to prevent her from falling. Stacey immediately felt tingles on her arms where his hands gripped her.

"O-oh, excuse me. I'm sorry..." she trailed off.

"For what?" he asked, looking at her intently and keeping his hands right where they were.

Stacey frowned in confusion. She watched his gaze move down to her lips and the usually light blue shade, darkened ever so slightly.

"F-for bumping into you," she responded.

"But it was my fault. I was waiting for you," he retorted honestly.

Stacey's eyebrows shot up. "You were waiting for me?"

Andre nodded, "Mhm, for the bathroom," he hedged.

Stacey's mood automatically deflated. "Oh, that's right. I'm sorry. It's all yours," she said stepping back out of his grip, trying to cover her embarrassment.

She remembered that the downstairs bathroom had been occupied. He probably came up here just like her in search of a free bathroom. Though she'd moved to the side to let him pass, Andre just stood there staring at her. She marveled at how his light blue pupils seemed to darken right before her eyes. When his pink tongue darted out to moisten his button lip, visions of sucking that lip into her own mouth danced around in her mind. She cleared her throat to break the tension.

"Well, I'm-"

"Is he your boyfriend?" he asked suddenly.

Stacey was taken aback by the question. "Wh-who?" she asked.

Andre stepped closer, crowding her space. "That man you came with," he said tersely. "Is he your boyfriend? He wasn't with you at the wedding so it can't be too serious if he is," he stated matter-of-factly.

Stacey was thrown, for one, because within the few seconds she'd been in Andre's presence she'd forgotten all about Damon. And secondly, his mentioning of the wedding meant that he had noticed her there, and had paid close enough attention to know she didn't have a date.

"No," she shook her head, "he's not my boyfriend," she responded.

"Good," was all he said.

"Good?" she inquired, giving him a curious look.

"Yeah, I'd hate to have to steal you from him. That could get messy, but...in this case I wouldn't mind a little mess," he said, looking her square in the eye to let her know he wasn't joking.

Stacey shook her head, still trying to wrap her mind around what he had just said. Mess? What did he mean by mess? And exactly how closely had he paid attention to her at the wedding? They'd barely spoken.

"H-how'd you know he wasn't with me at the wedding? You barely paid attention to me. You were with someone el—," she snapped her lips closed realizing she'd just revealed that she'd been watching him and his date at the wedding. Unfortunately, she wasn't fast enough as she watched Andre's lips turn up in a knowing grin.

"So, the watching wasn't one-sided. Good to know." Truth is, he'd already known she'd taken notice of him. He saw the sly glances she'd thrown his way when she thought he wasn't looking.

"I didn't speak much because I had a date with me. I didn't want to be rude to my uh, friend." He placed emphasis on the word "friend," referring to Maria who'd been his date for the wedding.

"Well, I have a date now. So, isn't you pushing up on me now a little rude?" she retorted, tilting her head to the side.

"So," he said shrugging his shoulder.

Again, Stacey was taken aback. She could already tell Andre had a way of keeping women on their toes whenever they were around him. Out of the two brothers, he appeared to be the more laidback, easy going one, but when he set sights on something or someone, they didn't stand a chance. Luckily, Stacey had spent years on her toes and masking even major discomfort behind a smile. She refused to let Andre see how much he affected her already.

"So?" she questioned, crossing her arms under her breasts. Wrong move.

The new position helped to lift her small, but already perky breasts. She watched as Andre's gaze shifted down to her cleavage and lingered for a second before he raised his eyes to meet hers, once again.

"Yeah, 'so'. He's of no significance to me and soon enough, not to you either," he said stepping closer.

"We don—"

"Stacey?"

Stacey jumped and turned to see Damon coming up the staircase with a concerned look on his face. She immediately stepped back from Andre, feeling as if she'd just been caught doing something she wasn't supposed to be doing.

"Da—" she cleared her throat, "Damon, what are you doing here?" she asked sounding guilty even to her own ears.

"I thought maybe you'd gotten lost in this big house. I think your friend Mercedes was looking for you. I see you got caught up talking. Hey, you probably came up here 'cause the bathroom downstairs was occupied too, right?" Damon asked directing his question to Andre.

"Not really," Andre stated, looking annoyed.

Stacey felt the tension radiating off Andre. He was clearly perturbed by Damon's presence. She didn't want to think about how she could already sense his change in mood while barely even looking at him. She decided to intervene in the tense standoff.

"Uh, Damon, this is Andre. Nikola's brother. We were, um, we were just...catching up," she said not knowing how else to explain their encounter to her date—a man Andre had just called insignificant not three minutes before.

"How about we go find Mercedes." She stepped away from Andre and moved towards the staircase. "It was nice, talking with you, Andre," she said over her shoulder. She noticed his scowl when Damon placed a hand on the small of her back to help her down the steps.

"You okay?" Damon asked as they descended the steps.

"Yes, I'm fine," she said, willing herself not to look back at Andre though she could feel his eyes burrowing holes into her back. She took a deep breath, grabbed her left hand with the other and rubbed her thumb across the faint scar.

"Let's go find Mercedes. I want to see how her honeymoon was," she said as they rounded the corner. She had to bite the inside of her cheek to keep from letting out a sigh of relief when she knew they were out of Andre's range of sight. Being around him for just that short period of time unnerved her in ways she hadn't felt unnerved in a long time. And he wasn't shy about making his intentions clear.

CHAPTER 4

"*Y*ou ready for the Jennings' meeting?" Nikola asked as he sat behind his large cherrywood desk in his corner office on the top floor of Excel's twenty story building.

Andre sat back in the chair and gave his brother a cocky look. "Who do you think you're talking to?" he asked, half-jokingly, half-serious. He knew Nikola knew him well enough to know he'd have his shit together for what was to be the final meeting before this deal went through.

"Don't get your panties in a bunch. I'm just making sure everything is how it should be. You'll let me know if you need me--"

Andre held his hand up, cutting Nikola off. "I won't. And they're boxer briefs."

Nikola lifted his eyebrow.

"My underwear. I don't wear panties. Boxer briefs. Ralph Lauren, in case you were wondering." A cocky grin spread over his face.

Nikola threw a crumpled up piece of paper at Andre. "Whatever, asshole. I don't need to know what type of underwear you're wearing. Just make sure you've got your shit together for this meeting," he said sternly.

Though Nikola's expression was serious, Andre could see a hint of laughter dancing around in his brother's eyes.

"My shit is together. You think I've spent months working on this deal to fuck it up now? Don't worry your pretty little head. Stress causes wrinkles. In fact, I think I see some forming already. Maybe you should ask mama for the name of a doctor who does Botox."

"Mama doesn't get Botox," Nikola reminded him.

"I know, but you know some of the women she does all the charity events with do. Maybe you should get their doctor's number."

"Keep talking, you'll be the one in need of a plastic surgeon," Nikola responded to Andre's teasing.

"Not even on your best day."

Nikola merely shook his head just as there was a knock at his door. They both turned to see Devyn standing in his doorway. She was dressed in a black pencil skirt, and a dark blue sleeveless top that was covered by a light, white button up sweater.

"Hey Andre, I didn't know you would be up here. Am I too early?" she asked. It was Wednesday, which was her day to leave early. Devyn ran an event planning business located on one of the lower floors. Wednesdays, she and Nikola usually had lunch together before she left for the day to relieve their nanny with the kids.

"No, he was just leaving," Nikola said rising from his chair to greet his wife.

Andre chuckled. "Just like that, you're kicking me out, huh?"

"Yes," Nikola stated as he pulled his wife towards his desk.

"It's okay. I imagine Devyn's better company than mine anyway," he joked. He gave Devyn a quick kiss on the cheek before turning to head out the door.

"Oh, before I go, Dev are you going to be at the Black Kitty this weekend?"

"Why?" Nikola asked, his eyebrows lowered, staring at his brother.

Andre just grinned. "Wouldn't you like to know," he laughed as the glower grew on Nikola's face. "Easy big brother. I just thought it might be time for me to check it out."

"Check it out or check *someone* out?" Devyn asked.

Now, it was Andre's turn to scowl while Devyn chuckled. He wondered if Stacey had told her about their brief exchange the previous week at the Labor Day barbecue. Andre thought of the look of guilt Stacey wore on her face as she descended the steps with her date. He doubted she would have said anything. No matter. Andre went after what he wanted. He just didn't want his sister-in-law or his brother looking at him like they could read him like a book, the way they were right now.

"You're getting just as bad as your husband," he grumbled.

She just laughed. "He's not so bad," she said defending her husband. "But to answer your question, yes Nikola and I are going to be at the club this weekend, but I'm not performing. This weekend is the return of the Black Dahlia since she got married." Black Dahlia was the stage name for Mercedes.

"Oh, and Stacey will be performing too," she said flippantly.

Andre already knew that piece of information. He may have spent some time on the club's website looking over the performers for the weekend, but he'd be damned if he'd let them know that.

"Oh, you don't say," he said offhandedly. "Well, I better go. I have a meeting in fifteen minutes and I want to double check everything before it starts."

"Alright, see you this weekend then," Devyn said.

"Close the door behind you," Nikola yelled to Andre's retreating back.

Andre looked over his shoulder to see Nikola pulling Devyn onto his lap. The last thing he heard was Devyn's giggles before he closed the door.

Forty-five minutes later, Andre found himself seated in one of Excel's conference rooms with a team full of lawyers, accountants, and consultants. He sat at the head of the long conference table, and at the opposite end sat Mitchell Jennings, current owner and president of Jennings Financial Services. Like Andre, Mitchell's company had been started by his father who'd passed it on to his son. However, unlike Andre and Nikola, Mitchell had nearly run his father's company into the ground. The company was hanging on by a thread.

Andre had gone over the financials for the company for months before even approaching Jennings for this deal. He knew the company still had a good foundation, but Jennings was lazy. He hired incompetent staff and had basically turned over the running of the company to employees who'd taken advantage of him, hiring unqualified staff simply because they were related. He had every intention of cleaning house once the company was his. That is, if Mitchell Jennings would quit bullshitting around.

"So you see, Andre, we're just not convinced that selling to you at fifty-dollars a share is the best deal for us. I'm sure you understand our hesitation," Mitchell said smugly as he sat across from Andre.

A muscle in Andre's jaw ticked as he attempted to reign in his growing anger. He knew Mitchell would try to pull some shit like this at the last minute. It was the type of sneak he was. He was a spoiled rich kid who rarely worked for anything in his life, and was handed the keys to a financial empire when his daddy died. He'd partied and snorted away much of his father's legacy and the reputation of his company, but here he sat here believing he could play games. He was in way over his head and didn't even know it.

Andre watched as one of Jennings lawyers leaned over and whispered something in his ear. Probably warning him to relax on the smugness, but Jennings wasn't smart enough to heed his lawyer's warning. Andre was done with this bullshit. He had plenty of other options for investment. He never put all his eggs in one basket.

"Then get out," he said before pushing back from the table, standing to his full height, and buttoning the dark blue suit jacket of his Burberry suit, gathering his papers and strolling towards the door.

You could hear a pin drop as almost everyone's jaw was on the floor. They all knew how long Andre had worked to get this deal done. They couldn't believe he would just up and walk away. But, they had another think coming if they believed Andre was one to back down. He wasn't about to be backed into a corner by some spoiled party-boy who barely knew the difference between an asset and a liability.

"Y-you've got to be kidding. You can't just walk away," Jennings sputtered just as Andre's hand reached the doorknob of the conference room.

"I can't?" Andre asked giving a sideways look to Jennings.

"Well no you-—"

"See, that's where you're wrong. Not only can I walk away, I can head straight to my office and pull up a list of financial companies who would happily take the deal we're offering you. Make no mistake, this deal we're offering you is generous considering the mess you've made with your father's company. Do you even know what your company grossed last year in revenues?"

"Why yes. It was..." Jennings trailed off as he flipped through the papers in front of him, searching for the answer to Andre's question.

"It was four million, three-hundred and fifty-five thousand, rounded off to the nearest thousand," Andre didn't blink as he ran the numbers, staring directly at Jennings,

"That's a pittance of your company's annual revenue five years before your father's death and each year since his death your revenues have steadily declined, last year's revenues being the lowest. And let's not even discuss your profit margin. It's dismal to say the least. So you coming in here with this self-righteous attitude, trying to throw months of labor that went into this deal down the drain is bullshit. You may have the desire to waste your employees' time with this nonsense, but I do not. I trust you have enough lawyers that can help you find your way out the door. Goodbye," he said dismissing Jennings.

He turned to the head of his acquisitions department, "Jeff, I'm sorry to have pulled you from your other engagements for this. Let's meet in my office later. Call my assistant to set up a time."

Jeffrey nodded and stood, knowing when his boss was and was not bullshitting around. The other Excel employees began gathering their things and rising to leave.

"Good day, gentlemen." And with that, Andre turned and walked out the conference room followed by his own team of lawyers and consultants.

A man's gotta know when to hold 'em and when to fold 'em. Andre remembered his father's words as he strolled down the hall to his office.

Jennings sat in his seat, a cold look in his eye. He didn't move, even after his own team realized Andre wasn't coming back and began gathering their things. After more urging from his lawyer, Jennings finally rose from his chair and followed his team out the door. When his lawyers encouraged him to go to Andre's office, he declined, feeling like a child who'd just been chastised in front of his peers. *You're not fit to run my company.* The taunts from his own father echoed in his mind. Jennings shook his head as he entered the elevator trying to devise a plan solve this mess and somehow still keep his father's company.

* * *

"THIS SHOW BETTER BE GOOD. And this woman you're dragging me to see perform better be worth the hype," Hwan said as he and Andre exited Andre's metallic brown, BMW ActiveHybrid 5.

"First of all, nobody dragged you anywhere. You decided to invite yourself when I told you where I was going tonight since your husband is away for the weekend," Andre reminded his friend.

Hwan waved his hand, dismissing Andre's statement. "Details, details. Listen, so tell me about this woman who has you so smitten that you've finally decided to check out a burlesque club."

Andre looked over at his friend who was only about two inches shorter than he was and shook his head. "Get it right. I'm not smitten. Just attracted. I haven't dated anyone new in a while, and now that I'm not traveling as much especially not back and forth to Boston, now's the time to pursue my options," he stated casually as they handed their tickets to the hostess at the front door, and made their way inside.

"Uh huh," Hwan said skeptically, squinting his dark eyes at Andre to let him know he wasn't fully buying what Andre was selling.

"And speaking of Boston, I can't believe Jennings tried that shit with you. You think he'll be back?" Hwan asked. The two men both had MBAs from Stanford. Hwan himself had made partner at PricewaterhouseCoopers a little over a year ago. He knew much of the ins and outs of the Jennings deal Andre had been working on.

"He's already comeback, but I haven't taken his calls yet, and when I do, I'm only offering forty a share," Andre stated seriously.

"Wow, he must have really pissed you off," Hwan whistled as the two men made their way to the bar.

"He did." Andre motioned for the bartender.

"Serves his ass right. He's been playing fast and loose with that business for too long," Hwan said, also aware of Jennings' reputation as a party boy. "Whatever, that's enough about work. Order me a martini please," he asked Andre.

Andre shook his head. "I can't believe I still hang with you ordering weak ass drinks like that," he chuckled. He ordered Hwan's martini and a Samuel Adams for himself. As their drinks arrived, Andre and Hwan were greeted by Nikola and Nikola's best friend, Raul.

Raul's wife, Mercedes was also performing tonight. Her first performance since getting married and spending the summer in Raul's native Brazil.

"Raul, you excited to see Mercedes back on stage tonight?" Andre asked.

Raul, who stood shoulder to shoulder next to Nikola, nodded as a grin spread across his face. Andre recognized it as the same type of grin Nikola wore when the topic of conversation was his wife. Andre thought of the many times he'd seen his typically stern father wear that same grin when he talked about Andre's mother.

The look of love. Count me out, He mused.

"Hell yeah," Raul responded, "she's excited to get back to it too, and a happy wife makes a happy home. A *very* happy home," he said wiggling his eyebrows. All the men laughed.

"Where's Dev? I thought she wasn't performing tonight?" Andre asked Nikola.

"She's not. She's just helping backstage." Devyn performed under the stage name Black Pearl, but this was her weekend off from performing.

"Let's go find a table," Nikola suggested.

As the men sat down, the lights in the club began to dim. Andre looked around the room as the audience members began to take their seats. The club was large, able to accommodate at least a hundred audience members. The hardwood stage at the front of the room drew his attention as the spotlight shone on it. A petite woman emerged from behind the curtain, known around the club as Mistress Coco, but Andre knew her real name was Diane. Apparently, she and his mother went way back when both of them had danced burlesque. Andre nor Nikola even knew their mother had ever danced burlesque until the night of Nikola's wedding.

The light shone, showing off Mistress Coco's smooth, latte-colored skin that contrasted perfectly with her silver hair. Andre suspected Mistress Coco had been the motivation behind Iris finally letting her hair go grey. Coco was dressed in a sleeveless, black chiffon dress adorned with beaded fringes that swayed with every step she took in her four-inch stilettos.

"Well, isn't she something?" Andre heard the approval in Hwan's voice. "I see why she and Iris are such good friends."

Andre had to admit, Mistress Coco and Iris were quite pair when they got together.

"Alright, let's get the show started!" Coco's voice came through the speakers. The crowd lit up in applause.

"Now, I know y'all been missing this first performer which is why I put her at the top of the show. Unfortunately for you horn dogs out there, this performer has recently married." Some male audience members booed at that, which made Raul chuckle.

"Oh, calm down! She wasn't ever going home with any of you anyway," Coco teased. The audience burst into laughter.

"Alright, I know you're all ready to see this old lady get off the stage. Ladies and gentlemen, please welcome back to the Black Kitty stage, the phenomenal, overwhelmingly sexy yet sinfully sweet, Black Dahhhhliaaaa!!!!" Mistress Coco announced before quickly exiting the stage.

Mariah Carey's *Emotions* began to play as Mercedes emerged

adorned in a blue, purple, and black peacock costume. She completed the look with a top hat and black cane. The audience roared.

Andre sat back and watched as Mercedes strutted across staged and shook what her mama gave her. He had to admit, she was good and had a way with the crowd. He could tell she enjoyed it. Still, as he peeked over at Raul who seemed to be enjoying the performance as much as his wife was, Andre shook his head. He couldn't imagine having his woman strut across a stage half-naked in a room full of men he just knew were itching to get their hands on her. Luckily, he wasn't in it to make Stacey his woman, just a couple of memorable jaunts in the sack and maybe some fun dates to get her out of his system.

As Mercedes finished her set, the crowd showed their enthusiastic appreciation. Andre watched as Raul rose to go greet his wife before she headed backstage. When he returned, a huge grin covered his face while his wife's glossy pink lipstick covered his lips. Andre shook his head and smiled. He knew what the newlywed couple would be doing later on that night.

After a brief intermission, Devyn and Mercedes greeted the men at the table. Their husbands immediately made room for them to sit and watch the rest of the performances from the audience.

Two performances later, it was Stacey's turn to hit the stage, or Jazmine Noir, as she was referred to in the club. This was the performance Andre had been waiting to see since he arrived at the club.

"Ladies and gentlemen, this next performer I like to call sexy flexxy 'cause she can bend and move in ways that will make you smack your own mama!" Mistress Coco's voice was filled with laughter and mischief. The audience, as usual, ate it up. "Ladies, you might want to take a few pointers for later, if you know what I mean," Coco teased, wiggling her eyebrows suggestively to the crowd.

"Without further ado, welcome to the stage, performing to MJ's Dirty Diana, the beautiful, the talented, the incredible, JAZMINE Noooiiiiir!!!" Coco shouted loudly as the audience clapped.

"Oh shoot, I thought you were sprung before. She's dancing to Michael Jackson? He's a goner," Hwan announced to the table. "Our boy Andre over here loves himself some Michael Jackson," Hwan said in response to the confusion on Mercedes' face.

"Yeah, he still takes off work on August 29th, MJ's birthday," Nikola smirked.

"That's because he was a God among men. Now, shut up while the King is singing," Andre barked at the table as the opening chords of the song began to play. He barely registered the snickers from the group as his senses were awakened not only by the music, but the figure emerging from behind the curtain.

Andre's heart nearly stopped when Stacey appeared on stage in a sky blue corset and bustle skirt set, paired with black peep-toe heels, black silk gloves that extended up to her elbow, and black stockings that reached mid-thigh and were connected by a garter belt to her corset.

Andre let his eyes roam over her creamy brown thighs as she floated across the stage. She had the grace of a gazelle, each move performed precisely but looking as if it took the least bit of effort. When she whipped those long twists around and rose up, her hands on the buttons of the corset, Andre felt his heart rate increase. He was torn between wanting to see more of her smooth skin and wanting to hide her from everyone in the audience. Andre's hand unconsciously clenched into fists each time the crowd roared or some randy male audience member called out "take it off."

The shouts of the crowd were overshadowed when Stacey removed her corset and threw it across the stage. Andre felt his arousal growing and had to shift in his seat. By the time Stacey's set ended, Andre was halfway out of his seat, adjusting himself as he stood so his partial erection wasn't obvious to the table.

"Where are you going?" Hwan asked.

"I'll be back." Andre didn't have an answer for where he was going or what he was going to do once he got there. He just needed to see Stacey.

"Whoa, whoa, young man where do you think you're going?" Andre found himself confronted by Mistress Coco as he attempted to enter the hallway he was told led to the changing rooms.

"I need to see Stac--uh Jazmine," he gave by way of explanation.

"And you think you can strut around my club without permission," she said folding her arms over her chest.

Yes, Andre thought, but figured it was best not to say out loud.

"I'll be quick. I just wanted to compliment her on a performance well done," he explained, giving Mistress Coco a grin he knew most women couldn't resist. "I won't be more than two, maybe three minutes. Promise." He threw her a wink, turning up the charm.

"Uh huh." Coco eyed him wearily. "Down the hall, second door on the right is my office. I'll let her know you're waiting," she said as she turned and proceeded down the hall.

Andre swore he heard her mumble something about "all she does for Iris and her pushy ass sons," but decided it was best not to ask her about it.

He strolled down the hallway, admiring the visuals of past burlesque performers on the walls. When he arrived at Coco's office, he took in the sight of the various posters of performers he knew who performed regularly at the Black Kitty. Among them were Mercedes, Devyn and Stacey's pictures, all the women posing in one of their performance costumes. Andre paced in the office for a few minutes as he waited, stuffing his hands in his pockets as his anticipation to see Stacey built. Within minutes, he heard the door creak open.

"Holy shit," he mumbled out.

Stacey was dressed in a pair of fishnet stockings and cream-colored short shorts that were covered in shiny rhinestones. The shorts hugged her firm upper thighs to perfection. The shorts had lace ruffling and were accompanied by a half-shirt that showed a considerable amount of cleavage. The shirt was also covered in rhinestones and around the back, a pair of fairy wings were attached. It showed off her flat, toned stomach to perfection. Her twists were now in a braid resting over her shoulder.

Andre's feet moved on their own accord. "You were amazing," he said reverently.

Stacey dipped her head and cleared her throat. "Thank you. What are you doing here?" she questioned looking back up at him.

"I wanted to tell you how wonderful you were out there," he said, stepping closer. "And to tell you I can't wait to get a play-by-play of your performance...in private."

Stacey's eyes widened before she placed her hands on her hips, and cocked her head to the side. "In private? What makes you th--"

"I don't think. I know." Andre stepped into Stacey's space and trailed his finger down the bridge of her nose. He felt her shiver at the contact. He had to resist the urge to cover her lips with his. He knew if he did that there was no way she was going to make it to her next performance.

"Tomorrow night. Dinner," he said pulling back slightly from her. He didn't want to ask to give her a chance to say no.

"I-I can't," Stacey said stuttering.

Andre lifted a questioning eyebrow. "Can't?"

"Yes. *Can't.*"

"You have plans already?"

"Maybe."

Andre smiled mischievously, stepping closer. "I like you." He smiled at his own admission. "I have no doubt you'd keep a man on his toes. What's so important you can't have dinner with me tomorrow night? I know it's not your date from the other week."

Stacey's perfectly sculpted eyebrows lowered. "And what makes you so certain?"

Andre's mirthful chuckle sounded around the room. "Because I know you're not turning down a date with me for a night out with him." He shook his head as if the thought were completely ridiculous.

Stacey's mouth opened in shock at how sure of himself he was. "Cocky much?"

"In more ways than one." He responded without hesitation.

Stacey lowered her head, not wanting him to see the smile she tried to hide. Andre didn't miss it, however. "Not that it's any of your business, but no. I have to study. I have a few assignments due this weekend," she said, folding her arms across her breasts.

Andre raised an eyebrow at her admission. "Studying? You're in school?"

"For what?" he asked when Stacey nodded.

"Nosy aren't you?"

"Answer the question, babe."

"I'm getting my BSW and MSW."

"Social Work?"

"Yup." Stacey smiled with pride.

Her smile made something akin to butterflies flutter in Andre's stomach. If he didn't know any better, he would have sworn he might have been feeling something slightly deeper than just a physical attraction to the woman in front of him. But, that was silly. He barely knew her. He probably was just feeling the excitement of a new dating prospect and the fact that she obviously excited about her education. Maybe they'd have more to talk about on a date besides the latest celebrity gossip or what finance company was taking over whom. It seemed most of his dates fell only into the two above categories. He'd been looking for something a little different to occupy his time lately. Maybe Stacey was it.

"Nice. You can tell me about it on our date. Monday at seven. I'll pick you up." Again, it wasn't a question.

"How can you pick me up? You don't even know where I live?" she asked again with her hands at her hips.

Andre found himself smirking. She looked cute standing there looking at him like he was half crazy. He had half a mind to show her what she could do with those perfect lips of hers. In fact, he took a step closer to do just that. He saw Stacey inhale deeply and her eyes widen as she realized his intentions.

That's right. I'm coming for you. His smirk widened.

Knock! Knock!

"Jazmine, girl! Shake a leg. You got ten minutes before you're on stage!" Mistress Coco shouted as she opened the door.

Dammit, Andre frowned at their interruption.

"And you, you're not in here molesting one of my girls are you?" Mistress Coco jutted her finger at Andre.

Stacey gasped at Coco's blunt question, but Andre was undeterred.

34

"Not yet, but soon." He winked at Stacey, letting her know he had every intention of following through on his word.

"Oh, you both shoo, now!" Mistress Coco said waving both Stacey and Andre out of her office.

"Alright," he conceded before turning to look at Stacey. "Monday at seven pm sharp. Do you like Moroccan food?" Andre asked catching Stacey off guard.

"Um, yes, I think. Yes," she said nodding her head.

"Good. Have another great performance. I'll be in the audience." He winked again before turning and leaving.

Again, he swore he heard Mistress Coco mumble something about him and Nik being "just like they daddy." He'd have to ask her what she meant later.

Andre decided to buy a drink at the bar before he went back to claim his seat at the table. He strolled over to the bar and took a seat at an empty stool, motioning for the bartender. When she looked over and saw him, Andre didn't miss the appreciative once-over she gave him. She sauntered over to where he was sitting, adding a little extra sway of her hips, no doubt for his benefit. She was dressed in a short black corset with a matching bustle skirt. Her long legs, long dark hair, and green eyes probably made most men sit up and take notice. Andre suspected she did very well in the tips department.

"What's your drink of choice, lover?" she asked suggestively.

Andre's lips quirked up into a grin. "I'll just have another Sam Adams. Thank you," he said, wanting to keep the flirtation to a minimum.

"Sure thing, lover. Anything else I can get you?" she asked wiggling her eyebrows.

He knew what she was asking, and any other night he might be interested, but not tonight. He'd come to the Black Kitty with a specific aim in mind and now that he'd accomplished it, he would stay for a few more performances and then head out.

"No thanks." He smiled as he tipped her and retrieved the beer she offered and stood.

"Damn, what took you so long and did you get me another martini?" Hwan asked as Andre sat back down at the table.

"Mind your business. And no, I didn't get you another martini. Your legs aren't broken."

"Um hmm, well did you at least get what you came for? Tell me you got a number, a date, something?" Hwan pushed for information.

Andre looked at him out of the side of his eye. "I told you to mind your business."

"Ha! That means he at least got a date. Good, maybe you will leave that Maria chick alone. I told you I don't know how many times I can't stand her." Hwan's face twisted into a mask of disgust.

"Whatever," Andre mumbled before taking a swig of his beer. He wasn't interested in thinking of Maria or any other woman tonight besides the woman who was getting ready to grace the stage again.

Andre sat back in his seat as he watched Mistress Coco saunter onto the stage. He knew Stacey's performance was next and he couldn't wait to see her again. He barely heard Mistress Coco's announcement as the image of Stacey in those thigh hugging short shorts played through his mind. He was so caught up in the image of Stacey's smooth thighs wrapped around him, he didn't even notice the seven foot dance pole that had been dragged onto the stage.

When the beat dropped for Ne-Yo and Juicy J's *She Knows* he saw Stacey emerge from behind the curtain and hop onto the small circular platform that held the pole. She walked enticingly around the pole before grabbing it with both hands and letting her body swing effortlessly around the pole. Andre's breath caught when he saw her do a flip and suddenly she was upside down, her legs wrapped around the pole and her arms free, moving in waves. Before he knew it, she flipped again and was back on her feet, presenting her barely covered ass to the crowd and winding it around.

What Andre wouldn't give to spank that ass, he thought as he adjusted himself in his seat. The room felt about ten degrees warmer.

Slowly, Stacey lowered the shorts revealing a sparkling, hot pink thong. She dipped it low and brought it back up slowly as she held on to the pole. She climbed onto the pole again, and did some acrobatic shit Andre could barely keep up with. She looked weightless, in the air as she performed a series of splits and moves while on the pole.

The applause and yells from the crowd brought Andre back to reality, and he had to refrain from the urge to go up on stage and cover Stacey with his jacket as he yanked her off. He felt relieved as the song ended and he saw Stacey, now dressed in only her fishnets, thong, and hot pink pasties with tassels, her tawny brown skin glowing in a sheen of body glitter, blow a kiss to the crowd as she exited the stage. He ran his fingers through his hair and blew out a breath as the audience applauded.

"I'm ready to go," he leaned over and told Hwan.

"Aww, the night's just getting started," Hwan half-whined.

"You can either leave with me now, or get a ride home from one of them," Andre insisted motioning towards Nikola and Raul's side of the table.

The men were now sitting and chatting with their wives, barely paying attention to Andre and Hwan.

"Ugh, fine. You can be such a spoil sport. Let's go," Hwan said draining the final sip of his martini and standing.

A little while later, after Andre had dropped Hwan off at home, he walked into his own twenty-fifth floor, luxury style condo. Andre remembered the image of seeing Stacey swinging around on the pole, her strong thighs holding her in place, and the flicker of arousal he thought had burned out began to rise again. He decided the only way he'd get to sleep that night was to work off this energy in the gym. Changing into a pair of workout shorts and sneakers, he headed to his personal gym for a few rounds on the punching bag, and ended it with a long run on the treadmill. By the time he finished his workout, showered, and climbed into bed, thoughts of Stacey had returned. He grunted in frustration, wanting to feel if her legs were as satiny smooth as they looked. He vowed he would get his question answered come this Monday night.

CHAPTER 5

Stacey sat back against the soft-cushioned couch. This hour of her week could be one of the most relaxing or one of the most stressful depending on the topic of conversation.

"Tell me how classes are going?" Stacey's therapist, Linda asked.

The response to that question was easy enough. "They're going well, just started, but I've already got some assignments I need to work on today and tomorrow. Nothing too stressful though," she replied happily.

"And what about your internship? How's that going?"

Stacey took a deep breath and looked at a spot over Linda's shoulder on the wall. She saw all the licenses and degrees Linda had hung up on her wall that attested to her professionalism. She'd been seeing Linda for about a year now, and felt comfortable opening up to her, but it was still difficult at times.

"It's going really well. I enjoy it, but it can get tough…" she trailed off.

"How so?" Linda asked.

Stacey knew Linda wouldn't let her get away with providing incomplete thoughts.

"The other day I was leading a group session and some of the women's shares just took be back to that place, you know? I felt their pain as they shared hiding their secret from their friends and family. I felt for them," she finished.

"Any good social worker or therapist feels for their clients. The question is, were you triggered?" Linda asked. "Feeling for someone and feeling triggered are two different things," she stated.

"I know." Stacey knew her triggers all too well by now. Luckily, she had come a long way in her recovery and being exposed to the stories of her clients didn't make her want to go back to the place she once was.

"It just makes me realize how broken I was and how far I've come. I want that for all the women I work with," she admitted honestly.

"I'm sure you're doing your best to give them what they need. And you have your strategies in place in case you ever are triggered. Now, anything else you want to share with me before our time is up?" Linda asked.

"I have a date this Monday," Stacey blurted out. She didn't even know where that came from, but ever since last night Andre had been on her mind. Heck, ever since their encounter on Labor Day, he'd been on her mind. Seeing him at the Black Kitty last night had her feeling a little off kilter.

"Oh, with Damon?" Linda smiled looking down at her notes.

"No," Stacey shook her head, "Someone else."

Linda's mahogany colored face became a mask of curiosity. "Oh, someone new?" she asked.

"Yes, he's the brother-in-law of a friend of mine. We've only met a couple of times…"

Stacey told Linda a few details of how she and Andre met and how he asked—well told her they were going out on a date. Stacey hated to admit it, but his take charge manner actually made him more attractive to her. In spite of hardly knowing Andre, she was really looking forward to their date. Though Stacey dated, it'd been a long time since a man had held her interest. And no man had ever made her feel as desired as Andre did with just one look, and a brief touch. She felt tingly just envisioning those brilliant blue eyes of his and the way they saw right through her.

"Alright, well that's it for today's session," Linda said, rising from her leather chair.

Stacey shook her head, reprimanding herself for getting so caught up in daydreaming about a man she hardly knew. She would definitely have to pull it together before Monday night.

* * *

At seven pm sharp, the buzzer for Stacey's fifth floor, one bedroom condo rung.

I do enjoy a man who knows how to be on time, she thought. She buzzed Andre up, telling him which floor to take the elevator to although she suspected he probably knew already. A few minutes later, she went to open the door to wait for his arrival. When she opened it, there stood Andre's well-built physique dressed in a dark blue slacks, a light blue button up shirt, and shiny black shoes. Though the outfit was rather understated, she knew it was name brand and tailored to fit his body to perfection. Stacey looked up into his eyes which held a bit mischief mixed with unmistakable desire. Stacey felt her stomach muscles tighten when Andre's tongue snaked out to lick his bottom lip.

"Good evening, beautiful." He smiled. "These are for you."

Stacey had been so caught up in staring at him, she missed the bouquet of flowers he held in his hand. She looked down to see a bouquet of purple jasmine flowers and smiled.

"Hi and thank you. These are beautiful," she said, taking the flowers from his outstretched arms.

"Not nearly as beautiful as you, but they'll do," he retorted.

Stacey's cheeks flamed when she saw Andre's gaze slowly trail down her body, taking in her curves that were encased in an electric blue, sleeveless wrap dress. Wearing her three-inch heels, the top of her head came to right below his chin.

"Um, come in. I'm just going to put these in water then we can go."

She held the door open for his entrance. She watched Andre as he looked around her condo's open floor plan with its teal colored walls and white and cream furnishings. She moved to the kitchen sink and removed a clear vase she kept in the cabinet. Filling the vase with water and placing the flowers in it, she sighed. She really loved Jasmine flowers. She found their scent really soothing.

"These are actually my favorite types of flowers," she said over her shoulder.

"I thought so," Andre said causing Stacey to jump.

She hadn't realized how close he was. He stood right behind her.

"I thought your stage name might have something to do with the flower, so I took a chance," he said, reaching over her shoulder to pluck one of the flowers from its stem.

"Turn around," he commanded softly.

Stacey's feet turned on their own volition. When they did, Andre lifted his hand and neatly tucked the flower in behind her ear where she had pinned back her twists into a braid.

"Beautiful," he said just above a whisper as he let his finger trail down her jaw.

"Come here," he said pulling her by her upper arms to him.

Before Stacey knew what was happening, his lips covered hers in a kiss that awakened all her senses. She felt Andre pull her in closer, deepening the kiss. She felt his tongue as it snaked into her mouth, tasting nearly every inch of her mouth. This kiss was demanding and held promise of what was to come. Before she knew it, the kiss ended just as quickly as it began.

"We need to go before I strip you naked and take you on this counter," Andre said.

Blinking to regain her bearings, Stacey took a step back to put some much needed distance between them. "You're mighty presumptuous, aren't you?" she asked leveling a look at him.

Andre just smirked confidently. "Yup. Now, go reapply your lip gloss so we can go," he said staring down at her with eyes darkened with passion.

The glint in his eyes let Stacey know he meant every word. Wordlessly, she sidestepped him and grabbed her purse before hurrying down the hall to her bathroom. When she closed the door behind her, she took a deep breath. Letting it out, she sagged against the bathroom door.

So much for pulling it together, she berated herself as she looked in the mirror. Her lips still tingled from the kiss. Not wanting to ruminate too long in the bathroom, she applied her lip gloss, smoothed down her dress, and lightly touched the flower Andre had placed in her hair. She smiled, took another deep breath, and exited the bathroom.

A while later, Andre's BMW pulled into the Imperial Fez parking lot. Stacey had heard about this restaurant. They served Moroccan food, and every night had a live show of belly dancers. She looked forward to the entertainment and the company.

"Mr. Collins, welcome! Your table is ready, sir," the hostess greeted them as they entered.

"Do you come here often?" Stacey asked.

He nodded. "A few business associates love eating here whenever they come into town." He put his hand at the small of her back, and they followed behind the hostess.

Stacey was relieved to hear that he'd been here with colleagues of his and not dates. As they entered the restaurant, Stacey took in the Middle Eastern style decor. The dining area was dimly lit, and the walls were adorned with a gold and red Middle Eastern pattern. The chairs sat only a few inches off the floor, and most of the seating was aligned against the wall with circular tables in front, leaving a large empty space in the center of the dining area that was covered in Persian rugs. Stacey figured the empty space was for the performers to dance and entertain the guests.

"You picked the perfect time. Our dancers begin at eight pm, so you have a little time to sit, talk, and order before the entertainment starts," the hostess gushed. "I'll send your waitress right over," she beamed before turning and leaving.

Andre helped Stacey into one of the seats along the wall, then moved to the opposite side of the table to sit.

"I've been wanting to come here for a while now," Stacey said. "I've heard great things about this restaurant."

A moment later, their waitress approached their table. "Hi, I'm Dominique and I'll be your waitress for the evening. Did you want to start with anything to drink?" she asked pleasantly.

Andre turned his gaze on Stacey. "Is there anything you don't drink?"

She smiled at his consideration of her drinking habits. "No, but I am partial to red wine."

"Great, then let's go with the bottle of your Dom Perignon," he told the waitress, handing her back the menu.

"How was your studying? Did you get everything done?" he asked when the waitress left.

Stacey took a sip of water their waitress had brought to the table. "Yes, I did. Thank you for asking." She smiled.

"Tell me about school. How much longer do you have to complete?" he asked sitting back in his chair.

Stacey smiled brightly. She'd been on a number of dates where the men barely seemed to take an interest in her. Instead opting to talk about themselves, not once asking her about her career ambitions.

"I'm actually in my last semester at Georgia State," she explained.

"And you'll have both your bachelor's and master's when you're done?" he asked staring at her as if she were the only person in the room.

"Um hm." She nodded. This was the part she hesitated explaining to most people. She knew that at twenty-eight, just getting one's bachelor's degree seemed a little late to some.

Andre cocked his head to the side as if trying to figure something out. "Please tell me you didn't go to college right after high school," he leveled a serious look at her.

Stacey smiled. She realized he was trying to discern just how old she was. She shook her head. "No, I uh, took a few years off between high school and college. Well, I took classes here and there, which is why I was able to complete my bachelor's in just over three and half years," she said happily.

"Your last semester. You've got to be excited about that," he said.

"I am, but enough about me tell me about you," she said changing the subject.

For a minute, Andre looked as if he wasn't going to allow her to change the subject. Eventually, he leaned in closer and propped his arms on the table. "What do you want to know?" he asked, staring deeply into her eyes. The intensity of his gaze shot all the way to Stacey's core. The way he looked at her had a way of making her feel completely exposed in a room full of people.

Thankfully, the stare off was interrupted when the waitress brought their wine and took their orders.

"So, you were asking about me," Andre asked after swallowing a bite of his grilled quail.

"Yes, tell me about you, Mr. Collins," Stacey teased taking a bite of her own shrimp kebab.

He shrugged. "Not much to tell. I grew up in Atlanta, went to school, and work at the company my father started," he said dismissively as if being the CFO of a huge financial conglomerate was no big deal.

It was Stacey's turn to cock her head to the side. "That's it? You grew up in Atlanta, went to college at Stanford, and now work at one of the most successful financial companies in the country?"

Andre smirked cockily. "I see I'm not the only one who's been asking questions." He laughed. "What else did you find out about me?" he asked, as if he just knew she'd been thinking about him just as much as he'd been thinking of her.

"That you're a consummate playboy," she let slip out her mouth before she had a chance to stop herself. She absolutely did not want him thinking she was spying on him or she was some sort of jealous woman.

Andre just grinned that cocky grin of his. "Oh yeah? Is that a problem?" he asked.

Stacey shrugged in an attempt to appear casual. "Not really. It's not like we're a couple or anything. This is only our first date—

"But not our last," he said cutting her off. "And just to be upfront, I date, but I'm always honest about what I do and when I'm with one person, I'm with them. And I don't share," he said that last part staring her directly in her eyes.

"Oh, okay. Well, glad you cleared that up," she murmured taking a sip of her wine to moisten her suddenly dry throat.

For the next few minutes, Andre and Stacey made chit chat about their careers and hobbies. Andre discovered that Stacey had been doing burlesque for about five years now. She sometimes traveled to different cities to perform, but school kept her pretty busy so she didn't have as much time to travel and perform as she would have liked. She told Andre that she'd been born in the Bronx, New York, but she'd moved down to Savannah, Georgia when she was twelve.

For his part, Andre opened up about growing up in Atlanta, going to private school and attending board meetings with his father and brother from the time he was six years old.

"No way! You're lying. You were not six years old dressed in a business suit at a board meeting," Stacey laughed.

"You think I'm kidding, I've got the pictures to prove it. My father swore there was no way in hell he was going to raise some spoiled rich kids who didn't know their asshole from their assets. He started us out early." He shrugged.

"Well, it definitely paid off. It's obvious you and your brother are very good at what you do. I bet he would be proud," Stacey said sincerely.

A look passed over Andre's face that Stacey couldn't quite place, but it tugged at her heart strings nonetheless. She'd lost both her parents relatively young, but could only muster real sadness for the loss of her mother. Without a conscious thought, she reached across the table and grabbed his hand. She watched as his expression changed. Even in the dimly lit restaurant, she could see his gaze darken as it zeroed in on her hand resting in his. When his eyes turned to her, Stacey's breath caught at the expression of emotion she saw there.

Andre gripped her hand and stroked the inside of her palm with his thumb. It was as if his mere touch served to increase her core temperature. Her heart rate picked up as his thumb continued to draw small circles around her wrist. Before she knew it, Andre released her hand, pushed his chair back and stood, coming over to her side of the table. Wide-eyed, she stared wondering what he was going to do next. When he looked like he was going to sit down, Stacey scooted over to give him some space. He sat so close to her she was practically in his lap.

"Show's starting soon," he said by way of explanation and giving her a wink.

Stacey had barely noticed the group of women who'd entered the dining area dressed in brightly colored, long, flowing satin skirts and tops that showed of much of their mid-sections, adorned with a series of rhinestones and jewelry. The volume of the music rose, and most of the diners grew silent, preparing to watch the show.

Stacey felt Andre's thigh brush against hers and her breath hitched. She could feel the strength in the muscles of his leg and fought like hell to not lean into him. Her battle was lost when he leaned back and threw his arm around her shoulders possessively. Instinctively, her body molded into his as if it belonged there. She inhaled his cologne which she recognized as Clive Christian 1872. While the cologne was a mix of spice and citrus, there was a scent she knew only belonged to Andre.

"It may not be quite as good as the show you put on the other night, but it's pretty entertaining," Andre leaned down and whispered in her ear as the women began dancing, causing shivers to run down her spine.

Stacey simply nodded her head and tried to focus on the dancers, even as Andre's fingers lightly caressed her up arm. In short order, Stacey found herself tucked into Andre's side but clapping to the beat of the music and enjoying the show. The women gyrated their hips and moved their midsections as if they were boneless. As a lover of all kind of dance, Stacey could appreciate passion it took to spend years practicing moves and skills to make them look effortless to the crowd. The crowd was in awe and a collective gasp washed through the diners as one of the belly dancers emerged balancing a sword that was set on fire on one end, on top of her head.

"Oh wow," she whispered to Andre, giddy with awe as they watched the woman lower herself down to the floor, moving her arms rhythmically in front of her dipping her head back until the flame almost touched the floor, then waving her body back upright. Stacey was in awe. She always became riveted when watching skilled dancers.

When Andre looked down at her through dark lashes, she smiled up at him in appreciation. She realized he probably brought her to this restaurant because she would appreciate the entertainment. He couldn't have been more correct. Without thinking, she reached up and pressed a kiss to his cheek. His consideration of what she would like warmed her heart. First the flowers that were her favorite, and now this wonderful date. For long moments, they stared in each other's eyes, forgetting everyone else in the room.

Suddenly Stacey felt someone touch her hand. She looked up to see one of the dancers encouraging her to the dance floor. She looked around to see all the dancers were at tables encouraging some of the female patrons to the dance floor. Stacey hesitated.

"Go ahead. Show 'em what you got," Andre urged her on.

The dancer, a beautiful woman with creamy, tanned skin and long dark hair, dressed in a green satin skirt and midriff top, pulled Stacey to the floor. Stacey immediately recognized Shakira's *Ojos Así* playing, and began to clap in time with the music. Before she knew it, she lifted her arms wide, stood on the balls of her feet and began bending and straightening her knees causing her hips to move in a shimmy. The dancer at her side smiled brightly and removed her waist belt, placing it around Stacey's hip. The hip scarf with gold coins began to dance relentlessly against Stacey's hips as she moved. She planted her left foot in front of her and began lifting and lowering her right hip in another famous belly dance move. At this point, even the other belly dancers and diners began watching her. She was a natural. She moved along to the music, mimicking the moves of the other dancers, laughing and clapping.

When Stacey looked back at the table where Andre sat, she saw he was riveted. His sole focus was on her and the movement of her body. A shiver ran down her core as they stared in one another's eyes and she danced only for him. When he licked his lips, Stacey felt the moisture pool in her panties. Not wanting to play too easy to get, she turned and shimmied, moving her body in a snake-like motion. When she threw a look back at Andre over her shoulder, she saw the look of promise in his eyes and shuddered.

Before long, the song ended, and she removed the hip scarf, handing it back to the dancer.

"You were very good," the woman gushed.

"Thank you, but you are fantastic in your own right," she complimented the woman, and headed back to her table.

As soon as she was within a foot of Andre, she felt his hand encircle her wrist and pull her down onto his lap. His arms wrapped around her waist, trapping her there. She couldn't help but laugh.

"I didn't know you belly-danced too," he said, his lips grazing the skin by her ear.

"There's a lot you don't know about me," she teased.

"I damn well intend to find out everything," he said right before his lips collided with hers.

Stacey sighed at the feel of his lips on hers. This was only their second kiss, but she was sure she was becoming addicted to his lips.

Again, Andre took control of the kiss, allowing his tongue to touch and explore every crevice of her mouth. He tasted of the wine they'd had with dinner and a taste that was unidentifiable, but addictive nonetheless. Andre moved his lips from hers and placed a small kiss to the corner of her mouth.

"We need to go." He shifted to pull out his wallet while still keeping one arm locked around Stacey's waist.

Stacey was still caught up in a haze from their kiss, and barely had time to register his words before Andre was thrusting his card into their waitress' hand. He quickly pulled out a handful of bills, tossed them on the table for the tip and stood, bringing Stacey with him. He helped her put on the grey shawl she'd brought to keep her warm as the weather was cooling down now that it was almost mid-September. When the waitress brought back his card, Andre quickly signed the receipt before placing it on the table with the bills, grabbed Stacey's hand, and practically dragged her out of the restaurant.

"Where are we going now?" she asked as she glanced at his tight grip on the steering wheel.

"Somewhere I can maul you in peace," he admitted.

Stacey gasped at his forwardness. "Maul me? What are you a lion?"

He looked at her out of the corner of his eye. "You have no idea," he growled.

Oh shit, Stacey thought as her stomach muscles tightened. It only took one look down towards Andre's lap to see he was clearly aroused and...big. Stacey swallowed a lump in her throat. Was she even ready to have sex with Andre? It had been a long time since she had been intimate with a man outside of some heavy petting.

Within minutes, they were pulling up to the parking lot of her building. Andre parked, rushed out his car door, and hurried to her door to open it before Stacey could even remove her seatbelt. When they reached the door to her condo, Andre took the keys from Stacey's hand and pressed her back against the door. He leaned over, his lips lightly touching hers.

"Invite me in," he said just above a whisper.

"Um, uh," Stacey sputtered. She couldn't think with his lips on hers. "I'm not sure—"

"I won't do anything you don't want me to. Invite me in," Andre insisted, cutting off her response with a kiss to her lips.

Hesitating, Stacey stared into his eyes. Though she wasn't sure how far she was ready to go with Andre just yet, something in his eyes told her she was safe with him. "Come in," she whispered.

Before the words were even out of her mouth, Andre had inserted her key in the lock and opened the door. Stacey entered, Andre following closely. She flicked on the lights.

"Um, do you want something to drink?" she asked. "I have water, tea, and coffee."

"Some coffee would be great. Black," he told her as he strolled to her living room area.

Stacey's shoulders' sagged in relief. Some distance between them was exactly what she needed to think clearly. She busied herself by preparing a couple of cups of coffee with her Keurig.

"I know you said black, but I brought creamer and sugar just in case," she called as she entered the living room.

He stood admiring her the books on her coffee table. When he saw her carrying the tray he strolled over, casually took the tray from her, and placed it on the table.

"Thank you," he said, lifting a coffee mug to his lips and sipping.

Stacey watched as his lips wrapped around the edge of the mug, and instantly her core grew warm. She bent picking up the mug and creamer, needing to distract herself from watching the movement of his lips.

Andre bent, picking up the book that laid on top of the magazines on her coffee table. "*A Life in Motion*. Misty Copeland. You're a fan?" he asked referring to her autobiography he held in his hand.

Stacey's lips quirked up into a reverent smile as she nodded. "She's marvelous," she said, smiling at the petite woman who stood *en pointe* in the photograph on her book cover. Stacey not only had the hard-cover version, but the e-book on her Kindle. She'd read the book at least three times and often reread her favorite excerpts.

"How long did you dance ballet?" Andre asked, bringing Stacey back from her reverie.

Her eyes widened. "How did you know?"

"You move like not even gravity itself can hold you down. You can dance just about any version of dance there is. Grace and poise pour out of you without you even trying. The same type of poise I've seen from some of the best ballerina dancers in the world as they performed on stage at the Met. How long were you a ballerina?"

Stacey was shocked. She had no idea he'd watched her so closely, but he seemed to know her without her telling him.

"From the age of two," she said answered.

"Until?" he asked with a raised eyebrow.

"A few years ago," she said bringing her coffee mug to her lips. Her former life wasn't one she opened up about easily. She lowered her mug and stared down into the light brown liquid, not wanting to think about how painful the end of her ballet career had been.

Noticing the far off look on her face, Andre put his own mug and the book down, and plucked Stacey's coffee cup out of her hand.

"Come here," he said pulling her to him. He nuzzled her neck with his nose, inhaling deeply.

"Have I told you how fucking good you smell?" His words brought on another shiver.

"No, but feel free to tell me," she joked. She felt the rumble in Andre's chest against her hand as he chuckled.

"You smell like the sweetest ambrosia ever created. I wonder if your lips taste as sweet," he said before taking her lips once again. He pulled her down onto her couch, pressed her back into the couch and covered her with his body.

Stacey felt his kiss all the way to her toes. She let her hands run up and down his strong back before she brought them to cup his face. She allowed her fingers to scrape against the hairs of his beard.

Andre pulled back, staring down at her. "Those lips are sweet, but they're not the lips I was talking about." The look he gave Stacey caused a saturation around the very lips he referred to. Moving swiftly, Andre eased himself down Stacey's body and moved his hands up her thighs under her dress until he reached her heated core.

"I want to taste you here." He cupped her wet mound.

At the touch of his hand on her so intimately, Stacey moaned and spread her legs wider. She saw the look in Andre's eyes as he bent his head while lifting her dress up her waist. In that moment, Stacey didn't care about how long she'd known Andre, or whether or not this was just a one-time thing for him. She wanted what his eyes were promising.

He bent his head and grasped the edge of her black lace panties with his teeth, pulling them down her thighs all the while keeping his eyes on hers. When he completely removed her panties, instead of discarding them on the floor, he stuffed them in his back pocket and winked at her.

"I like souvenirs," he said.

Stacey nearly came from wanton expression in his face. "Andre," she moaned just above a whisper.

"Louder," he demanded, dipping his head lower.

Stacey blinked, "Wha-what?" she asked.

"Say my name louder," he commanded just before he let his lips make contact with her pussy lips.

"Ooh," Stacey gasped when she felt his fingers spread her labia, and his tongue made first contact with her throbbing clit.

Andre must have liked what he tasted because as soon as he made first contact, he ate her like a man starving. He sucked and allowed his mouth to make love to her most sensitive spot, causing Stacey to see stars.

"Andre!" she yelled as her back arched off the couch. She could barely keep her hips still.

"That's it. Call my name," he encouraged in between licks. He began making a figure eight motion with his tongue before he drew her clit completely into his mouth. He rolled it between his lips before releasing it, and diving in for more. When he felt Stacey's thighs tremble, he knew she was close. He doubled his efforts and soon, he felt the dam open as her orgasm shot through her.

"Ahhh, Andre!" she shouted.

Andre licked and slurped all her juices before diving in for more. He had no intention of stopping at just one orgasm. He slid one finger into her wet pussy while he let his mouth continue its assault on her still trembling core. He moaned against her pussy lips, enjoying eating her out just as much as she was.

"Andre, I can't. Nooo," she moaned, trying to push his head away, feeling as if a second orgasm might kill her.

Andre pushed her hand away and placed a strong hand on her hips to keep her from moving away. He had every intention of seeing her come again. He licked, and inserted a second finger into her wetness.

"Shit, you're so tight," he growled. He pumped his fingers in and out of her while he allowed his mouth to eat her. Andre sucked and ate her until he felt the now familiar tremble of her thighs.

"Aaaanndreee!" Stacey gasped as she came again.

Not until the last tremor passed through her did Andre finally pull back. He sat up and looked down on her with heavily lidded gaze.

"I knew your taste would be addictive," he said as he leaned down so his lips hovered just above hers.

When she opened her mouth, allowing him access, Stacey could taste herself on him. The moans coming from Andre's mouth turned her on more than she thought possible. She was ravenous and wanted to have him inside her, but Andre pulled back.

He lowered her dress, straightening it for her, before he stood and adjusted himself. Stacey could see from the sizeable bulge in his pants that he was just as turned on. Instead of unbuttoning his pants however, he pulled Stacey up from the couch.

He pulled her into him and stared down into her amber colored eyes for a long moment before placing a tender kiss to her lips. "Walk me to the door, babe," he said placing his arm around her waist.

"What, but you—" she was cut off by his kiss.

"I plan on writing my name on every inch of your delectable pussy. Just not tonight. You're not ready."

Stacey stood there stunned, staring in his eyes that had now darkened to almost a navy blue. She found she could stare in his eyes all day.

"I have a business dinner tomorrow, but are you free Wednesday night?" he asked, breaking into her thoughts.

Stacey shook her head, causing a few of her twists to fall free from her braid. "No, I work Wednesday evenings from five to ten," she said looking at him. Stacey watched as his brows furrowed.

"That's late." His concern was obvious. "Where do you work? Do you always get out so late?"

Stacey was surprised by the concern she saw etched on his face. His brows furrowed and his gaze narrowed on her eyes. The desire she saw there only moments before was now underscored with worry.

"Um, I teach yoga and a pole dancing class a couple of days a week. Wednesday is my late class," she told him.

"So, you don't get out until well after dark every Wednesday?" he asked.

Stacey nodded. "Yes, but I've done it for more than a year—"

"Anything could happen. What studio do you teach at?"

Stacey's eyebrows raised. "Why, you thinking of taking up pole dancing?" she joked.

Andre's face remained serious. "No, it could be dangerous getting out so late. Is there security at this studio?" he asked glaring at her.

Stacey rolled her eyes. "No and it's fine. I've never had a problem. I carry pepper spray in my purse." She smirked at him hoping he'd lighten up.

"Gimme your phone," he said, ignoring her little quip.

"For what?" Stacey wanted to know.

"I'm going to program my number in it and you'll call me before you leave the studio and talk to me on your way out, so I know you're safe," he said looking around for her purse.

Stacey remained stunned.

"Your phone," Andre insisted.

Stacey could tell by the look in his eyes that he was very serious about calling her to make sure she got home safely. She knew he wasn't leaving without getting assurances from her that she'd call him. Stacey stepped around Andre and proceeded to the kitchen where she'd placed her purse. Pulling out her phone, she entered the passcode and passed it to Andre who was right behind her.

Andre entered his number and immediately dialed his own so he had her number.

"Now that that's out of the way, we're on for Thursday instead. We can have an early dinner and do something afterwards. I'll pick you up at six," he told her before reaching down to pull her into his arms. Pressing a quick kiss to his lips, he took another moment to stare down into her eyes before releasing her and turning towards the door.

"Don't forget to lock up behind me," he said over his shoulder.

Stacey followed him to the door. "Okay, and text or call me when you get in. Just so I know you got in safely," she instructed.

Andre turned and smirked at her. "Will do," he said before stealing another kiss and heading out the door.

Stacey watched as he strolled down the hall, his head held high and one hand in his pocket as if he owned the world. Just before he stepped onto the elevator, he turned and winked at her, sending a jolt of arousal through her body. She closed her eyes, inhaling deeply and remembering the bliss he'd just given her with his skilled mouth. It wasn't until long after she stepped back into her condo, closed, and locked her door did she realize the reason for his smile as his hand rested in his pocket. He'd left with her panties.

CHAPTER 6

"Forty-dollars a share? Come one, Dre. That's highway robbery!" Jennings insisted, spilling a few drops of his scotch on the sleeve of his dark grey suit jacket as they dined over their steak dinner.

Jennings had called Andre's office numerous times after Andre and his team walked out on him almost two weeks ago. Andre had ignored his calls until this week. Jennings finally seemed to come to his senses and realized how much he needed this deal. Now, Andre found himself at dinner with Jennings and two attorneys, each from either side of the aisle trying to broker this deal. Andre told his own lawyer beforehand he was not buying Jennings & Co. for more than forty dollars a share, especially since he'd found out the depth of the company's debt since the younger Jennings took over.

"Maybe we should speak with Nikola about this. I mean, he is the CEO," Jennings tried one last time to press his luck.

This asshole just doesn't learn, Andre chuckled to himself. This was a tactic a few other potential business partners had tried with Andre. They figured since Nikola was the CEO, and Andre the CFO, Nik's opinion had more weight. They tried to go over Andre's head. What they didn't know, and what Jennings was soon to find out, was that speaking to Andre was just as good as speaking to Nik. Both brothers owned an equitable share in the company's shares. Andre held just as much weight as Nikola in the running of Excel.

"Oh, really? You think that's a good idea? Let's call him right now," Andre said removing his phone from his pocket.

"What are you doing?" Jennings asked, the once brash look on his face dropping.

"I'm calling the CEO of Excel so he can tell you exactly what the fuck I just told you." Andre sent Jennings a glare before staring down at his phone to dial Nikola.

Jennings must have sensed that Andre wasn't bluffing because he soon changed his tone. "I-I don't think that's necessary," he said, his shoulders now slumping a bit.

"Why? 'Cause you know that forty-dollars a share is generous and that you have no other choice?" Andre asked, placing the phone to his ear as it rang.

"I just think the company is worth more than that," Jennings defended.

"Oh right, like you knew your company's earnings last year? You and I both know you're full of shit. You wouldn't be here if you didn't need this deal. You know it, I know it, and the expression on your lawyer's face tells me he knows it," Andre said, motioning towards the man sitting at the right of Jennings whose face was turning an interesting shade of red. "Cut the shit. Sign the papers so we can all go home," Andre finished just as Nikola answered the phone.

"What?" Nikola answered, seeing it was his brother on the line.

"Well, hello to you too," Andre stated sarcastically as he watched Jennings' expression turn to one of resignation, just before he picked up the pen that sat in the middle of the table.

Jennings began going through the paperwork and signing where his signature was required, finally sealing the deal.

"Hello, Andre. Got any news for me?" Nikola asked just as sarcastically as Andre's previous response had been.

"Yup, just wanted to let you know the Jennings deal is done for forty a share." He sat back, brought his own drink of scotch on the rocks to his lips, and stared over the brim at Jennings.

"Good. I've got some bedtime stories to go read. Bye," Nikola said abruptly hanging up the phone.

Andre chuckled again as he hung up the phone. "Nik, says it was a pleasure doing business with you," he said putting his phone back in his pocket. "I'll have my attorney file the paperwork and send you the copies once they're all filed. Now, if you'll excuse me," Andre said gathering the signed documents, sticking them in his briefcase and standing.

"So, you're just going to rush off?" Jennings asked looking half shocked, half angered.

Andre was too preoccupied to care. He'd spent months on this deal to almost have that time wasted by a spoiled rich kid whose father was probably rolling over in his grave right now. Andre was about business, and now that business was over, it was time to go.

"Sure am. I'm sure I won't be missed. I've left my tab open with the waitress, tip included, so enjoy yourselves on me. Night, gentlemen," Andre finished, adjusting his silver suit jacket, shaking hands with all the men at the table and heading out.

Andre missed the look of contempt Jennings threw his way as he left.

On his way out the restaurant, Andre's cell rang. Retrieving his phone from his pocket, he saw it was Maria calling and immediately hit the ignore button. He scrolled through his contacts to call the other woman he was itching to speak with.

"Didn't you just get off the phone with my husband?"

Andre could hear the smile in Devyn's voice as she answered the phone. "Sure did, and he's a poor conversationalist," he responded and smiled at Devyn's laughter on the other end.

"What's up?" she asked.

"I need a favor," he said, tossing his briefcase in the passenger seat and sliding in behind the steering wheel.

"What do you need?" she asked skeptically.

"I know it's gonna cost me, but I need some very important information about a certain someone," he hedged.

"I was wondering when this call was gonna come. What do you want to know about Stacey and what are you willing to give up to get it?" she asked.

"How's a free weekend of babysitting services sound?"

"Sounds like you really want this information. Tell me what you want to know first and I'll tell you my answer," she hedged.

"Alright..." he began as he pulled out of the restaurant's parking lot and pointed his car in the direction of his condo.

* * *

STACEY PUSHED through the glass door of the dance studio, reaching one hand in her bag to pull out her phone as she turned to lock the door with the set of keys in her other hand.

"Get home safe, Stace," one of her dance students called as she walked to her car.

"Thanks, you too, Tasha." Stacey waved as she pressed the name of the person she intended to call. As the phone began to ring, she heard a noise not too far from her own car, which she'd just reached.

"Calling me?" she heard someone say over her shoulder. Gasping, she turned ready to either strike or run until she saw who it was.

"Andre! You nearly scared me half to death! What are you doing here?" she asked, blowing out a relieved breath.

"You're late," he frowned, ignoring her question.

Stacey cocked her head to the side, staring up at him perplexed. "Class ran over a little bit. Again, what are you doing here?" she said placing her hand on her hip.

Stacey noticed the frown on his face as he took in their surroundings. The neighborhood they were in wasn't particularly bad, but it was somewhat reclusive and the lighting wasn't the best. Stacey watched as Andre's frown deepened when he took in the pair of leggings she wore, and the workout t-shirt she threw over the half shirt she wore during class.

"You come out alone every Wednesday night?" he asked, that same concern from the other night etched on his face.

"I told you it's not that bad. And how did you know where I taught?" she asked again.

"I have my ways," he answered. "Are you going home now?"

"Why?" she asked, irritated he wasn't giving straight answers.

"I want to take you somewhere," he said.

Stacey's face scrunched in confusion. "It's late, isn't it? And I'm not dressed to go out anywhere," she said motioning towards her outfit. "And you still haven't answered any of my questions."

"I know this really good ice cream spot that's open pretty late. I can drive there, bring you back when we're done, and follow you home to make sure you get in safely," he reassured her.

"Ice cream?" she asked.

"They have really great butter pecan," he said smirking.

She could tell he'd done his research. Butter pecan was her favorite ice cream and she always kept at least one pint in her freezer throughout the year. She felt kind of silly being so suspicious of him now. The man already knew where she lived and had already had his face buried between her legs. It was probably a little too late to play coy now.

"Okay, but it better be as good as you say," she said, lowering her car keys into her bag and allowing Andre to escort her to his car.

As they drove, Andre asked Stacey how class was and how long she'd been teaching pole dancing and yoga. She told him she'd been teaching for a couple of years, but her hours had decreased now that she was interning as part of her last semester requirements.

At the ice cream parlor, Stacey ordered her butter pecan while Andre went with his favorite mint chocolate chip. Andre asked her about her internship and the career she planned to pursue after completing school. She told him she wanted to work in as a mental health counselor specializing in eating disorders. While she told him a little about her current internship, she avoided going into detail about the special significance the location held for her. They were just getting to know each other, and it took her a while to warm up to most people. She hadn't even shared all the details of her past with Mercedes or Devyn. Unfortunately, some of her early life experiences had taught her to keep people at arm's length. It was something she continued to work on with her own therapist. Plus, she didn't know how serious Andre was about her. She knew he was interested in her sexually, maybe even more than sexually, but was he interested in a relationship? If so, how serious?

"Ask me."

Stacey looked up from her ice cream to see Andre's penetrating gaze on her. She had to look away, feeling as if he might be able to read her very thoughts.

"Ask you what?" she asked.

"You were just wondering what was going on between us. What I want from you, right?" he asked nonchalantly.

"How do you know what I was thinking? I could have been wondering about the exam I have later this week," she defiantly stated.

"But you weren't, were you?" he asked using his finger to tilt her chin so she had nowhere to look but into his eyes.

"No," she answered honestly. "Okay then, what's going on between us?"

"Isn't it obvious?" he asked.

"Yes. I mean no. I just...are we dating are you just looking for some fun? A few nights in your bed and then you're on to the next woman? I'm not asking you to declare us in a relationship or anything because we just met and this is like, only our second time out together, but what happened between us the other night is not something I usually do. I mean, not on the first date. Hell, not even on the tenth date with most men I've been out with. And I know that's something some women say to not make themselves appear *hoish* or whatever, but it's true. Anyway, all I'm asking is...hell I don't know what I'm asking," she finished, worrying her bottom lip.

She looked up expecting to see Andre staring at her as if she were crazy after that rant, but he wore a sideways grin on his gorgeous face. Stacey didn't know if she was more annoyed at the delight she saw on his face or turned on at the way his eyes glinted with mischief.

She'd bet more than one woman had lost their entire soul just by looking in those eyes for too long.

Andre gripped Stacey's chin between his thumb and forefinger, and pulled her in to meet his lips. He methodically outlined her lips with his tongue before urging them apart to take her mouth in a mouthwatering kiss. The now-familiar tingles of arousal that were only brought on by this man began to oscillate in her belly. Stacey threw her arms around his neck, needing to gain more contact.

"Mmm." She moaned at the feeling of his tongue stroking hers, forgetting all about the other patrons in the ice cream shop.

Andre pulled back from the kiss, allowing his lips to graze hers. "You feel that?" he asked, his fingers still holding her chin in place.

"Yes." She nodded.

"That's all you need to remember about what's going on between us," he said before dipping his head to take her lips in another breath-stealing kiss. When he finally released her lips for much needed oxygen, Stacey was so dazed she forgot all about her previous thoughts.

"Come on, let's get you home before it gets too late," Andre said as he stood, bringing Stacey with him.

"You still haven't told me how you found out where I worked at," Stacey said as she pushed her key into her door lock, an hour later.

"And I'm not going to," he smirked, pressing a kiss to her cheek and pushing her door open wider. "Go inside and don't forget to lock it and put the chain on the door," he insisted.

Stacey gave him an, "are you serious" look. "You know, I was born and grew up in the Bronx and I've lived by myself for many years now. I don't need you to remind me to lock my doors. Plus, I've got a mean right hook. My sister taught me to fight," she joked.

"Your sister, huh? I'm sure your right hook is not to be messed with. Still, don't forget to lock the door," he reminded her again.

Stacey sighed and shook her head, stepping in her apartment.

"See you tomorrow night," Andre said referring to their date. When he heard the click of the door lock and the rattling of the chain as she put it on the hinge, he strolled down the hall smirking. When he stepped off the elevator, his cell phone buzzed. It was a text from Stacey asking him to text her when he got in to let her know he got home safely. Andre's smile deepened at the message. Few women he dated asked him to check-in with them. Truthfully, he would have balked at the idea had it been any other woman, but the thought of Stacey being concerned about him didn't draw the same ire for relationships and attachments he'd become accustomed to.

When he arrived home, he willingly sent the text letting her know he was home before heading for the shower. Climbing into bed thirty minutes later, he was happy to see she'd responded, letting him know she'd waited up for his message. Andre was more satisfied with this knowledge than he cared to admit. That night he drifted off to sleep with a smirk on his face and an image of Stacey's succulent, slightly swollen lips right after he'd kissed her.

CHAPTER 7

ring! Bring!

Stacey knew there was only one person bold enough to call her before eight am on a Saturday morning. Even her aunt never called her this early.

"Morning, sis," Stacey yawned into the phone.

"Did I wake you?" Stacey's sister, Coral asked innocently.

Stacey knew it was all a show. Coral knew good and goddamn well her sister usually slept in later on Saturdays and she had a habit of always waking her. Even years ago when Stacey was dancing ballet and she'd had performances late into the night on Fridays, Coral would call early on Saturdays just to catch up. The one reason Stacey obliged her sister's call was because she hardly ever knew where in the world her sister was. Though Coral wasn't as guarded of her whereabouts these days, she rarely remained in one place for too long.

"No, I'm always awake at," Stacey paused and pulled her cell from her ear to check the time, "six-thirty in the morning on a Saturday," she said sarcastically around another yawn.

"Oh, good then I didn't wake you," Coral answered sweetly. "Tell me what's new," Coral retorted ignoring her sister's clear annoyance.

Despite herself, Stacey half-smiled a she stretched in bed. Her sister was one of a kind and had been the mother to her they'd never had growing up. She was her first protector and confidant even when Coral herself was young and should have been protected from the very person she protected Stacey from.

"Let's see," Stacey said, sitting back against the white tufted headboard of her queen-sized bed. "Classes are going well. I only have two actual classes this semester, but my internship counts as six credits," she supplied happily.

"And how's the internship going?" Coral asked a hint of worry in her voice.

Stacey knew to be nothing short of honest with her sister. The woman could read her like a book. Heck, she could read most people like a book, which was what made her so valuable when she worked in army intelligence and her jobs afterwards.

"It's going well. The women I work with have been through so much, you know? I just want to make sure I am giving them the services they need." Stacey had spent the last month interning as a clinical counselor at a major center for eating disorders.

"I understand. I know no one can help those women like you since you probably know their struggle better than anyone," Coral stated sincerely. "And how are you feeling being back there?"

At that question, Stacey rested the phone between her head and shoulder, and placed both hands in her lap. She absentmindedly began rubbing her thumb over the tiny scar on her hand. If Coral had seen the faraway look on her face, she would have known her sister was thinking back to a time when she was on the receiving end of help instead of being the one providing the help.

As it stood, the silence spoke volumes and Stacey's perceptive sister understood what hadn't been said out loud.

"I know it can be tough. No one expects you to be a robot. If you're not feeling up to being back th—"

"No, no, it's not that," Stacey said cutting her sister off. "I wouldn't change it for the world. It's just taking a little getting used to. I'm fine.

And I've been talking about it with Linda. It's just a process," Stacey admitted.

"Okay, but you'll let me know if it gets too much, right?" her sister warned.

Stacey sighed. "Of course," she promised. Stacey knew her sister would be there for her if she needed anything. Though she was feeling strong now and didn't feel as if she needed big sis to come to her rescue any longer, it felt good knowing someone as strong and capable as Coral had her back. Strangely enough, this thought made her think of Andre and she smiled.

It'd been two weeks since their first date and she was supposed to have dinner with him tonight before her performance at the Black Kitty. They'd been out numerous times and had talked or texted on the phone daily. For their third date, he'd taken her out to eat at a delicious steakhouse and then they'd played a few rounds of miniature golf. It had been Stacey's first time playing and Andre had graciously showed her how to swing her clubs properly, although Stacey was sure his instruction was due more to wanting to feel her up, which he'd done plenty of. Presumptuous as he was in the liberties he took in kissing her or grabbing at her, she didn't mind. Every touch sent a warming sensation through her body and inflamed her senses. She even looked forward to his showing up at her job every Wednesday evening to escort her home. It now turned into their late night ice cream tradition in which he then followed her home, and walked her to the door to make sure she got in safely. Stacey sighed thinking about the way he'd kissed her just last night after he reminded her to lock and put the chain on her door.

"Oh shit, I know that sigh. Spill it," Coral said bringing Stacey back to the present moment. "What's his name?" she asked.

Can't put anything past Coral Coleman, Stacey thought as she began telling her sister about the new man in her life. She figured telling her sister now would help her avoid Coral showing up at her apartment unannounced, waiting on an explanation when Stacey got home from work one day. It had happened before and Stacey knew Coral wasn't opposed to doing it again, especially if she was concerned about Stacey.

The women spent the next thirty minutes talking and catching up. Stacey told Coral about Andre and how they'd met. When Coral told her she knew Andre's brother and his friend Raul from her army days, Stacey wasn't surprised. Nor was she particularly stunned to learn Coral had worked with Raul since. Stacey was even less surprised to learn that her sister was calling from somewhere in the Caribbean, though she wouldn't be specific. Coral's home base was Savannah, Georgia now that she'd begun working with their two cousins, but she was rarely in Savannah long enough for anyone to consider it her home.

After ending the phone conversation with Coral, Stacey decided against trying to get back to sleep. Instead she got up, dressed only in a pair of white boy shorts and a light pink tank top, and decided to practice on her nine-foot dance pole for a little while.

Clicking on some music, she began doing some basic stretches. When Janet Jackson's No Sleep began playing, she gripped the pole with both arms extended, swinging herself around freely. She spun and performed a number of tricks on the pole feeling weightless the higher she rose on the pole. Stacey discovered pole dancing around the same time she begun burlesque, and both appealed to her love of dance and performance. Poling also helped her keep in shape without putting too much stress on her bad knee. She loved burlesque but performing too much, especially in heels, could cause her old injury to act up which could land her on bed rest for a few days at the least, which was not an option. Thus, Stacey limited her performing to two weekends a month and she mixed them up between dancing in heels, poling, and some ballet sprinkled in for good measure. Although this style of dance and performing was nothing like what she envisioned for herself, after all those years of training and practice, she'd reached a place where she accepted it and was happy where she was in her life.

An hour later when Stacey stepped out of the shower, she had a text message from Andre. Her lips spread into a satisfied grin when she read his message.

Good morning, beautiful. Can't wait to see you later today. Wear something short to show off those killer legs of yours.

Later that evening, Andre was taking Stacey out to dinner before her performance that night. She needed to spend the day studying and preparing some case notes for her internship after her therapy session, but she couldn't let the entire day go by without talking Andre. She decided to tease him a little bit. She snapped a picture of her freshly shaved and moisturized legs she sent him the picture with a message that read:

You mean these legs?

It took only a few moments to get Andre's response.

Yes, those legs spread eagle on my bed and your voice hoarse from yelling my name as my cock makes your pussy mine.

Stacey's entire body stiffened as she read his explicit response. Never had a man been so forthcoming sexually, and never had her body been so responsive. Stacey could feel the evidence of how much his message turned her on by the increasing wetness between her legs. She should have known Andre would pull no punches. If she didn't know she was playing with fire, his next text said it all.

Don't play with fire unless you're looking to get burned, baby. Now, go study.

He had the nerve to end the message with a winky-eyed emoji. Stacey pictured the winking expression he always gave her with that cocky head tilt and her body, once again, spoke to exactly how receptive it was to his wanton talk. She already knew another sexual encounter between them would be explosive. The man ate pussy like it was going out of style. Stacey shivered at the prospect of being in his bed. How the hell was she supposed to go to her therapy session and study with Andre's message now foremost in her mind?

* * *

"THIS IS the second time you've been here in three weeks. Can't stay away?" Nikola asked Andre as he pulled out a chair at his table. Their table sat only a few feet from the stage in the Black Kitty.

"Maybe I have a growing appreciation for the art form?" Andre retorted like the smart ass he was.

"Or for a certain performer," Nikola said looking at Andre over the rim of his glass.

"Mind your business. Raul's not here tonight?" he asked looking around for his brother's friend.

Nikola shook his head. "Not tonight. Mercedes isn't performing."

The two men conversed for a little while about who was performing that night and in what order. Both Devyn and Stacey were performing tonight. Andre watched as the different performers took their turn on stage. Again, he was impressed by their style and appeal but he was most anxious to see Stacey get on stage. Looking around the room, he saw a number of men in the audience hooting and hollering. The thought of those men seeing his Stacey on stage in a few straps of cloth had his jaw tightening. He continued to look around and saw a man off to the side of the stage talking to a few of the other performers. He was video-recording their conversation. Andre sat up in his seat as he took in the scene of the two dancers dressed in short shorts, half-shirts and makeup, being recorded.

"Who's that?" he asked Nikola, not taking his eyes off the man.

"That's Sean. Sean Stevens. He's doing a documentary on the club," Nikola answered, following the direction of Andre's gaze.

"You checked him out?" Andre asked still staring at the sandy-blond haired man.

"You think I'd let someone film in here while my wife is here and I didn't check him out? He's on the up and up," Nikola retorted.

"I want his info," Andre said still not looking at his brother.

"I said he's fine," Nikola responded.

"And I said I want his info," Andre said finally turning his attention back to his brother and leveling a serious look at him.

Nikola's own usually serious face lightened with amusement as he smirked at his younger brother. It was evident to Andre that Nikola was reading more into this than was necessary. He just wanted to make sure the man was who he said he was, with his own eyes. In fact, maybe it was time to go have a talk with this Sean character instead of looking at Nikola's goofy grin.

"I'll be back." Andre stood and left the table before Nikola had a chance to respond.

Andre strolled over to the man, analyzing him. He was about five-nine, and had tanned skin. He wore a pair of casual jeans and a button up shirt. He stood a respectful distance from the women when speaking. He looked at their faces when discussing their burlesque performances. All in all, he acted like a respectable documentarian. Still, this guy might be coming in contact with Stacey, which meant Andre needed to check him out.

"I hear you're doing a documentary on the Black Kitty," Andre said not even bothering to introduce himself. "Sean, right?"

Sean nodded. "Uh, yeah, I am doing a documentary on the club. And you are?"

"Why are you doing a documentary on the club?" Andre asked.

"Um, well," Sean hesitated, obviously thrown by Andre's brusque manner, "there's been a resurgence in the last few decades of burlesque, and the Black Kitty is one of the most popular clubs here in Atlanta. Anyone interested in the goings on in the entertainment industry would be interested."

Andre nodded. "And you have written permission from the owner and all the women you interview right?" he asked in the same tone he would closing a business deal.

"Yes, of course. Diane, uh, Mistress Coco has given her blessing and granted me access, albeit limited access, to her club," Sean answered. "I'm sorry, you are?" he asked.

"Me? Consider me a concerned citizen. Just make sure you're following the rules laid out to you," Andre advised before strolling back to his seat.

"Got what you needed?" Nikola asked over the rim of his beer.

"Maybe. Just make sure you send me that information on him," he reminded Nikola.

Seconds later, the lights dimmed and Mistress Coco emerged from behind the curtain, this time dressed in a gold shimmery dress. Her short, silver locks were pinned back on one side and a large black flower was tucked behind her ear.

"Give it up for our last performer!" she yelled to the applauding crowd. "Now, next to the stage is a young lady whose dancing will set your soul on fire and cripple even the strongest of men! Put your hands together and make some noise for the one...the only...Jazmine Noirrrrr!" Mistress Coco's voice reverberated across the audience as she made her way to the edge of the stage to exit.

Even in the dimly lit room, Andre could make out the grace with which Stacey walked as she entered from the right of the stage carrying a wooden chair. She was dressed in a long, fifties style red dress that flared out at the bottom. Sade's *Is It A Crime* began to play as Stacey took her seat. She began moving her shoulders in time with the music, then lifting a leg, spreading them wide, and closing to tantalize the audience.

Andre sat transfixed as he watched Stacey's fingers trail up her sides to her neck and tug ever so gently at the strings that tied the back of her dress. Standing and gliding across the stage as she teased the audience with a shoulder here and another there, she sat back down with her back to the audience, straddling the chair. Andre's cock stirred in his pants when she slowly let the edges of her dress drop, and he saw the muscles of her back flex with every movement. Tightening his fists, he just barely managed to refrain from rushing the stage and throwing her over his shoulder to take her away from the prying eyes of the men in the room. He knew they were imagining doing things to her only he wanted to do to her.

Andre chanced a sideways glance at his brother and sure enough, a knowing smirk lined his face as he stared back at Andre. *Fuck you,* Andre mouthed to Nikola before turning his attention back to Stacey. By now she was out of her dress and down to a pair of red satin boy shorts and a pair of black and red pasties. As the song ended, she sat in the chair with her back to the audience again and threw her arm up, dipped her head back to create a perfect arch along her spine. Andre was out of his seat before the final notes ended.

When her beautifully lithe body bounded down the stairs in

nothing but a pair of fishnets, short shorts, and pasties, Andre was the first face she saw. He immediately grabbed her in his arms and placed a crushing kiss to her lips. Andre ignored the few gasps he heard from onlookers and deepened the kiss. When his tongue made contact with Stacey's, the entire room disappeared. The tightness in his groin grew and he knew he wouldn't last for much longer. He needed to be inside her now.

"Go get your shit," he demanded as he pulled back from her.

Still stunned by his sudden appearance and that all-consuming kiss, Stacey was speechless. Her hands still latched onto his shoulders, she blinked a few times and looked around. Remembering they were still in the company of the performers and some audience members, Stacey tried to step back but Andre only tightened his grip.

"Andre, I still have to change and I thought we were going to stay to catch the rest of the performers," she tried to remind him of their plans. She should have known by the look in his eyes that he was not changing his mind.

"Plans changed. I'm giving you five minutes to change, grab your stuff, and meet me right here or I'm coming to get you," he said, finally releasing her.

Stacey couldn't ignore the way her pulse increased at his commanding attitude and threats. Still, she refused to make it too easy for him. Placing her hand on her hip, she threw him a serious look of her own. "Andre, you can't just order me around whenever you want—"

"Wrong, baby. I can and will. You now have four minutes or I'm going to turn you around, bend you over on that stage, and give this fucking audience a real damn show," he growled low in her ear.

He took a step forward, allowing his bulging cock to brush against the hood of her pussy. Stacey's breath hitched as she realized just how serious Andre was in following through with this threat.

"F-fine," she stated, trying to sound more confident than she felt. Stepping around Andre, she went towards the direction of the dressing room, ignoring the stares and giggles of the few performers who'd overheard their little exchange. She pulled out the dress she'd worn earlier on her date with Andre and closed her locker. It was a long-sleeved, flowing pink dress with a lace overlay. She stepped into the black, three-inch ankle boots she'd worn earlier, and packed up her discarded costume that had been brought back by one of the stage kittens. She threw her bag over her shoulder and headed out of the locker room towards the bathroom.

"Hey, you're Jazmine aren't you?" she heard a male voice ask behind her as she exited the bathroom. Turning and looking over her shoulder, she saw man only a few inches taller than her approach.

"Yes, I am. Enjoying the show?" she asked casually as the man stepped closer. She figured he was an audience member.

"Oh yeah," he said looking her up and down with a look in his eyes that made her skin crawl.

"Good. Hope you enjoy the rest of the show." She forced a smile and turned to leave, but was stopped when he caught her arm.

"What's the rush sweetie? You performing again tonight?" he asked not letting go of her arm.

"Take your hands off me," she said trying to tug her arm from his grip.

"Why, is there some—uff!"

He grunted as Stacey felt his grip being ripped from her arm. When she turned around, she saw the man slumped on the floor and Andre standing over him, breathing heavy with a dangerous look in his eye.

"Didn't she fucking tell you to take your hands off of her?!" he snarled as he took another threatening step looking as if he was ready to finish the man off.

Stacey's feet remained stuck to the floor, stunned at Andre's anger. He had a cold look in his eye. The stranger was already down on the floor holding his hand up to try and keep Andre at bay, but Stacey knew it was of no use. She watched as he leaned down and grabbed the man by the collar of his button down shirt.

"Next time a woman tells you to take your hands off of her, do it asshole!" he said before pushing the man back into the wall.

Stacey heard loud talking and footsteps behind her.

"What the hell is going on here!?" she heard Mistress Coco's raspy voice demand. She looked at Andre who still looked poised to beat this man to a pulp right in front of Mistress Coco, security and everyone else. Stepping closer to him, she placed a reassuring hand on his arm.

"Andre, it's fine. Just let it go, please," Stacey urged, trying to turn pull Andre away from the man as the club's security guard attempted to intervene. "Come on," Stacey continued to encourage him. Stroking her hand up and down his arm, she felt the tension relieve ever so slightly from his body. He looked down at her with such a blazing fire in his eyes, Stacey shivered. Without saying a word, Andre wrapped his arm around Stacey's waist and guided them down the hallway and out the club without a backwards glance.

* * *

THE MAN, now sporting a swollen and bruised eye, was tossed out of the club. He attempted to convince the bouncers at the Black Kitty that he'd just wanted to talk with Jazmine, but they weren't trying to hear anything he had to say.

"Whatever," he mumbled to himself as he slid behind the wheel of his black sedan. As soon as he closed the door, he knew he wasn't alone in the vehicle. In the next instant, his feeling was confirmed.

"Did you get close to him?" the man in the backseat asked.

"Did I get close to him? What does this fucking look like?" he asked, turning so the man could see his swelling eye in plain sight.

"Shit. I didn't know he'd hit you. So, he's protective of the girl, huh?"

"You fucking think?" the first man nearly shouted. "Listen, you didn't tell me this would require me getting hit. I don't appreciate this shit, Jennings."

"Just calm down. A little bit of ice and you'll be fine in a day or two, but what I just found out could be helpful later on. If the girl is his weakness, I can use her to make him regret the day he ever fucked with me and my family's legacy. Go take care of that eye. I'll be in touch," Jennings threw over his shoulder, unconcerned about the man's injury as he slid from the backseat out the car. Jennings walked briskly to his own car, not wanting to be seen in the parking lot. He climbed in the backseat of his waiting limousine and snickered to himself.

"I'll see you soon, Andre," he mumbled as they pulled off.

CHAPTER 8

"*A*ndre, slow down. I have on heels remember?" Stacey said as Andre half-dragged, half-carried her through the doors of building that housed his top floor condo. When the attendant saw Andre coming through the door, he hit the button for Andre's private elevator. Only Andre and the attendant had the code for the elevator that went directly to his suite

"Good evening, Mr. Collins," the attendant called.

Andre merely nodded to acknowledge the man's greeting, and pulled Stacey onto the elevator. He'd just barely managed to keep his hands off of her as he drove home. Seeing her on stage made him mad with lust and already impatient to take her, but seeing that asshole patron back at the club with his hands on her made him want to both break bones, and bury himself so deep inside her she wouldn't be able to walk straight for the next few days.

He tried to breathe deeply to gain control over himself, but that was a bad decision. All it did was serve to fill his nose with the jasmine-scented perfume she wore. Andre looked down at her amber-colored eyes and his arms moved on their own accord, wrapping around her small waist. He looked down at her arm where that prick had gripped her hand. His hand moved up to massage the spot as if trying to erase the memory of the vision of seeing another man's hand on her.

"I'm okay, really," she said. "But you might need some ice for that hand of yours."

She smiled up at him.

"All I need is you, naked. In my bed," he said before capturing her lips for a soul-stealing kiss. Before he could even enjoy the kiss fully, the elevator dinged, signaling their arrival at his condo. He didn't allow Stacey time to take in the light grey and black modern style furnishings in his condo, the huge floor to ceiling windows, or the black patio chairs that sat in front of those windows. Within seconds, he had Stacey's back pressed against the wall in his living room as he sunk down to his knees. With his face right in front of her mound, he inhaled deeply, smelling her arousal. He reached underneath her dress and pulled at the thong panties she wore. Andre made quick work of discarding the panties then threw one of Stacey's legs over a broad shoulder, pushed her dress up to her hips, and stroked her wet lips with his tongue.

Stacey's hips jerked forward at the contact and she threw her head against the wall, trapped by her leg on Andre's shoulder and his strong arms around her waist.

"Huh, Andre!" she yelped when he picked up her second leg to place over his other shoulder and stood completely, taking her off her feet as he held her against the wall using only his hands and body, her pussy completely open and exposed to him.

"You have the prettiest pussy I've ever seen," his hoarse voice whispered against her labia as he stared at her shaved pussy with such awe.

Stacey creamed at the deep wonder she saw etched in the lines of his face as he stared at her most intimate spot.

When his tongue darted out and licked her from taint to clit, Stacey already felt the first tingles of her climax began to rise. She reached around and placed both hands in Andre's hair urging him on. She soon felt his hot mouth completely cover her as he began sucking her clit, rolling it between his lips before releasing, and doing it all over again. Stacey ground her hips against Andre's face, her senses heightened by the feeling of her inner thighs being tickled by the hairs from his beard.

"Andre, that feels so good!" she moaned, her fingers tightening their grip in his hair.

Andre continued to hum and moan against her pussy, causing tiny vibrations to reverberate through her core. Stacey couldn't hold out much longer and soon she found herself falling over the cliff.

"Ahhhh!" she yelled as she came.

Even as she came, Andre continued to eat her like a man possessed. Before the tremors of her first orgasm ceased, she was already feeling the sensations of another impending orgasm. Andre refused to let her down even as she tried to pull his head away.

"Andre! I-I-Mmmmmmm, AHHHH," she ended her protest on a moan as he did a move with his tongue that made her forget her first name. Her second orgasm was even more powerful than the first. She screamed Andre's name, begging him to stop as she pulled at his hair. Finally, he relented as the final tremors of her orgasm ended.

Andre pulled back slightly, lowering her legs from his shoulder but catching them around his waist.

Now they were at eye level, Stacey could see the lingering wetness that remained on Andre's beard. The gleam of wetness on his lips and beard and the glint in his eyes were irresistible. When he licked his lips and smiled, looking her in the eye, she couldn't keep her mouth off him any longer. This time she was the one moving in for a deep kiss. Their tongues immediately touched, dancing together in a rhythm only made for one another. Stacey felt cool air against her back when Andre pulled her from the wall and began walking with her legs still wrapped around his waist. She assumed to his bedroom. She was so ready.

Stacey heard a "thud" as Andre kicked his bedroom door open, flicked on a light, and proceeded to lay her down on huge bed. Stacey felt as if she was being laid in a bed of clouds when the Egyptian cotton sheets touched her back. She reached up to grab Andre, but he caught her hand and pressed a kiss to the inside of her wrist before releasing it and stepping back.

"I want to see you." Andre's voice was thick with need. "Sit up and remove your dress," he said authoritatively. He continued to glare at her expectantly.

Stacey felt the heat of his gaze on her and felt completely naked already. She let her own gaze drift over his body. She noticed his labored breathing and spotted the very evident bulge in his pants and smiled. She decided to tease him a little bit.

"This dress, you mean?" she asked, sitting up on her knees in the middle of his bed, toying with the edges of her dress. She slowly lifted the edges of her dress, exposing the tops of her thighs, and spread her legs to show the remaining moisture from her previous two orgasms.

"I wouldn't tease me right now if I were you." His voice was low, dangerous.

Stacey heard the warning in his voice and wanted to tease it even more. "Why, lover? Something I should be concerned about?" she asked, turning around so her back was facing him. She reached up and let one hand slowly remove a sleeve of her dress before she stopped, tugging it back up.

"Hm, maybe, I'll ju—Huh!" she gasped, when she heard the sudden ripping of material and found herself lying flat on her back staring up into a pair of passion-filled blue eyes.

"I told you not to tease me. I hope that wasn't one of your favorite dresses," Andre declared before reaching down and capturing her lips before she could answer. Andre let a hand reach under her body and grip the back of her hair, capturing a bunch of her twists in a tight fist. He moved down her jaw before reaching her neck, licking first then sucking at the tender flesh of her neck. Andre used his grip on her hair to pull her head back, exposing more of her neck to his lips.

Stacey moaned at the feeling of his big body on top of hers, while his hand gripped her hair and his lips sent ripples of pleasure through her body. She reach up and began pulling his shirt from his pants, trying to unbutton it. She needed to feel his skin against hers.

But before she could undo the first button, Andre pulled back and sat up to stare down at her. Settling himself in between her legs, he stared down at her breasts heaving up and down. Reaching both hands to cup each breast that fit perfectly into his hand, he looked between both as if he had trouble figuring out which one he wanted to taste first.

"Andre, please!" Stacey moaned, needing him to do something. She saw his smirk as he leaned down, pressing both her breasts together.

"I like it when you beg," he said, looking her directly in the eye right before his tongue snaked out to lick both her nipples. "Do it again," he commanded.

Stacey could do nothing but comply, "Please," she pleaded again just above a whisper. Before she knew it, Andre sucked one of her brown pebbles into his mouth, taking small nips and bites in between sucking, giving her just a hint of pain with her pleasure to heighten the sensations rippling through her. Andre let his hand trail down her toned stomach to reach her slippery core. He inserted two fingers into her, making her back arch up off the bed.

"Aaanndre," she said around a moan, making his already hard as a rock cock stand at complete attention. Andre knew if he didn't get out of his clothes soon, he would likely embarrass himself by coming in his pants. Reluctantly, he withdrew his fingers from her pussy, released her breast, and sat up between her legs. With speed he didn't know he possessed, Andre removed his shirt, throwing it over his shoulder before moving to his pants.

Stacey soon sat up and replaced his hands with her own. "Let me," she said, unbuckling his belt and unzipping his pants. When his cock sprang loose, Stacey gasped at the sheer size of him. She attempted to wrap her hand around him and could barely fit her fingers all the way around. She swallowed nervously. It'd been a long time since she'd had sex and never with anyone this size.

"You'll be okay," he told her, noting the way she stared at his size.

"Andre," she whispered as he pressed his lips against her.

"Are you on birth control?"

"Y-yes."

"Good. I don't want any barriers between us. I've been tested and am clean," he told her.

"I-I haven't been with anyone in a long time and my last test was clean," she told him.

Andre nodded as he captured her wrists, pressing her back into the bed and raising them above her head. When his stiff cock made contact with her wetness, they both groaned. Andre reached down, wrapped his free hand round his hardness, and rubbed the tip of his cock against her lips. With her hands still bound with his much larger one, Stacey could do nothing but jerk her hips forward.

Andre chuckled as he toyed with her. "You want this?" he asked as he smacked his cock against her wet pussy.

"Ahhh," Stacey cried out in agony and frustration. "Dammit Andre, why are you teasing me?" she asked.

"Turnabout is fair play, babe," he reminded her of her teasing from earlier.

Stacey wasn't planning on taking his toying without some payback of her own. She widened her knees, putting her sopping wet pussy on full display. "I'm sooo wet," she moaned. "Take me. Make me--Ahhhh" her words were cut off when Andre inserted himself to the hilt in her passage.

"Shit!" he shouted. "Is this what you wanted?" he asked as he moved his hips in and out of her.

"Yes, yes! Give it to me!" Stacey shouted over the loud slaps of their bodies coming together.

"Fuck!" Andre yelled as he felt every ridge of her pussy grip his cock like a vice. Andre gripped her leg up high on his waist and dove in deeper. He alternated between short strokes and long strokes that had Stacey barely able to catch her breath.

"So. fucking. tight," he growled in her ear before sucking her earlobe into his mouth. He continued to pump and rotate his hips, making sure to hit every corner of her inner channel.

"Andre! That's it! Right there, don't stop please!" Stacey wailed as he drove himself in and out of her. "Andre, I need to touch you, please!" she begged, trying to wriggle her wrists from his tight grasp.

Andre finally released her wrists, and immediately used both hands to grip her ass cheeks to pull her off the bed and further down his cock.

Stacey wrapped her arms around his broad shoulders, pressing her nails into his back. She knew they both would have marks in the morning from their passionate encounter, but she couldn't care less.

"Oh Fuck!" she called out when he hit the sensitive spot inside her core. Her back arched off the bed and her nails dug even deeper into his skin.

Andre positioned himself so his cock hit both her g-spot and rubbed against her clit as he moved in and out.

"I'm coooomming!" she called out as she couldn't hold out any longer and the ripples in her core turned into tidal waves of sensation and she came.

Stacey's orgasm and the squeezing of her already tightness against his bare cock caused Andre to come as well.

"Oooh," Stacey moaned at seeing the wanton expression on his face as he came with his eyes half shut, lips parted and a pained, yet pleasure filled look of strain on his handsome face.

"Ahh, Fuuuuuck!" he shouted as he came.

Stacey watched as Andre jerked and shook as he came before collapsing to the bed, sated. He rose from on top of her, pulled himself out of her, and lay down at her side. He pulled her into his side, placing a kiss to her temple. Stacey snuggled deep into his embrace and was half asleep before she felt him release her and leave the bed. When she opened one eye to see where he was going, she saw his perfectly round ass as he strolled into the bathroom. She heard him relieve himself and water running before he returned with a warm washcloth in his hand. He wiped her down and himself before climbing back in bed.

Both Andre and Stacey soon drifted off in a very sated sleep, with Stacey tucked tightly in Andre's embrace.

* * *

A FEW HOURS LATER, Stacey awoke in the dark still wrapped in Andre's embrace. Her mouth felt cottony and she needed to pee. Remembering his bedroom also had its own bathroom, she attempted to wiggle out of Andre's embrace, only for his grip to tighten.

"Where're you going?" his groggy voice asked.

"To the bathroom."

His grip loosened and she eased from the bed. Looking around for something to put on, she found the remains of her shredded dress on the floor next to the bed.

Poor thing never stood a chance against Andre.

Leaving the dress, she found his dress shirt and put it over her naked body before going to the bathroom. After doing her business, she decided to go to the kitchen for a glass of water to aid her parched throat. As much as she'd screamed out his name, it was no wonder her throat felt like the Sahara.

Tiptoeing out of the bedroom to not disturb Andre, she headed in the direction she hoped the kitchen was. Andre hadn't given her any time to check out the rest of his condo, so she assumed his kitchen was somewhere around the front of the condo. Rounding the corner, she realized his condo had an open floor plan and that she could see straight into the kitchen from the hallway. Opening the sub-zero fridge, she was shocked to find a completely stocked fridge, neatly ordered and separated by fruits, vegetables, meats, condiments, and beverages. Pulling out a bottle of water and closing the fridge, she eyed the rest of his condo over the brim of the water as she sipped. The huge floor to ceiling windows caught her eye as she padded across the room to admire the view. He had a great view of the Atlanta skyline.

"Oh," she yelped as she felt Andre's hands wrap around her waist.

"I got thirsty," she said, giving him an explanation. "And I got caught up in this view," she said, tilting her head to the side as his warms lips made contact.

"Mm, I got hungry and I'm sure I have the best view in the city right now," he told her, his lips against her skin and his hands easing up the sides of his shirt. Cupping her breasts, he rubbed his growing cock against her ass cheeks. Stepping into her, he removed one hand from her breast to pluck the water bottle from her hand, unbuttoned and removed his shirt, letting is slide to the floor.

"Put your hands on the window and spread your legs," he commanded.

Stacey immediately complied as his hand reached down to spread her pussy lips. She shivered when she felt his hot tongue outline the butterfly tattoo on the back of her shoulder. She threw her head back when his strong fingers circled and teased her clit. Andre didn't give her time to catch her breathe before he was pushing his way inside her hot channel.

"Ooohh," she groaned as he filled her.

Gripping her at the waist, Andre began pounding her relentlessly. The sound of flesh slapping against flesh echoed around the room. Andre pulled her head back by her hair and placed a hard kiss to her lips as he continued to pound into her.

Pulling away, Andre looked down into Stacey's face mixed with so much pleasure and passion etched on it. Her eyes were closed tightly as her fist pounded on the window. That would not do.

"Open your eyes. Let me see you," he said, yanking her head back even further so their gazes could meet. When she opened her eyes, Andre saw a mirror of his own lust in her eyes.

"Aww, fuck! Andre, you're so deep," she moaned.

Andre released her hair and allowed his fingers to dig into the skin at her waist as he flexed his hips, pumping in and out of her. She was so wet, every in and out movement of his cock created a suction noise. Andre moved his hand around to massage her clit again when he began to feel her thighs quake.

"Come on my cock!" he demanded in her ear and within seconds, she was screaming his name and coming all over him. Andre quickly followed behind her, pressing his big body against her as he came.

"Fuck!" he yelled in a hoarse voice as he expended into her. "Shit," he breathed heavily against the back of her neck as he panted against her back.

They both took long moments to regain their regular course of breathing. Andre pulled back, extracting himself from her and swooping down to pick her up and carry her back to his bed.

Stacey wrapped her arms around his neck and rested her head on his chest as he carried her. She heard the wild rhythm of his heartbeat and knew it probably mimicked her own erratic pulse. Although Stacey assumed they were going back to sleep, when they reached his bedroom, Andre threw her on the bed causing her to bounce. A giggle sprang from her lips.

"What was that—ooh," she gasped as she looked down and saw his quickly growing erection. The man was like a damn jack rabbit.

"Haven't had enough yet?" she asked sitting back on her elbows and spreading her legs. When Andre moaned, the sound had her creaming yet again.

"Not yet," he said licking his lips. And for the rest of the night, he showed her exactly what the term *all night man* was all about.

CHAPTER 9

"What are you studying over there?" Andre asked, bringing Stacey a glass of red wine as she sat on his very cozy, light grey colored shag rug in front of his coffee table. She was surrounded by a pile of textbooks while her laptop rested on the table.

They'd spent most of the rainy day nestled in his condo. That was only after Stacey had to practically threaten Andre to take her home so she could get a change of clothes and her books. After the previous night's events, the only decent dress she'd had with her remained torn on his bedroom floor. She'd had her burlesque costumes, but those weren't *lay around in the house* or *go out to eat lunch* clothes. Andre tried to give her his shirt to wear after she told him she refused to walk around completely nude in his home, but she'd refused, insisting on needing her own clothes.

Only after she reminded him that she had schoolwork to complete before Monday did he relent and take her home for a change of clothes, her books, and her laptop so she could get some work done at his place. After that, they'd had lunch at a bistro not too far from his condo, and then went to the grocery store so Andre could pick up some items to make dinner. They spent the rest of the day both doing some work and watching movies.

"Just the riveting world of research methods for social workers. You sure you know what you're doing in the kitchen?" she asked a smirk on her face.

"You doubt my cooking abilities?" he asked a grin on his jovial face.

Stacey laughed. "Maybe. It's just that Devyn's told me Nikola can't boil water, and you telling me how your father preferred you in the boardroom rather than the kitchen makes it a little hard for me to not question your cooking skills," she answered honestly.

"Alright," he said, turning and heading back to the kitchen. Before long, he was returning with a spoon with sauce in it, holding his hand underneath so it didn't drip on the floor. "Try this," he ordered holding the spoon to her lips.

Stacey parted her lips and Andre slid the silver spoon in. As soon as the delicious alfredo sauce hit her tongue, she closed her eyes. "Mmmm," she moaned. When she opened her eyes it was to see Andre staring intently at her lips. She smiled as she read the thoughts running through his head. "That is delicious. I stand corrected."

"Just a little fettuccine alfredo with shrimp, broccoli, and mush-rooms and some homemade butter pecan to top it off."

Stacey's eyes widened. She had no idea he made ice cream too. "You have an ice cream maker?"

"Is there any other way to make homemade ice cream?" he asked in his usual cocky manner.

"How did you learn to cook so well?" she asked.

Andre took a seat on the floor next to Stacey, and she moved her books out of the way to make room for his long legs.

"Uh well, a few years ago I decided it was time to take up cooking classes. No sense in being a grown ass man who couldn't at least prepare the basics, right? I found I really enjoyed it and at the end of a stressful day at work, it helped to relax me. To my mother's shame, I can cook more Italian dishes than Greek, but I'm still learning," he half-smiled before taking a sip of his own glass of wine.

Stacey saw a look pass over his face that she couldn't quite read. It looked almost like look of sadness, as if he was remembering something he didn't want to think about. Ironically, for Stacey, food had at one time in her life been a source of stress and resentment. She was glad to no longer be in the place where she looked at food as the enemy. Now, she wanted to help other women do the same.

"Tell me about your family," Andre suddenly requested, interrupting her thoughts.

She was caught off guard by the sudden change in topic, but quickly recovered. "What do you want to know?" she asked.

"Everything," he said looking directly into her eyes.

A shiver ran down her spine as she saw the intense gaze he gave her. Her family story was a bit complicated and one she rarely shared with people she wasn't close to. "Um, let's see, you know my Aunt Ruth and Uncle Gerald raised me from the age of twelve in Savannah, Georgia. They have two sons, Quincy and Jabari, who are a few years older than me but they're like my brothers. And of course, there's my older sister," she answered giving the standard answer she gave most people when she talked about her family, but Andre wouldn't let up.

"What about your parents? Why did you go to live with your Aunt and Uncle at twelve?" he asked seriously.

Stacey sighed. This was the less appealing part about her family she rarely shared. She wasn't ashamed of her past, but she hated seeing the look of pity some gave her when she talked about her parents. Turning and resting her elbow on the couch to look at him directly, she began, "My mother died when I was five. Breast cancer. She battled it for a few years before she died, so most of my young life I was cared for by my sister. My sister was the one who walked me to and from school every day. She walked me to dance classes at our local Boys and Girls Club. My dad was….he wasn't the best," she told him, not wanting to go into depth about the abuse she, but mostly her sister endured at the hands of their father. "He died in a car accident a few months after I turned twelve. That's when we, Coral and I, went to live with Aunt Ruth and Uncle Gerry. We hadn't even met them before then. Aunt Ruth is my mother's sister—her twin actually, but they hadn't spoken in years before my mom died. It's a long story, but that's the gist of my family life." She shrugged.

"And you're pretty close with your aunt and uncle?" Andre asked.

Stacey nodded. "Hmmhm, it was an adjustment at first, but now I think of them as my parents. I know they'd do anything for me. It's because of them I have a place to live," she answered. "They own the building I live in," she told him in response to the questioning look he gave her.

Andre nodded and pressed his lips to her forehead in an endearing kiss. "Thank you for sharing that with me," he said sitting back. His fingers trailed down her leg, which remained uncovered due to the shorts she wore.

When his fingers lingered over a spot on her knee, it took everything in her not to push his hand away. She knew the question was coming and she wasn't ready to share all of that with him just yet.

But, perceptive as he always was, Andre saw the look in her eye. The wave of sadness that appeared when his fingers touched the scar on her knee. He'd noticed it the very first time he'd seen her bare legs, but didn't ask. He knew by looking at her that this scar and whatever brokenness it healed over was the reason she no longer was a ballerina.

"Come on, dinner's ready," he said, standing and extending his hand to her, pulling her up. He saw her shoulders slump with relief and knew he'd made the right decision not to push just yet.

"ARE YOU READY FOR YOUR TRIP?" Nikola asked as he, Raul, and Andre settled in for lunch at an Italian restaurant only a few blocks from Excel's offices. Andre was going to Boston in a few days due to some issues with the Jennings' merger. Apparently, some of the top-level executives were threatening to abandon ship because of the merger. Andre couldn't be sure, but he believed the employees were being fed wrong information. The last thing he or Nikola wanted was for disgruntled employees to abandon ship and take their knowledge to one of their competitor firms. Andre was hoping to only be gone a few days, but he'd likely have to do some house-cleaning while in Boston which could extend his trip longer than he'd anticipated.

What he was not looking forward to mostly, was leaving Stacey. It'd been a few weeks since their first night together after her show, and they hadn't gone a day without seeing each other since. She ended up spending the night at his place at least two to three nights during the week and on weekends. It was as if he couldn't get enough of being around her. His usual rule of never spending the night with a woman or letting a woman spend the night just didn't apply where she was concerned. He sighed at the thought of possibly going a whole week or more without her in his bed.

Unbeknownst to Andre, his thoughts played out all over his face. His emotions did not escape Nikola and Raul's perceptive eyes, but both men remained silent, simply passing a look between one another.

"Yeah, I'm ready. I think Jennings is trying to play games," Andre said shrugging off his thoughts about Stacey for the moment.

"How so?" Nikola inquired.

"Not sure exactly, but I think he's been in the ear of some of the execs. I'm sure the knowledgeable ones realize what a sham he is, but some still have loyalty to his father and think following the son is the right thing to do. No worries, I'll handle it. Did you do what I asked?" Andre asked, shifting his focus from Nikola to Raul.

Raul's brown eyes met Andre's as he nodded. "Yup, my guy's set to go. Wednesday evening, right?"

"Yup," Andre answered. He wouldn't be there to escort Stacey home after her late dance class on Wednesday, so he'd arranged for one of Raul's employees to do it in his stead.

"Are you sure it's necessary though? I mean, she has been working at that studio for a while and never had any problems," Raul commented.

Andre cocked his head to the side in disbelief. This is the man who'd followed Mercedes around for an entire summer when a stalker had threatened her. Andre couldn't believe he would question the need for safety for his woman.

Raul must have noticed Andre's look. Throwing up his hands in defense he said, "Whoa, I'm just asking a question. Calm down there, Junior." He laughed at the incredulity written all over Andre's face.

"Yes, I'm sure. I don't like her leaving work so late without anyone watching her back. She carries mace and says she has a mean right hook. Her sister supposedly taught her." He gave a cynical snort at that statement. "Anyway, since I won't be there, I want someone watching her."

Andre did catch the look that passed between Raul and Nikola this time. The two men clearly had something on their mind.

"What?" he asked almost defensively.

Nikola sat up in his seat and fixed his dark blue Tom Ford suit jacket before turning his blue eyes that were so much like Andre's on his brother. "Andre, if she says her sister taught her to fight, I would believe her about that right hook," Nikola stated cryptically.

Andre turned his gaze to Raul who was nodding in agreement. Obviously, the two men knew Stacey's sister.

"Army?" he guessed.

Raul and Nikola had met at West Point and had become instant friends. The years after graduating were spent in the U.S. Army, and serving overseas in both Iraq and Afghanistan. After retiring, Nikola went to work at Excel and Raul opened his own security firm there in Atlanta.

"Yup, the army and some...other stuff," Raul answered.

Andre narrowed his gaze as he pondered Raul's meaning. He wondered if Raul was hinting he or Nikola had had a relationship with Stacey's sister, but that thought was dismissed with Nikola's next words.

"Nothing like that. She works in the same industry as Raul so their paths have crossed from time to time," Nikola stated, answering Andre's unasked question.

"Oh." Andre nodded. "Anyway, I still want that security detail on her while I'm gone," Andre told Raul.

Raul nodded. "Consider it done."

The men spent the rest of their lunch talking about work, life, and the upcoming gala that was to be hosted by Andre and their mother, Iris. It was a Mother's Against Drunk Driving fundraiser that Iris worked closely with. Andre helped to sponsor the event and raise funds for it. He was glad of the awareness the event would bring to the issue of drunk driving and the destruction it could cause. He knew all about that pain.

* * *

ANDRE'S COULDN'T HELP LOOKING at the clock for the third time in only the last five minutes. He sat in his office as the head of the accounting department talked about the latest reports and upcoming changes in accounting systems. Though Andre usually lived for these kinds of meetings, he was more anxious to see the woman he'd made plans to share his lunch with.

Since it was Friday, Stacey got out of her internship a little early and he'd convinced her to swing by his office for a late lunch. Unfortunately, his meeting had run a little over and he had to call her to come about thirty minutes later than their planned time. Now, he was regretting that decision, wanting nothing more than to see her. He'd be leaving for Boston early Sunday morning so they had only another day and a half to spend together before he'd be gone for at least a week.

Sighing, Andre ran his fingers through his hair and dragged his hand down through his beard. When his phone rang, his hand darted out to pick it up without even asking Charlie—his head of accounting—to hold on.

"Mr. Collins, a Ms. Stacey Coleman is here to see you," the security guard on the first floor told Andre on the other end. Andre had called down to security to let them know to call him as soon as she arrived.

Standing with the receiver of the phone tucked into his ear, Andre didn't hesitate. "Okay, I'll be right down," he said hanging up the phone. "Charlie, I'm sorry we have to cut this short. I have another meeting. We'll talk more about this when I get back from Boston," he said, shaking the other man's hand and escorting him out of his office.

"No problem, Andre. Have a safe trip," Charlie responded as both men headed past Andre's assistant and out the double doors.

When Andre stepped off the elevator, the smile that touched his lips was instantaneous. He stared at Stacey, taking in every detail of her presence as she stood with her head down, scrolling through her phone. Her twists were piled on top of her head in a neat, high bun. He wondered how she got all of that hair to stay up like that. She wore a knee-length black pinstripe skirt and a white button up top. Andre let his eyes travel over her toned legs that bowed back ever so slightly, the small swell of her ass, small waist and the roundness of her breasts. She looked perfectly professional, but good enough to devour at the same time.

Andre noticed movement out of the corner of his eye, and his gaze traveled to the security guard who stood at the desk behind Stacey. He noticed the guard's eyes were doing the same perusing Andre's just had. When the man, who stood a few inches shorter than Andre, licked his pink lips while ogling Stacey, Andre's jaw tightened and his fists clenched. Andre strolled over to Stacey, who still remained oblivious to either man's attention. Her beautiful face was still looking down at her phone as her fingers typed away.

"I hope whatever you're reading is interesting," Andre whispered in her ear, causing Stacey to jump.

"Oh my goodness! Andre, you scared me," she admonished, swatting his arm playfully.

"Hey, beautiful," he said, leaning down to press a quick peck to her luscious lips.

"Mm, hey yourself," she moaned when their lips separated.

Andre's stomach muscles clenched at hearing her low moan, and his eyes flew to the security guard who was now pretending to not notice the couple in front of him.

That's right, keep your damn eyes to yourself, Andre thought as he wrapped his arm around Stacey's waist and began escorting her to the elevator.

"Thanks, Gus," Andre threw over his shoulder to the security guard and continued walking.

"No problem, Mr. Collins," Gus said, avoiding eye contact with Andre.

"What were you reading on your phone?" Andre asked as they stepped into the elevator.

"Just some of my client notes and making more notes for next week."

Andre admired the way she lit up when she talked about her internship. He knew she was hoping to get hired at the institution she interned with after completing school.

"Hey, Madelyn, this is Stacey," Andre introduced her to his administrative assistant.

The middle aged woman looked up from her desk and smiled when she saw Stacey. "Hi Stacey, it's a pleasure to meet you," she said extending her hand.

"Same here," Stacey said grasping the older woman's hand and smiling.

"Andre, your lunch was delivered while you were downstairs. I placed it on the table in your office," she directed at Andre.

"Thanks, Madelyn. Hold all my calls for the next hour," he said, pulling Stacey into his office.

She gave one last wave to his assistant before she disappeared behind the door as Andre shut it. Andre immediately pulled her into his arms, cupping her face and letting his lips meld into hers. Prying her mouth open with his tongue, he deepened the kiss, using his tongue to devour every available space in her mouth.

"Mmm," she moaned into his mouth.

Andre's cock twitched at the sound and feel of her lips on his. Before long, he pulled away. "Hi," he smiled down at her.

"Hi," she said just above a whisper.

"You hungry?" he asked, releasing her face and pulling her to the table where a spread of sandwiches, fresh fruit, soda, and bottles of water waited.

"Yes!" Stacey said excitedly. "I haven't eaten since breakfast this morning."

Andre frowned. It was close to three o'clock in the afternoon. She'd nearly gone the entire day without eating. "Why haven't you eaten anything?" he asked, pulling out one of his mesh chairs for her to sit. When she did, he began plating her food.

Stacey shrugged. "It's not big deal. I just got really busy at work and didn't bring anything to snack on since we were meeting for lunch," she told him. "Anyway, how did your meeting go?" she asked accepting the plate of food he handed her.

"Well, you should have told me you hadn't eaten. We could have met somewhere closer, or I could have changed my meeting," he said still frowning, and ignoring her question.

"Andre, it's no big deal. I'm not actually starving. Tell me about your meeting," she retorted, stroking his hand as he sat. She enjoyed the way he seemed to always take her needs into consideration. She'd never had a man she was dating be so concerned about her well-being. It felt good to know he cared.

Andre's face didn't relax until he saw her take a bite of her turkey club sandwich. He'd ordered her favorite sandwich from a small shop around the corner that often catered meetings at their office. Andre sat back and began eating his own roast beef sandwich. He knew she was trying to get him off her back about not eating by asking about his meeting, but he couldn't help his concern. He'd never felt this way about a woman so early on. He just wanted to make sure she was taking care of herself. He couldn't hold back his protective instinct when it came to her. He was feeling especially protective since he would be leaving her soon.

"My meeting was fine," he grumbled.

"Don't sound so ornery," she teased, lightly tapping him on the leg. "Tell me about this trip you're going on."

Andre couldn't help but give a sideways smile as she winked at him and took another bite of her sandwich.

"It's just to tie up some loose ends with this merger," he told her. She eagerly listened to him talk about the merger he'd been working on for months as she ate. She often interjected with insightful questions about the deal or matters he was having with employees.

"You're going to be a great social worker," he told her honestly as they finished their lunch. The shocked look on her face told him she wasn't expecting that.

"Wh-what makes you say that?" she asked almost shyly.

Andre found himself amused by her coyness when it came to talking about herself as a social worker. It was almost as if she wanted it so bad, she couldn't allow herself to believe she was would be one, one day.

He pulled her up from her seat and pulled her to sit on his lap in his large leather chair behind his desk. He kissed her the crook of her neck before responding. He enjoyed the feeling of the small hitch of breath she took when he placed his lips on her skin and nuzzled her neck.

"Because I've been talking about boring ass numbers and business shit for the last twenty minutes, and you didn't seem bored or yawned once. Your attention remained on me and what I was saying and I know this shit is boring to most. I live it. If you give your clients half the attention you just gave me, they're going to love you," he told her honestly still nuzzling her neck. He felt her arm encircle his waist and squeeze.

"Thank you," she said just above a whisper.

"Thank me properly," he growled as he pulled her lips down to meet his. Within seconds, he became lost in the kiss as their tongues stroked one another and his lips nibbled at hers. His cock began to stand at attention as her hand moved around his waist to massage him through his pants. He moved his hand to her leg, pushing her skirt up her hips.

"Wait, Andre," Stacey said breathing heavily as she broke away from the kiss. "Are you sure this is okay? I mean, what if someone walks in?" she asked worriedly, turning her head to look at his door.

"It's locked," he responded, darting his tongue out to lick her neck. He smiled when he felt her shiver.

"Are you sure?" she moaned as he sucked on her earlobe and let his hand move up, spreading her legs wider and palming her hot core.

"Yes. Come here," he growled, catching the back of her neck and pulling her lips to meet his for another blistering kiss. Andre let his fingers maneuver around her stockings and panties, pulling them down just enough to leave room for his fingers to enter her. He inserted one finger at first, feeling her already wet. When she widened her legs, he entered a second finger.

Andre pumped his fingers in and out of her at the same rate he allowed his tongue to stroke her mouth. He angled his fingers upward to make contact with the sensitive spot inside her wet channel, bending his thumb to massage her budding clit.

Stacey threw her head back and began pumping her hips against his hand. "Shit," she whispered not wanting to be too loud, remembering they were in Andre's office.

"You can't speak louder than that?" Andre taunted. "I must not be doing it good enough," he said before inserting a third finger and pumping his fingers even faster in and out of her growing wetness. He increased pressure on her clit as he slanted his fingers in a curling motion, hitting both her sensitive spots at one time. When Stacey's hips began moving even more vigorously, he knew she was close.

"Come, now!" he growled and slammed his lips to hers.

Stacey moaned loudly into his mouth as her body exploded. She clutched her fingers tightly around his shoulders as she let the shudders pass over her one by one. Regaining her breath, she picked her head up from his neck and smiled down at him.

"Your turn," she said naughtily.

Andre barely registered her words before she slid off his lap and was on her knees in front of him. With trembling fingers, Stacey reached up, unbuttoned, and unzipped Andre's pants. She reached inside his pants, pushed down his black Calvin Klein boxer briefs, and pulled out his massive erection.

Stacey gave Andre a seductive smiled before lowering her head and wrapping his cock with her lips. Letting her mouth slide down his long shaft, Stacey heard Andre moan above her. Slowly, she licked her way back up his cock, stopping to suck and lick around the tip before lowering her mouth onto his cock again.

"That's it. Just like that. Fuck yeah," Andre grunted in the sexiest voice Stacey had ever heard.

She quickened her pace on his cock as she bobbed her head up and down, wanting to bring him as much pleasure as he'd brought her moments before. She let her hand reach into his pants to cuff his heavy sac, massaging and stroking him as her mouth slurped and sucked his thick cock. Moving her hand from his pants to his shaft, she enveloped the base of his shaft with her hand and began bobbing her head vigorously on the top half of his cock, desperate for the taste of his seed on her tongue. She felt a trickle of precum at the tip of his cock and used her tongue to spread it around the entire tip of his shaft. When she went to dive in again, she found herself stopped by Andre's hands on her shoulders.

"No," he said, his voice strained. "I want to come inside you," he said, pulling her up as he stood.

Stacey felt his hands roughly pull her skirt up and push her stockings even further down her smooth thighs. She heard a thud behind her as Andre pushed a stack of papers and folders from his desk and picked Stacey up, placing her on the desk.

Stepping between her legs, Andre nudged her knees apart even more and gripped her by the hips. He took his time sliding into her wetness while staring her directly in the eye. Stacey felt transfixed by the need she saw in his eyes that had darkened to a teal blue with lust. Stacey parted her lips just as Andre's mouth made contact with hers, and he seated himself fully inside her. He gripped her waist tightly, pumping his hips and sawing in and out of her. Stacey grabbed the back of his neck with one hand and placed the other on his desk to hold herself up under his vigorous stroking.

"Oh God, Andre! Don't stop, please, baby. Just like that," she begged as she wrapped her legs around his waist, pulling him in closer.

"You like that, baby?" he panted, his head buried in her neck as he licked and sucked. "Tell me how much you love this cock!" he demanded, rotating his hips to hit every inch of her channel.

"Oh, shit! I love it soooo much," she moaned, "Oohh, I'm gonna come," she panted knowing she couldn't hold on much longer.

"Come with me, baby!" Andre ordered, again sealing her lips with his. They both moaned into each other's' mouths as they came, pumping their hips against one another.

"Damn. I don't think I can get enough of you," Andre panted in between breaths as they came down from their orgasms.

"Tell me about it," Stacey laughed as her head lolled against his shoulder, "Mmm," she moaned as he pulled himself from her.

Andre grabbed a few tissues from his desk, quickly cleaning himself and Stacey up before placing her feet on the floor and fixing her clothes. She helped him put all the papers back on his desk as they had been before their sexual encounter.

"I think I'll leave early today," Andre said picking up his suit jacket and shutting down his computer.

Stacey looked at him confused. "I thought you had more work to do today."

"I do have more work to do. In that pussy," he teased, grabbing her to him and placing kisses down her jaw to her neck.

"You're so nasty," she laughed.

"You like it," he teased, smacking her on the ass. "Let's go. I'll follow you to my condo. I'm going to be gone for about a week so we gotta make up for lost time before I go," he told her.

Stacey just smiled and shook her head. She couldn't think of a better way to spend the rest of the day than being wrapped in this man's arms, his cock stroking her insides while he moved over top of her. She was already missing him and he hadn't even left yet. She knew whatever was growing between them had the potential to be serious. To say that unnerved her would be an understatement.

* * *

"ALRIGHT Y'ALL, that's it for tonight," Stacey told her pole dancing students as they completed their end of class stretches. As her class of about fifteen women began gathering their belongings, Stacey unfurled her yoga mat. Over the last few weeks, she'd grown accustomed to seeing Andre waiting for her on the other side of the door as she exited with her last student. Tonight, however, she knew he wouldn't be waiting since he was still in Boston. Instead, she opted to do some yoga to unwind from the last few days. The last of her students filed out of the studio, leaving Stacey alone. After locking the door, she turned on some relaxing meditation music, lowered the volume, and began with her opening sun salutations.

After about a half an hour, Stacy sat cross-legged in the center of her yoga mat. Closing her eyes to end her yoga session, she felt the hairs on the back of her neck stand up. An eerie feeling began to creep into her belly. She pried one eye open and then the other, looking around. She was alone in the studio and with it being dark, she couldn't see outside, but she got the distinct feeling she was being watched.

Deciding to end her night, she grabbed her Nike sports bag, rifled around for her cell phone and keys, which held a small jar of mace, placed the bag over her shoulder and headed out the door. Making sure to keep her eyes open and alert, she quickly strode to her car. She reached her car door and just as she placed her key in the lock, she saw the image of a man in the window's reflection.

Moving quickly, Stacey yanked her key out of the lock, spun around, and shot off a spray of mace before swinging with her right arm.

"Uff!" she heard the man grunt when he fist made contact with his ribs. "Shit," he said, coughing and backing up. The man, who appeared to be about six-feet tall with tanned skin and dark hair, coughed and sputtered, holding up his hand. "Wait, wait," he said trying to stop Stacey she held up her mace again, aiming at his face, which she'd missed last time.

"Who the fuck are you?" she demanded angrily. She was now more pissed than afraid.

"Ma'am, my name is Lorenzo. I work for Raul Santiago. I was hired by Mr. Collins to escort you home," he said still holding his hands up.

Stacey's eyes narrowed on him. She looked hard into his dark eyes as he stood under the streetlight. His stance showed that he was giving her space and time to appraise him, attempting to come across as non-threatening.

"Prove it," she said still holding up the can of mace and remaining in a defensive stance.

Lorenzo nodded. "Okay, I'm going to reach for my phone and call Mr. Collins."

He reached into his jacket pocket to go for his cell phone.

"Other hand stays up," she ordered when his second hand began to drop.

Lorenzo put his other hand back up and nodded. He pulled his cell phone from his pocket, holding it up for her to see. He pressed in his code, dialed the number, and placed the phone to his ear.

"Hello, Mr. Collins. I'm here with Ms. Coleman who almost maced and assaulted me," he said in a deadpan tone. "Apparently, you forgot to tell her you hired me to escort her home," Lorenzo frowned.

Stacey almost laughed. Almost. She still wasn't sure this guy was for real and after feeling as if she were being watched in the studio not too long ago, she wasn't taking any chances.

"He wants to speak with you," Lorenzo said taking a step forward and holding the phone out in front of him.

"Put it on speaker," she told him, holding up the mace again and bracing herself.

To her surprise, Lorenzo's face softened into an almost impressed expression as he nodded. Remaining where he was, he pressed the button to put the phone on speaker and within seconds, a feeling of relief washed over Stacey as she heard Andre's voice.

"Stacey, did you really hit and mace him?" he asked, his voice laced with laughter.

Stacey, whose eyes never left Lorenzo's, didn't look as pleased to hear the laughter in Andre's voice. "Maybe," she said, finally relaxing and placing her hands on her hips. "Why didn't you tell me you hired someone to follow me? I nearly took this guy's head off."

The vibrant sound of Andre's laughter came through the speaker loud and clear in the quietness of the still night. "I'm sorry, baby. I just forgot. As I recall, we got sidetracked doing other...things before I left," he laughed.

"Andre!" she yelled, peeking at Lorenzo's face to see if he picked up on the innuendo. His impassive face belied the glint in his eyes that told her he had picked up on it.

"Okay, okay. I'm sorry you got scared. I just wanted to make sure you got home safe since I wasn't there," he told her.

Stacey opened her mouth to remind him that she had worked at that studio, and had worked those hours for more than a year before she met him, but he cut her off.

"And don't tell me how long you worked there before we met. I'm not letting my—" he paused and cleared his throat, "—*you* leave late at night from anywhere without someone watching your back. Now, get in your car and drive safe back home. Lorenzo will follow and make sure you get in safely. Call me when you make it home," he told her. "Lorenzo make sure she gets in safely."

"Will do," Lorenzo stated before giving Stacey a reassuring smile.

Stacey felt the tenseness in her muscles begin to fade. She knew Raul owned and operated a security firm, and now that she looked at Lorenzo, he did look familiar. She probably had seen him at Mercedes and Raul's wedding, but at night while she was already on edge, those few details were hard to remember. She heard Lorenzo saying some last minute words to Andre before hanging up. She felt a little guilty for almost macing and hitting him.

"I'm sorry about—"

Lorenzo waved her off, shaking his head. "Don't worry about it. I've been maced before. Luckily, I've got quick instincts. I wish my sisters had your chutzpah." He smirked. "Go ahead get in your car. I'll follow you home," he said ushering her to her car door.

Before turning, Stacey had one question to ask. "Um, did you, by chance get here a little early and sit out here for a little while?" she asked, hoping that it was Lorenzo who'd given her that feeling of being watched earlier.

Stacey's hope deflated when Lorenzo shook his head. "No, actually I got caught up with another client and got here later than I was supposed to. I arrived only a few minutes before you exited the studio. I intentionally planned to come in the studio and introduce myself to avoid scaring you. Obviously that didn't turn out so well." He sighed.

"Oh, okay," she said trying to hide her frown as she got in the car. All the way home, Stacey couldn't get past the feeling of being watched from earlier. She was actually grateful that Andre had hired Lorenzo to see her home safely, although she wouldn't admit that to anyone.

CHAPTER 10

*E*venings like this, Andre was grateful he had a chauffeured vehicle to drive him from his Boston office to his hotel. He was so tired, it was a struggle to keep his eyes open as he rode past the buildings in the downtown Boston area. It'd been a long five days in Boston. In addition to dealing with the executive who'd threatened to abandon ship, he'd had to sort out financial and recording issues with the accounting team and work with a few of the top level executives to weed out clients who were not serving the business' bottom line. Then it was another matter altogether to inform those clients that they would not be renewing their contracts. Even though he was dog tired, Andre felt good about what he'd gotten done in a short period of time. Now, as he returned to his hotel room, the only voice he wanted to hear was that of the woman with a dancer's lithe body and amber colored eyes, who was, unfortunately in Atlanta while he was in Boston. He began pulling out his phone just as the car stopped in front of his hotel.

Seconds later, Andre's door was opened by the hotel's doorman. As he greeted and tipped the serviceman, Andre began scrolling through his text messages, stopping at one in particular. The message read:

Hope you had a good day. Call me no matter what time you get in, if you're not too tired.

Andre's mood instantly perked up as he read the message. That one message was like a jolt of caffeine to his tired body, and suddenly he couldn't wait to get up to his room and call Stacey. The smirk that appeared on Andre's face wasn't missed by any of the female guests in the lobby as they eyed him openly, and some more subtly. Nearing the elevator, Andre finally looked up from his phone to see the last person he wanted to see. His smile faltered.

"Maria," he stated plainly, stopping short. Tucking his hands in his pockets, he wondered how she even knew he was going to be there. "What are you doing here?" he asked, barely attempting to conceal his impatience.

"Is that any way to greet me after I've been waiting for nearly an hour and a half for you?" she asked, batting her long, dark eyelashes at him and attempting to give a coy smile. She was dressed in a red trench coat that stopped a few inches above her knee. Her long legs were adorned in black stockings, and Andre bet she didn't have on much under the coat. Heck, he knew, looking around, most of the men in the lobby could tell she wasn't wearing much under the coat. But unlike the other men, Andre wasn't turned on. He was irritated.

"How did you know I was here?" he asked, making no attempt to hide his irritation.

Maria's smile faltered a little and she tried a more flirty approach, stepping closer and running a Rouge Vernis tipped fingernail up his arm while looking up at him through her lashes.

"I asked around," she answered cryptically. "You haven't been answering my calls."

Andre grabbed her hand to halt her caress. He would admit that she was a beautiful woman, but he was not feeling her tonight.

"I know, I haven't answered your calls. That should have been your first clue," he said rather dryly. It was late, he was tired, and the only woman he wanted to talk to was in Atlanta, so a phone call would have to do. Unfortunately, Maria was getting in the way of said phone call, causing his patience to wear thin.

The seductive smile Maria wore dropped immediately and she yanked her hand from his, her own irritation shining through. "So, you're seeing someone," she accused.

Andre's eyebrow shot up. Where the hell did she get off questioning him? They weren't and never had been exclusive. Hell, they weren't even really dating. They'd just been someone to warm each other's beds or wear on an arm at an event when the need arose. They often went for long periods of time without speaking when the other was seeing someone. So, why was she trying to get all territorial now?

Not wanting to drag this out any longer, Andre simply nodded. "Yes, I am. Not that it's really any business of yours." He shrugged and placed his hands in his pockets.

Maria looked affronted as if he'd just told her he'd run off, gotten married, and was starting a family. "Who is she?" she demanded.

Apparently, Maria forgot who she was talking to and dealing with. No one questioned him about what he did with his own life. Especially, not someone he wasn't related to or had any serious commitment with.

"First, who she is, is none of your damn business." Andre watched as Maria's eyes grew wide with shock at the way he was speaking to her. "Second, don't ever, show up here like this out of the blue when you weren't invited. Third, it's late. I'm tired and going up to my room. Alone. Goodnight."

He walked off without giving her a backwards glance. Andre strode to the elevators and got on as soon as the first arrived to deliver him to his private suite.

* * *

MARIA STOMPED out of the hotel and back to her off-white BMW, slamming the door when she got in. Pulling out her phone, she punched in the first number in her most recent contacts list.

"Jennings!" she shouted when he answered the phone. "You didn't tell me he was seeing someone else!"

"Oh Maria, how wonderful it is to hear from you again. I take it the evening didn't go as expected." Jennings' cocky tone relayed the smile he likely wore on his face.

In that moment, Maria knew he probably had known Andre was seeing someone and would have likely rejected her advances. "You knew didn't you, you son of a bitch!" she snarled.

"Now, now, Maria, we don't want such ugly language coming from such a beautiful woman, do we? I merely thought you'd want to know your lover was in town. How was I to know he'd drop you like last week's trash?" he taunted.

"Fuck you!"

The two had run in the same social circles in Boston for years and had always had a hate-hate relationship, even though they had many friends in common. When Jennings had called her out of the blue earlier in the day and "accidentally" let it be known that Andre was in town due to his recent acquisition of Jennings' company, Maria hadn't thought twice about showing up at his hotel. Now, she knew Jennings had something else up his sleeve.

"Tell me who she is," she demanded.

"Now why would I do that?" he questioned.

"Because you still owe me for getting you out of trouble with the police last year." Maria knew all about Jennings' nasty drug habit, and had even covered for him one night while they happened to be out at the same club.

"Oh fine, since you want to bring up the past," he relented.

Somehow, Maria knew that despite his seeming reluctance, Jennings was more than happy to give her this bit of information. But, she wouldn't question his motive. Maria just wanted to know how much of a threat this woman was to her plan to have Andre all to herself. She'd be damned if she let another woman come in this late in the game and swoop in on her territory. Sitting back in her car, she intently listened as Jennings told her what he knew about one Stacey Coleman.

* * *

MEANWHILE, Andre sighed in relief as he entered his hotel suite. He tossed his briefcase onto the couch in the living room before heading the large bedroom. It took everything in him not to collapse into bed, but he wanted a shower before he called Stacey.

Showering quickly and throwing on a pair of boxers, Andre crawled into the king-sized bed and stretched out as he reached for his phone. Checking the time, he saw it was close to midnight. It was Thursday night and he knew Stacey had to get up early to be at her internship the next day. He hesitated for a second before pressing the button to call her. He was feeling particularly selfish and just wanted to hear her voice before conking out for the night. Even if it was just a few minutes.

"Hello," Stacey's groggy voice came through the line as she answered.

"Hey, babe," Andre smiled, more happy than he cared to admit that she'd answered.

"Hi," Stacey said around a yawn. "How was your day?"

Andre could hear some ruffling in the background as if she were sitting up in bed. He felt a slight twinge of guilt at waking her. "Hey, I'm sorry for calling so late. I should let you get back to sleep," he told her.

"No, no," Stacey rushed. "I said you could call anytime. I wanted to talk to you. Tell me about your day."

"My day was boring, bunch of talk about quarterly projections, annual revenues, return on investment, and a bunch of other bullshit that would put you back to sleep in a heartbeat," he admitted.

Stacey laughed. "But you love it."

"I sure do. Enough about work, tell me something interesting, like what are you wearing?" he asked playfully.

The timbre of Stacey's laugh shot directly to his cock.

"What? You can't be serious," she admonished.

"Oh, baby, I'm very serious. It's been five days since I've felt your tight pussy walls wrapped around my cock, gripping it for all it's worth," he said in a low, seductive voice.

"Dammit, Andre! You say stuff like that and get me all hot and bothered," Stacey nearly moaned.

"Good, now we're both hot and bothered. Touch your pussy and tell me how wet you are," he commanded.

"Andre," Stacey warned.

"Do it," he ordered again. "Tell me how wet you are." He could hear Stacey's labored breathing as his words turned her on.

"Mm, sooo wet," she moaned.

Andre's free hand moved to the inside of his boxers, releasing his straining cock. He closed his eyes and pictured Stacey naked in his bed, fingering herself.

"I'm so hard right now. Tell me what you're doing," he requested.

"I-I," she stuttered.

"Tell me."

"I'm fingering my pussy pretending it's your cock inside me," she groaned.

"Add another finger," he ordered. "Tell me how good I feel inside you."

He used the drop of precum at the tip to moisten and stroke his cock.

"You feel soooo goood," she panted.

"Pinch your nipples," he ordered, picturing her heaving breasts.

"Oooohh," she groaned.

"Fuck, baby that sounds so hot," he growled, his own stroking growing more erratic. "I feel your pussy muscles clamping around my cock. Your thighs are beginning to quiver and your growing wetness is making it easier to glide in and out of you. Are you about to come?"

"Y-yes," she answered.

"No. Not until I say," he commanded. "Remove your hand."

"A-andre," Stacey moaned in impatience.

"Put your fingers in your mouth," he told her. "Suck them like they're my cock. Let me hear it," he grunted, still stroking his cock and feeling its weight grow heavier as the need to orgasm loomed over him.

"Mmmm, Ahhhh." He heard Stacey's groans as she sucked her fingers.

"Put your fingers back in your pussy. I want you to come with me," he ordered as he picked up the pace in his own stroking, lifting his hips wildly. "Come now, baby! Fuck!" he yelled as his orgasm rushed over him, causing his cum to spill out.

"Fuuuuuuck, Andreee!" He heard Stacey yell and groan on the other end, causing his own orgasm to heighten.

"Damn," he panted as his senses returned.

"Damn is right," Stacey giggled on the other end. "That was the first time I've ever had phone sex," she admitted in a shy tone.

"I'm glad I could pop that cherry for you," he retorted.

"Shut up," she laughed and sighed. "I miss you," she said in a low tone.

"I miss you too," Andre admitted without missing a beat. He'd missed her a great deal in the last few days he was gone. It had been just about a month they were seeing each other and he couldn't believe how much he thought about her already. Andre opted not to let his thoughts travel to how much mental space thinking of her was taking up in his mind.

"How's studying coming along?" he asked, changing the subject.

Stacey's semester was in full swing and she had midterms in a couple of weeks. She wanted to get an early start on studying, so she was using her free time to get ahead in her classes and turn in work early.

"It's going well," she said around a yawn.

They talked for a few more minutes, catching up on each other's days before hanging up. Andre made sure to insist she get some rest. There were times where she'd spent the night and he'd woken up in the middle of the night to find her studying in bed, or at his desk with the laptop, typing away on a paper. She'd told him it was what she did when she couldn't sleep, but sometimes, he worried she was burning herself out. Even though he worried, he was proud of how dedicated she was to her profession. He felt the same passion for his own work, so he didn't try to dissuade her from doing what she felt she needed to do. He realized that the years she'd spent dedicated to and practicing dance likely instilled a drive in her to succeed that she would carry for the rest of her life.

Andre went to bed that night satisfied. Though he couldn't wait to get back home, that intimate time on the phone with Stacey had been enough to invigorate him for the next few days. He planned to tie up some loose ends with this acquisition and get back home and to the woman in his life who was becoming even more special to him with each passing day.

CHAPTER 11

A *dancer's body is the instrument with which she makes music, the* *loom with which she weaves magic. But we take our bodies to* *places they would naturally never go...we subject ourselves to unbelievable* *strain. And sometimes we stumble. We break.*

Stacey read that passage again for a third time out of Misty Copeland's, *Life in Motion* as she sat in the dressing room at the Black Kitty. She was all too familiar with the stumble and breaks that came from dancing. Subconsciously, she reached down to rub the scar on her knee, which was covered by her fishnet stockings. She was scheduled to perform later tonight.

"What are you reading, Stace?"

Stacey looked up to see Mercedes enter the dressing room. "Hey, Mercedes. I didn't even hear you come in. I'm reading Misty Copeland's book." She rose to give her friend a hug.

"Oh, I heard it was good. You look really into it. You know she just became a principal with ABT?" Mercedes asked.

Stacey nodded, smiling. ABT stood for American Ballet Company, arguably the top ballet company in the nation. Principal was the highest ranking a dancer could receive and Misty was the first African-American woman to reach such a level. It was a proud moment for Stacey who'd once had those aspirations. It was what had inspired her to pick up the book again for a fourth reading.

"I know. It's so exciting. She's earned it," Stacey admitted happily.

"I see you're in your *en pointe* shoes tonight. Are you dedicating your performance to Misty tonight?" Mercedes asked, referring to the white ballerina shoes Stacey wore.

"Maybe. You'll just have to wait and see," Stacey teased.

"I can't wait," Mercedes said as she moved past Stacey to begin changing her own clothes for her performance.

A while later, Stacey braced herself as she smoothed the scrunched parts of her fuchsia satin gloves that extended all the way to her elbows. She wore her fuchsia *en pointe* shoes, and a matching fuchsia and gold colored corset and short shorts. The corset had a long extended tail trailing behind.

"Help me welcome this next performer to the stage to shake her money maker! Give it up for Jazmine Nooooiiireee!!" Mistress Coco's voice boomed over the raucous applause.

The opening chords of Goapele's *Strong As Glass* began to play, and Stacey sauntered on stage on her tiptoes. She didn't often perform ballet sets, but reading Misty Copeland's book put her in the mood to revisit her past life for a little while.

She whirled around the stage like the dervish Misty's book referred to ballerinas as, leaping across the stage performing a *jete*, completing a full split in mid-air. The audience cheered and hooted their appreciation. The leap wasn't nearly as high as the *jetes* she'd performed years ago, but it felt great nonetheless. She spun, pausing to stick her finger in her mouth, clutched the glove and then slowly pulled her hand out, leaving it exposed. She did the same for the second glove and then fluttered her arms out to her sides like wings as she rose on her toes once more. She paused, lifted onto her toes, and then slowly extended one leg straight up so she was in a perfect split still standing on one leg.

A collective gasp was heard around the crowd as they marveled at her flexibility and poise. Releasing her foot down to the ground, she performed a series of steps, gliding across the stage as she reached around and pulled the strings that attached her corset. Slowly, she removed the corset to show off her bared breasts covered only by a set fuchsia pasties. She slowly swiveled her hips in time with the music, seductively slid her shorts town her smooth brown thighs, and ended her set with the classic ballerina bow—her left foot forward turned outward and her right foot behind her, bent at the waist, head down, arms held high.

Stacey took in the crowd's applause and cheers as she caught her breath before exiting the stage. While these performances were vastly different from her formal ballet performances, it felt just as good. As she sauntered off the stage, she had to admit what would have made her exit from the stage even better was knowing Andre was in the audience, but he was still away in Boston. She missed his presence at her shows more than she cared to admit.

She bounded down the stairs, and after throwing a thumbs up and to the next performer, she turned to head towards the dressing room.

"You were amazing, babe." Stacey heard the voice that sent shivers of joy down her spine. Turning, she saw all six-feet two inches of her fantasy, dressed casually in a pair of dark jeans and a pale blue Burberry button up, holding her favorite flowers. The best part was the shit eating grin he wore as he stared at her.

Stacey didn't hesitate to throw her arms around his neck, squeezing tightly. Luckily, Andre's reflexes were quick enough that he moved his arms just in time to avoid the crushing of the flowers. Not that they would have cared too much; he'd finished work up early just so he could hold this woman in his arms again.

"I thought you weren't supposed to be back until Monday," Stacey mumbled into his ear.

"I wasn't, but I—" he paused, clearing his throat for some reason not wanting to completely reveal the extent of how much he'd missed her. "We, uh, got done early. These are for you," he said holding out the flowers to her when she finally released him.

"They're beautiful. Thank you," she said accepting the flowers.

"You're beautiful. Do you have to perform again or are you done for the night?" he asked.

Stacey shook her head. "No, I was—"

"Get dressed and come with me," he ordered not even giving her time to finish her sentence.

"Where're we going?" she asked, confused.

"I've got a taste for butter pecan ice cream and *you*," he stated, giving Stacey a scorching look.

The sides of Stacey's mouth kicked up into an instant lascivious smile of her own. "Lucky for you, I'm craving the same thing." She winked. "Let me go change and I'll be ready in—"

"Five minutes," Andre ordered impatiently. "Or I'm coming in after you."

"Tsk, tsk, so impatient," Stacey teased.

"You have no idea. Hurry up," he retorted.

At the serious look he gave her, Stacey turned and strode down the hallway to the dressing room. Dressing quickly, she threw on a pair of dark blue skinny jeans, a green three-quarter length top, and a pair of black ballet flats before gathering her discarded costume. Within minutes, she was heading out the door with her belongings in tow. Usually, she liked to stay and support the other dancers, but when she turned and saw Andre standing there, looking as good as sin, all thoughts of being anywhere but in his arms fled.

A while later, Andre pulled in after Stacey into their favorite ice cream shop, or what was becoming known as "their spot." Since Stacey had driven her car to the Black Kitty, Andre opted to follow her to the parlor and then she'd follow him to his place. Entering the shop, Stacey noticed the place was kind of busy. It was a Saturday night after all, and one of the last few weeks the parlor would be open before closing for the fall and winter months.

"Tell me about your trip." Stacey nudged Andre when he wrapped his arms around her from behind as they waited in line. She felt his arms tighten as he shrugged his shoulders.

"Not much to tell. Got done what needed to get done. Had to let a few people go, but we'll be better off for it. Hopefully, this trip fixed most of the human resources problems. Though, I might have to make a few more trips."

"Can I help who's next?" the young woman behind the counter called. Andre ordered their ice cream to go, wanting to get home quickly to be alone with Stacey.

"Take this, I need to use the restroom," he told Stacey, handing her money to pay for their order.

"That's, okay, I c—"

"Take it," he said, giving her the serious eye.

She knew he wouldn't let her pay for anything while they were out together, but she still tried on occasion. Begrudgingly, she took the money and Andre pressed a kiss to her lips before strolling to the bathroom.

Stacey smiled at his retreating back. Even seeing a few of the other women eyeing Andre as he walked away filled her with a sense of pride instead of jealousy. She turned to watch the clerk scoop their ice cream into bowls, still smiling and reveling in the feeling of being with Andre. Though they still hadn't solidified what they were, she believed they were in a relationship. She hadn't seen anyone since they began dating, not even Damon. Although Andre never said he wasn't dating anyone else, she couldn't see how he would have had time, as much time as they spent together. She hated the idea of having to have the dreaded "what are we" conversation, but for her peace of mind, she decided she needed to ask tonight.

Lost in her own thoughts, Stacey didn't notice the man who stood a little too closely behind her.

"Jazmine, right?" she heard a deep baritone voice ask just a few inches behind her.

Turning, she had to look up a few inches. He was around six-foot and towered over her. The way his brown eyes assessed her made Stacey uneasy. Unconsciously, she took a step back, bumping into the counter behind her.

"I thought that was you." He leered down at her. "I caught one of your shows the other week. *Very* hot. So, how much for a private show?" He lowered his voice and wiggled his eyebrows.

Stacey's eyes widened. Did he just proposition her?

"What?" she asked incredulously.

"Oh come on, don't act like that. Not when you do what you do on a stage in front of perfect strangers. So, how much?"

"Look, you better get the hell away from me before—"

"Before what?" he questioned, his face turning into a sneer as he attempted to grab onto her arm.

Stacey saw the move and pivoted out of his reach, grabbed his hands, and twisted, causing him to hunch over in pain.

"What the fuck?!" she heard Andre's voice yell as he approached.

Before she could even release the man, Andre picked him up by his collar and spun him so they were face to face. "What the fuck did you do to her?!" he growled at the man so fiercely it sent a cold shiver down Stacey's back, but she was pissed in her own right.

"H-hey man, I was just asking about her services. I didn't know she was taken for the night," the stupid man tried to defend himself.

When Andre realized exactly what the man was referring to, his eyes narrowed in a ferocious stare and he sent a hard punch to the man's gut, causing him to fall to his knees.

"Oooh, what hell?!" the man cried out, just as Andre attempted to swing again.

Stacey moved to his side, pulling him away. "Andre, enough. We're causing a scene," she said in a low voice, not wanting to make more of a deal out of this man's disgusting behavior.

"I don't give a shit about a scene. This bastard tried to proposition you like some common whore," he railed, his hand still gripping the man's collar.

"Something I bet he'll never do again. He's just an overzealous fan who got carried away. Please don't let this ruin our night," she tried to cajole.

"Get me your manager," Andre barked at the poor clerk who stood wide-eyed behind the counter. She ran to the back and a few moments later, a stout, older man came out of the back of the store.

"Oh Mr. Collins, we're so sorry for the inconvenience," the older man apologized as soon as he reached Andre. Only after a long while of cajoling did Andre finally release the man. He made him apologize to Stacey, and the owner assured him the man was never to be allowed back in the store.

Finally, after convincing Andre that she was okay, they left the parlor. Stacey couldn't even look at the other patrons as they departed. She hated gaining the attention of onlookers unless she was on stage, but she understood Andre's anger. She was just as shocked and disgusted by the man's proposition as Andre was.

"And after all that, we didn't get our ice cream," she teased, trying to interject some levity into moment. She could feel Andre's tension as he walked her to the car.

"This isn't funny. That asshole could have harmed you. You need to quit burlesque dancing," he demanded.

"First of all, he wouldn't have hurt me—wait did you just demand I quit performing?" she asked, finally realizing what he'd just demanded she do.

"You heard me loud and clear. You. need. to. quit!" he reiterated, crossing his arms over his chest.

"What the hell? So, one asshole goes full asshole and you think you can tell me what the hell to do with my damn life?" she asked, her own anger rising.

"Two assholes in the last few weeks, if you remember correctly. This is the second damn time I've come up to find some jackass with his hands on you," he said through gritted teeth.

"And that's my fault how? Just because some guy thinks it's okay to proposition me doesn't mean I need to quit something I enjoy," she retorted.

"These assholes wouldn't be coming out the woodwork if you didn't take your damn clothes off for money. I'm not dealing with this shit. You need to quit. End of discussion," he said pushing past her to open her car door.

"End of discussion?! I'm not a damn puppy you can just lead around. And after you just insulted me, basically implying I'm some kind of whore like that man in there just did, I'm not even sure I want anything to do with you. Asshole!" she furiously spat at him.

Andre stiffened, his eyes widening for a nanosecond before they narrowed on her face.

"You should know I don't respond well to threats," he gritted out.

"And you should know I don't make threats. That was a promise. You can either drop this stupid argument and apologize for insulting me, or you don't have to worry about seeing me again," she bit out.

Andre stared at her for a few seconds, but Stacey wasn't backing down. She was not about to give up a second dancing career she enjoyed for someone who wasn't even her boyfriend. When she saw Andre straighten and fold his arms across his broad chest again, she had her answer.

"I'm not changing my mind," he said with finality.

Stacey ignored the pang of hurt she felt in her chest at his words. She wasn't going to back down for someone she'd been dating just over a month.

"Fine," she said shrugging and turning to get into her car. She felt Andre's penetrating gaze on her back as she fumbled with her keys to open her car door. A big part of her hoped he would change his mind and stop her. Tell her that he was sorry for what he said in anger and give up his silly notion that he could make her quit an activity she loved, but that moment never came. The disappointment rushed through her as she slammed her car door. She refused to even look in Andre's direction as she yanked at her seatbelt across her lap, started her car, and backed out her parking space, speeding out of the parking lot.

ANDRE ANGRILY WATCHED as Stacey's car peeled out of the parking lot. He too ignored the pang of disappointed in his chest that grew the further away her car got. No matter how disappointed he was, he would not change his mind. She was putting herself in danger by performing. Assholes were coming out of the woodwork and propositioning her because of her performing. Why the hell couldn't she see how that was an issue? The thought of some jackass making a pass at her, or worse, putting his hands on her because he saw her on stage, made him see red. He'd been ready to beat the shit out of the man in the store. Hell, the way he was feeling right now, he had it in his mind to head back to the store to finish what he'd started before. Somebody needed to pay for the way he was feeling right now.

"Fuck!" he cursed out loud before pulling his keys from his pocket and striding angrily to his car. Slamming his own car door, he sped out of the parking lot. Before he hit the corner, his phone rang. Andre quickly reached for his pants' pocket hoping it was Stacey calling to apologize to him for being so damn stubborn. When he pulled out his phone, he saw Maria's name come up. Pressing ignore, he threw his phone into the passenger seat.

"Not tonight," he mumbled crossly before pressing on the gas, speeding through a green light. He couldn't believe how Stacey had stormed off, effectively ending their budding relationship when he clearly was just trying to keep her safe.

"Whatever," he said dismissively. But no matter how hard he tried, he couldn't tamp down the twinge of regret that began to bubble up in his chest as he drove home.

CHAPTER 12

"Anything else you want to share? You're looking down in the dumps," Stacey's therapist, Linda observed.

It had been nearly two weeks since her break up with Andre and she was still feeling hurt and angry over it. He hadn't called her and although she'd picked up the phone many times in the two weeks to call him, remembering his angry words and his demand that she quit ultimately stopped her. She figured since she hadn't heard from him, he couldn't care less. That was what had hurt most, thinking that he could just throw her away without a care in the world.

"Is it your mid-terms? Are you nervous about how you did?" Linda asked when Stacey didn't respond.

Stacey shook her head. "No, mid-terms are fine. I've gotten my grades back on those already. I guess I'm still feeling this break up, or whatever it was. I'm not sure we were even a real couple." Stacey sighed.

"Tell me about it," Linda encouraged.

For the next ten minutes, Stacey told Linda about her relationship with Andre and how much she'd missed him when he was in Boston. She told her how happy she had been to see him at the Black Kitty that night, and then how it all had gone wrong when they'd stopped just to get some ice cream. She hated the tremor in her voice she felt when she talked about his demanding she quit burlesque, and how her refusal to do so ended their short time together.

"I see. And has this set off any triggers for you?" Linda asked perceptively.

Stacey wanted to lie and say that she'd been fine. That she was too distracted by school and work to even think about how her break up with Andre left her, but that wasn't the case. She had been feeling withdrawn and noticed small bad habits creeping back in.

Stacey reluctantly nodded. "I skipped lunch a couple times this past week. Then at night, I'd find myself stuffing my face with a carton of ice cream," she confessed.

"And how did you handle that?" Linda asked.

Linda's non-judgmental tone helped Stacey to relax and tell the truth. Stacey knew better than anyone that being honest about her behaviors was the best way to avoid spiraling out of control down a very long and ugly road…a road she'd been down before and had to fight like hell to come back from. The stress of her last semester of school, mid-terms, and her feelings about her break up with Andre were beginning to get to her. She realized all this while talking with Linda.

"And what can you do to take care of yourself today?" Linda asked, sincerely.

"I have plans to meet Devyn and Mercedes at a spa later this morning. We're doing the full treatment, massages, facials, manis and pedis," she said feeling relieved just thinking about the outing with her friends. She hadn't hung out with her girls in a few weeks. Devyn's husband and three kids, and being owner of an event planning business, kept her pretty busy. Being a new wife and full-time assistant principal kept Mercedes busy as well. Not to mention, Stacey had a lot going on in her own right, but she was ready to have a fun day out with her friends.

"That sounds really good. And if you're feeling like you need to talk, you have my cell number, right?" Linda questioned.

"Yes. I'll call if I need to," Stacey agreed.

"Good. Have fun with your friends," Linda told her as they ended their session.

Stacey looked forward to her spa treatments with her friends. Maybe a day out with friends was exactly what she needed to shrug off the funk she'd been in since that night with Andre.

* * *

"Mmmm, ahhhh. This was so needed," Devyn moaned as she laid her head against the black leather headrest and placed her feet in the bubbling water.

Stacey sat to Devyn's left and Mercedes sat on the other side of her, her head laying against the headrest as well. Stacey smiled at how relaxed the two women appeared. She wished she could feel as relaxed, but seeing these two women who were blissfully in love and happy in life made her miss Andre even more.

Just get over it, she scolded herself, trying to force herself to enjoy the moment.

"Mmm, you can say that again," Mercedes commented in response to Devyn's earlier statement.

"I could, except our friend here doesn't appear too happy," Devyn astutely acknowledged, peering over at Stacey. "What's up, Stace? You look like someone just kicked your puppy."

"Mhmmm, we know what's wrong. Same thing that's wrong with your brother-in-law, Dev. They haven't spoken in days probably. What happened?" Mercedes asked, bluntly.

Stacey sighed and shrugged. "It just didn't work out," she said, not wanting to go into full detail of what happened between her and Andre, especially since she didn't want them to know he'd essentially insulted burlesque dancers. Even though they'd broken up, a part of her felt protective over him. She didn't want to distort his image in their eyes.

"Don't give us that bullshit. What'd he do?" Mercedes pushed, sitting up in her seat like she was just waiting for a juicy story.

"Ugh, fine. The night he came back from Boston, he surprised me at the Black Kitty," she began.

"Awww," Devyn interjected.

"Yeah aww, until we went out for ice cream. Some jackass comes up and propositions me while Andre was in the bathroom. Apparently, he'd seen me perform and thought I'd be interested in giving him a private show," she said using air quotes. "The guy tries to grab for me after I curse him out, and I do a finger lock my sister taught me just as Andre comes out of the bathroom. Long story short, after I had to restrain him from beating the guy down, he insists that I quit burlesque," she told them.

"What?!" both Devyn and Mercedes exclaimed.

Stacey nodded. "Yup, he said these men wouldn't get the wrong idea if I wasn't a glorified whore."

"Oh my God! He said that?!" Devyn's gasped.

"Not in so many words, but he insinuated it," Stacey said feeling her anger rise all over again.

"So, you told him to kiss you where the sun don't shine, right?" Mercedes asked.

Stacey giggled. "Not in so many words, but...that was the gist."

"Good!" Mercedes nodded.

"I can't believe he would say something like that. Maybe he was just having a bad day or something. I know he really liked you," Devyn defended, "but what he said was out of line."

"I could tell he was feeling you too. I saw all those forehead kisses he gave you when you came off stage after performing," Mercedes teased.

Stacey shrugged. "No big deal. A few forehead kisses doesn't mean he really liked me all that much," Stacey said trying to downplay her relationship with Andre.

She saw as Devyn and Mercedes both sat up, looking over her and at one another. They made eye contact and burst out laughing. Stacey was confused.

"What? What's so funny?" she asked wanting to be let in on the joke.

"Girl, forehead kisses are the damn reason I have three kids now!" Devyn laughed, wiping tears from her eyes.

"Hmhm, and they're damn sure the reason my last name changed from Holmes to Santiago. Forehead kisses are a prelude to...well, I'm sure you've figured it out," Mercedes whooped, wiping her own eyes from the tears that formed.

Stacey's lips turned up into a half-smile as she thought about how affectionate Andre had been. She'd admittedly enjoyed any time his lips touched any part of her body, but forehead kisses while in public had a way of making her crave his touch.

"Anyway, are you going to the MADD gala next week? Iris wanted me to ask if you were coming. She and Andre host it every year," Devyn asked.

Stacey had heard about the Mothers Against Drunk Driving event from Mercedes but had no intention of going. Andre had never mentioned it, another indication he wasn't all that serious about her.

She shook her head. "I hadn't planned on it."

"You have to come" Devyn pushed.

"I don't have a dress or a date. I can't show up to something like that alone," Stacey explained.

"Don't worry about that." Mercedes waved her concerns off. "We can go shopping one day this week, and there's a single teacher at my school I think would be perfect for you."

Stacey shifted in her seat, feeling uncomfortable. Could she go to an event she knew Andre would be hosting on the arm of another man? How would that look? And how would she feel seeing him again? But Devyn and Mercedes wouldn't take no for an answer. In fact, after their spa treatments ended, instead of going out for an early dinner as planned, the women dragged Stacey to Neiman Marcus to shop for dresses. After trying on six different dresses, they decided on a long-sleeved Herve Leger jacquard mid-thigh dress. The dress was a pink champagne color that perfectly showed off Stacey's long legs. They paired the dress with some strappy black heels, and Devyn insisted on paying for her purchases.

"Just consider it an early graduation gift," Devyn told her, smiling and holding up the bags for Stacey.

"Now, that that's settled, let's go eat. I'm starving!" Mercedes interjected.

Stacey had to admit her day with her friends had been exactly what she'd needed. She still missed Andre and now she was even more nervous about seeing him at the gala the next week, but laughing and shopping with her friends had taken her mind off him for a little while. She just had to figure out a way to make it through next week's gala without making a fool out of herself, pining away for a man she was supposed to be done with.

* * *

"ANDRE." Nikola knocked on his brother's door before entering.

"What!?" Andre barked at him without looking up.

"I see your panties are still in a knot." Nikola sighed, stepped into Andre's office, and folded his arms across his chest.

I don't need this shit today, Andre thought giving his brother a frown. "Did you need something?" he asked.

"Yeah, I'd like for you deal with whatever the hell is bothering you. You've been acting short with the staff and me for weeks now," Nikola growled.

"Whatever. I don't need a damn lecture on my attitude. I'm busy," Andre stated turning his attention to his computer.

"If you say so. I came to bring these documents for your approval and signature. Get 'em back to me as soon as possible," Nikola said placing the folders on Andre's desk.

"Fine," was all Andre said, effectively dismissing his brother.

Nikola simply shook his head as he walked out of Andre's office. He knew how bullheaded his brother could be when he was in one of his moods, and he'd been in this mood for weeks now.

Andre didn't even bother to look up as Nikola walked out. He felt a twinge of guilt at the way he'd been treating his staff and brother lately. He made a mental note to send his assistant some flowers and let her leave a few hours early later in the week to make up for it. His mood had been shit since the night he'd last seen Stacey.

Andre pounded his desk with his fist. Just the thought of her caused his blood to boil. He didn't know if it was with anger, lust, longing, or some combination of the three. He couldn't stop thinking about her, how she was doing, or if was she seeing someone else. He spent a number of restless nights thinking of picking up the phone to call her, but his pride wouldn't let him do it. He'd kept himself busy with work, often not leaving the office until nine or ten o'clock at night. He'd avoided hanging out with Hwan as he knew his friend would question his foul mood, and he wasn't up for talking about it.

Andre turned his attention back to his computer just as he heard another knock on the door.

"Dammit, Nik, I'll get the papers to you soon enough," he said without looking up.

"That's nice, but I don't need any papers," Devyn said as she entered his office.

Andre abruptly turned his attention from his computer towards his doorway to see his sister-in-law strolling into his office and taking a seat in the chair in front of his desk. It briefly reminded him of the days when Devyn was his assistant.

"Sorry, Dev. I thought you were Nik," he said, feeling a slight bit of remorse at having raised his voice at her.

"No problem, brother-in-law." She smiled, but it didn't quite reach her eyes.

Oh shit, Andre thought knowing this would not be a social call. The only time Devyn referred to him as "brother-in-law" was when she was about to ream him about something. Like the time he'd fed the boys cake and ice cream for dinner while babysitting, and they'd spent the entire night up with crying with stomachaches. It took him months to live that down, and before Nik or Devyn would let him babysit again. He could probably guess what was coming, but he decided to ask anyway.

"What did I do now?"

"Who says you did something? Feeling guilty?" she questioned, raising one perfectly arched eyebrow.

I can play this game too, he thought. "Not particularly, no," he said sitting back in his seat and resting his palms on the sides of his chair.

"You probably should over the way you've been treating your staff the last few weeks. You nearly took poor Margaret's head off because she brought you two creams instead of three the other day," Devyn shot back at him. "Or, maybe you should feel guilty for implying that burlesque dancers are whores."

She folded her arms and eyed him. He should have known that comment would make its way back to Devyn. He could admit he regretted saying that in anger. And now as he looked into Devyn's eyes, he could see she was pissed with him. She had a right to be.

"Dev, you know—"

"Save it," she said waving him off, "You know, your brother asked me to quit burlesque too. Well, he didn't ask, he demanded I quit. Seems to be a trait with you Collins men."

Andre sat up in his chair. He hadn't known Nikola ever had a problem with Devyn's dancing. He'd never told Andre anything negative about his attitude towards her performing.

"What happened?" Andre asked, wondering how Devyn and Nikola made it over that hump in their relationship.

"I said no." She shrugged. "You don't know about my relationship before Nikola and I, but my ex was an ass. Anyway, when I got out of that relationship, I promised to never change who I was or stop doing something I enjoyed and that made me happy for another man. I'd made too many sacrifices in my previous relationship to give up that part of myself. I don't know everything about Stacey's past, but I know she used to be a ballet dancer, and I know performing is in her soul. You can see it when she's on stage. If you cared about her, really cared, you wouldn't ask her to give that up."

Devyn stood and Andre sat back in his seat, letting her words sink in. He knew of Stacey's dance past. One could see she was a natural performer, but seeing so many men ogle her on stage got under his skin.

"I'm sorry, Devyn. You know I didn't really mean what I said about burlesque dancers," he finally said just as Devyn reached the door.

Devyn stopped and turned to him. "I know. Don't worry about it. We're good. And maybe you'll get a chance to apologize to Stacey this weekend at the gala."

Devyn smiled innocently at him.

Andre raised his eyebrow questioningly. "She's going?" Andre had planned to ask her to accompany him to the gala that night, but things hadn't worked out. When he saw the saccharine sweet look on Devyn's face, he knew something was up. Narrowing his eyes on her, he asked, "Is she going alone?"

When Devyn shook her head, Andre's heart dropped. Who the hell was she going to *his* gala with?

"Mercedes offered to introduce her to a co-worker friend of hers. I think they're going to the gala. Isn't that nice?" Devyn asked. "Oh, maybe now you can tell Lorenzo he doesn't have to follow her every Wednesday or after her performances now. You know, since she might be seeing someone else."

Devyn waved and headed out. Andre was floored. Not only was Stacey going to his gala, but she wasn't going alone? She was going with some schmuck? And how the hell did Devyn know he still had Lorenzo watching over Stacey? Even though they technically weren't together, he still worried about her safety. The thought of Stacey leaving work in the dark and no one watching over her filled him with a sense of anxiety he'd rather not think about. So, he'd hired Lorenzo to make sure she was okay.

Bring!

His cell phone went off, interrupting his thoughts. Looking down, he saw it was Maria. She'd been calling every day for the past two weeks. He'd send her straight to voicemail, but today was different. Hearing Stacey had a date to his gala irritated him beyond rational thought. He made his decision without a second thought.

"Hey, Maria. What are you doing this Friday night?" he asked without preamble as he answered the phone.

CHAPTER 13

*I*ris Collins was in a good mood as she stood under the handcrafted plaster relief ceilings and crystal chandeliers of the Imperial Ballroom at the Biltmore. Tonight, she was hosting one of her most cherished charities. Dressed in a navy blue, Badgley Mischka lace cape sheath cocktail dress, and a pair of silver strappy heels, she felt proud of the work she'd done with MADD over the past five years. Annually, this gala would bring hundreds of thousands of dollars to the organization, and help spread the word about the dangers of drunk driving, as well as provide assistance to those who'd had their lives altered by it. She knew all too well how drunk driving could take a life and ruin a family.

Iris watched as many of the movers and shakers in the sports, music and business world in Atlanta mingled and entered the ballroom. Checking her watch, she noted the time. It was just after eight-thirty, and she'd just received word from her personal assistant that Nikola and Devyn had just arrived. She smiled at that bit of news, but she was really waiting for her youngest son to arrive. She was expecting fireworks to go off tonight with her stubborn, youngest child.

"Iris, don't you look fancy tonight?" Iris heard the raspy voice of her dear friend, Diane, from behind her. To most, Diane was known as Mistress Coco, especially around her club, the Black Kitty, but Diane and Iris went back decades, long before there ever was a Black Kitty. Iris' pink colored lips turned up into an even more brilliant smile.

"Diane, it's about time you showed up. Did you get lost?" Iris teased as she swiped two glasses of champagne from the passing waiter, handing one to Diane. Diane was dressed in a black, form-fitting Carmen Marc Valvo cocktail dress with sleeve lace trim, which stopped a few inches below the knee. Her short, natural silver hair was styled in a tapered cut.

"I sure didn't. I got um....distracted." Diane answered slyly, glancing over at her date who stood at the other side of the room.

Iris peeked around Diane's shoulder and admired the six-foot-four, broad shouldered, caramel complected man who'd drawn the attention of her friend. He appeared to be in his mid-forties, which was just Diane's speed. She liked her men young and virile, as she would say.

"I see," Iris eyed her friend, "luckily, you haven't missed anything. Oop, wait, here comes Stacey now. Isn't she lovely?" Iris turned her attention towards the entranceway where Stacey stood.

"Of course, she is. She's one of my girls," Diane answered arrogantly. Diane was very protective over her dancers and would tell anyone who would listen that her club had the best dancers this side of the Mississippi.

"I thought you said she was bringing a date. Why is she alone?" Diane asked, her face a mask of confusion.

"She was supposed to come with a teacher from Mercedes' school, but he couldn't make it. No matter, there are plenty of eligible men here who would walk through fire to get next to her, which is perfect." Iris clapped giddily.

"Iris, one day those children of yours are gonna turn on you for all your meddling in their lives," Diane giggled conspiratorially with her friend.

"Oh please, like you wouldn't do the same thing for your kids.

Remember when you tried to get me to introduce Leslie to the Mayor's son?" Iris questioned, referring to Diane's twenty-four year old daughter, a lead dancer for one of the world's leading pop stars.

"Psshh," Diane snorted, waving off Iris' comments. "That was when the fire department was trying to cite me for some type of violation. I needed an in and the Mayor's son is cute. And Beau lucked up and found his own wife without meddling from me," Diane defended herself, referring to her thirty-six year old son.

"Diane, you're ridiculous." Iris giggled at her friend's antics.

"What do you have planned for tonight?" Diane asked after they regained their composure.

"It's going to be good," Iris said, wiggling her eyebrows before leaning in and lowering her voice to tell Diane her plan.

* * *

"ANDRE, slow down! I'm wearing five inch heels. I can't keep up with your long strides," Maria complained as he strolled through the double doors of the Biltmore.

"I wouldn't be rushing if you had been ready at eight o'clock like I'd specified," he chided as he held the door open for Maria. Andre was beyond irritated, and Maria's lateness had only served to irk him even more. Knowing he would see Stacey again for the first time in three weeks had him on edge. The thought of her showing up on the arm of another man made his fingers itch to wrap around the bastard's throat. When he felt Maria's fingers wrap around his upper arm, he resisted the urge to shake her off of him. After all, he was the one who'd invited her. His foul mood wasn't entirely her fault.

"I'm sorry, but I wanted to look my best for you," she purred close to his ear. She was dressed in a long cream and black, sleeveless gown that grazed the floor as she walked. Her long, dark hair was pulled back in an elegant bun. She looked beautiful, and most men would be happy to have her on their arm.

But Andre wasn't most men.

"Then you should have gotten dressed earlier so we wouldn't have been late," he stated bluntly. "Let's find my mother." He turned his attention to all the guests in the ballroom.

"Great," he heard Maria mumble under her breath.

They walked through the ballroom, Andre greeting business associates, politicians and other important people in attendance. Everyone wanted a piece of Andre. He graciously talked about the charity they were hosting, but held firm on keeping talk of business for the office. Many guests passed their business cards and tried to set up a meeting with him, which he easily deflected and referred them to call his office on Monday to schedule a meeting. He was in no mood to talk about work or business right now. This event was special to him, and especially to his mother.

"Hi, mama." He greeted her with a kiss on her cheek when he spotted her. "You remember, Maria, right?"

Andre watched as his mother's smile faltered almost imperceptibly, but he knew his mother well enough to know when she was faking it, and he knew that she wasn't the biggest fan of Maria's.

"Of course. How are you, dear?" Iris asked, greeting Maria.

"I'm well, Mrs. Collins. Pleasure to meet you again."

Andre could tell the smile on Maria's face was just as phony as his mother's. The two women had never really hit it off although they'd met on numerous occasions, but they kept it cordial. Andre half listened as his mother and Maria made small talk. He let his gaze drift from his mother and Maria to the other guests. There was one person in particular he was looking for, and when his eyes landed on her, he felt the blood rush from his head to other parts of his body. He eyed her from head to toe as he took in the way her dress showed off her long legs, and the V-neck of the collar highlighted the delicate column of her neck. Her hair was different from the last time he'd seen her. Gone were the long twists, and it hung in curly ringlets that fell a few inches past her shoulder. She looked delectable.

Without thinking, Andre instinctively turned to walk towards her. It was as if her body had a magnetic pull and he couldn't resist the urge to be near her.

"Oh, Andre, the mayor wanted to speak with you," his mother told him halting his movements.

"O-okay, sure thing," he reluctantly acquiesced, taking a step to follow his mother. He'd forgotten all about Maria's presence until her fingers wrapped around his bicep as she trailed him.

* * *

STACEY COULDN'T EXPLAIN IT, but she felt his presence as soon as he entered the ballroom. She hadn't seen Andre, but she felt him. She'd arrived at the gala a half an hour prior, alone. Apparently, Mercedes' teacher friend was unavailable on such short notice. When she tried to tell Devyn and Mercedes she couldn't show up alone and tried to cancel, they wouldn't hear of it. Devyn arranged for a town car to pick her up from her condo and take her to the gala. Now, she stood looking around for either Devyn or Mercedes. Instead of finding her friends, her eyes first made contact with Andre's. He was staring directly at her, and Stacey couldn't move as those blue eyes perused up and down her body.

Stacey allowed her own eyes to do an assessing gaze of Andre in his tailored black and white tuxedo, which had probably cost a small fortune, but damn if it wasn't worth every penny. Time stood still as they stared at each other from across the room. Stacey smiled as her heart rate increased. She couldn't deny how happy she was to see him. When the side of Andre's mouth tipped up into a half-smile, she blew out the breath she'd been holding. Maybe coming hadn't been such a bad thing after all.

Just as that thought had passed through her mind, she noticed cherry red fingernails grip his bicep, and a woman dressed in a cream and black gown lean in and whisper something in his ear. Stacey's smile instantly turned to a frown as the woman stepped even closer to Andre's side. They were clearly there together and the woman was staking her territory. Stacey recognized the woman as the one he'd attended Mercedes' wedding with.

Stacey felt as if she'd been sucker punched in the gut seeing the woman's hands all over Andre. She instantly turned away, looking to find Devyn and Mercedes to make her hellos and then hightail it out of there. She'd be damned if she stayed at this gala all night and watched some other woman with her hands all over Andre.

"Stacey, there you are," she heard over her shoulder. Turning, Stacey saw Andre's mother, who wore a bright smile on her elegant face.

"Are you enjoying yourself?" Iris asked.

Hell no, Stacey wanted to say, but held her tongue. She nodded.

"Yes, Mrs. Collins. Thank you for inviting me. This is a beautiful event," she said instead.

"No problem. I wanted to introduce you to someone," Iris rushed on. "This is David. David works at one of the top law firms in the city." Iris gestured to the man at her side.

"Oh," Stacey said, stunned. She was unsure how to reply as she looked over the man who was about five-foot ten, and had tan skin, blond hair and green eyes. His strong, chiseled jaw and scruffy beard gave him a roughish appeal. Stacey could admit that he was a very handsome man.

"It's a pleasure to meet you, Stacey," David said taking her hand and pressing a kiss to the outside of her palm.

Unbeknownst to Stacey, Andre saw the kiss and his gaze narrowed. Without bothering to excuse himself from the conversation with the mayor and his associates, Andre angrily strode over to where Stacey, his mother, and the schmuck stood.

Who the hell does he think he is putting his damn lips on her like that? Andre angrily questioned to no one. He didn't even hear the click-clack of Maria's stilettos as she scurried to catch up to him.

"Oh, An—"

"Who the hell is this?!" he testily spat towards Stacey, interrupting the little pow wow the three of them seemed to have going on.

"Andre!" Both Iris and Maria gasped.

"I'm sorry, David. Something has seemed to come over my son this evening," Iris interjected. "Andre, this is David. I was just introducing him to Stacey."

"This is who the hell you came here with tonight?!" he questioned Stacey, not even registering his mother's words. Andre saw red when he saw that asshole's lips make contact with Stacey's hand. A possessiveness he'd never felt before came over him.

"Since when do I have to explain myself to you?" Stacey spat at him just as bitterly.

"Since you showed up to my Goddamn gala with this schmuck on your arm!" he retorted.

"Andre that's enough!" Iris interrupted their little spat. "David I am so sorry. This is not how he usually is."

"No, I'm sorry Mrs. Collins. I'm sure you raised your son better than this," Stacey said eyeing Andre with cold eyes. "David, would you care for a dance?" Stacey threw on a sickly sweet smile, effectively dismissing Andre.

When David nodded, she tucked her arms around his as he led her to the dance floor. She could feel Andre's heated gaze on her back as they strolled to the dance floor.

"You know what? I need to use the ladies' room. Would you excuse me?" Stacey asked once her dance with David ended. She'd barely been able to concentrate on their dance. She was so angry, she couldn't think of anything but that confrontation with Andre she'd just had. She needed a moment to compose herself.

"Sure, I'll be right here." David smiled and stepped back to release her from his embrace.

"Thank you." She smiled and nodded before rushing off to the bathroom.

* * *

STACEY WAS livid as she pushed her way into the marble tiled bathroom. She barely noticed the bathroom attendant standing outside. Luckily, the bathroom was empty. She was so angered she nearly took one of the stall doors off its hinges pushing it open.

Who the hell did he think he was? He had no damn right questioning her about who she was or wasn't there with. Especially not as that woman clung to his arm like a second damn skin!

"To hell with him!" she angrily mumbled to herself as she flushed and exited the stall. "He can kiss my ass!" she continued to rant under her breath as she washed and dried her hands. With her back turned to the door, she didn't realize someone had entered the bathroom until she heard the loud "click" of the lock. Turning quickly, she saw the source of her ire. He had the damn audacity to stand there in his perfectly tailored tuxedo, spit shined shoes, and an irate expression on his own gorgeous face.

He has the nerve to be angry? Stacey thought.

"What the hell are you doing in here?!" she demanded.

Andre just stared at her with that angry look on his face, frowning and taking shallow breaths as if he was trying compose himself.

"Who the fuck was that?" he asked in a low voice riddled with acrimony. He began approaching her slowly, reminding her of a panther stalking its prey.

Even though she was pissed, her traitorous body began to tingle at the mere thought of being this close to him after three weeks of not seeing or talking to him. Nevertheless, she wouldn't let her longing for him get in the way of a good cursing out.

She threw her hands to her hips. "Are you serious? Where the hell do *you* get off asking me," she pointed her finger towards her chest, "who that was when you're here with some tramp clinging to you like white on rice. Who the hell is that!?"

By this time, Andre was only a few inches from her. "She doesn't matter. Are you fucking him?"

Andre knew the question was way out of line, but he was past the point of no return. No woman had ever made him so damn possessive. The last few weeks without seeing or touching her had been torturous. When he heard from Devyn she was bringing a date to tonight's gala, he'd nearly lost it. When Maria called at the last moment, he'd thought he could take her and ignore Stacey. Now, he knew that was a mistake.

"Did you...are you..." Stacey sputtered, looking as if she could spit nails. "Am I fucking him?? You know what? YES! I'm fucking him 'cause that's what women who take their clothes off for money do right? We fuck everyone who—" Stacey couldn't even get the last words out before Andre slammed his mouth over hers. Her hands came up to his chest to push him away, but when he reached around to grab her ass and pull her into his growing hardness, her hands moved up his firm chest and wrapped around the back of his head, pulling him in closer.

Andre pulled Stacey's head back by her hair, giving him a better angle to take control of the kiss and her body.

Stacey felt herself being lifted and instinctively wrapped her legs around Andre's waist as he carried her to the sink and placed her on it. Pulling back, Andre looked her square in the eyes and said the one word that made Stacey's panties moist with need.

"Mine," he growled before lifting her to push her dress up to her waist, and slamming his lips back over hers. Stacey felt his fingers as they gripped the edges of her black lace panties and pulled. She heard the tearing sound of her panties before Andre pulled her back down from the counter, placed her feet on the floor, and spun her around so her back was to him. With deft movements, Andre inserted his foot between her legs, pushing them wider. Gripping her waist with one hand and pulling her head back by her hair so she had no choice but to look at them both in the huge bathroom mirror, he looked her directly in the eye as he pushed his hard cock into her wet core.

"You. are. mine!" He claimed her with each thrust of his hips. "Say it!" he demanded as he stared at her in the mirror.

Stacey was so far gone, she couldn't do anything but stare at his handsome face in the mirror and receive all that he was giving her. The absolute look of possession in his eyes made her cream even more.

"Ohhhh, Fuck, Andre!" she yelled when he adjusted his hips to hit her g-spot.

The hand that rested on her hip moved around to pluck and rub her clit. "Say it!" he demanded again, yanking her head back and biting her earlobe.

"Andre!" Stacey yelled, still not giving him what he wanted.

He began thrusting into her with even more wild abandon. They both moaned and groaned, not caring that they were at a gala and people could possibly hear them.

Andre let the hand that was in Stacey's hair move around to wrap around her neck from the front. He squeezed, applying pressure to the sides of her neck as he continued to pound into her while rubbing her clit.

Stacey couldn't feel anything but the pleasure he was giving her. Her entire world shrunk down to the places on her body where Andre was touching her.

"Ooohhhh, Gooood," she moaned when the pleasure became almost unbearable as he squeezed her neck again.

"Say it, dammit!" he growled in her ear when he released some of the pressure off her neck, still holding onto it.

"Yours! I'm yours!" she screamed as wave after wave of intense euphoria rippled through her body. Everything in front of Stacey went black as the orgasm took over her entire body.

"Fuuuuck! I'm yours Andre!" she yelled.

"Mine!" Andre yelled before releasing her neck and pulling her head back to press another hard kiss to her lips as he came. He pumped wildly as he spilled his seed into her.

When he was done, he let his arms fall to her waist and rested his head in the crook of her neck. Both were panting as they struggled to catch their breath.

After a long while, Andre finally withdrew from her and stepped back, giving her space to adjust her dress. He grabbed a few paper towels and went to wipe Stacey down.

"I can do that," she said half embarrassed by the lewd way she'd just behaved.

Andre couldn't give a shit though. "No," he said simply, pushing her hand away and stooping down on one knee to wipe away their mixed fluids that dripped from her body. Finishing that task, he picked up her shredded panties from the floor and stuffed them into his pocket. For the first time that night, he gave her his signature smirk and wink.

"Your driver will drop off your...date," he spit out the last word, "and deliver you to my condo once you leave." He adjusted his own clothing.

"And what about your date?" Stacey asked, saying the last word just as tersely, not even mentioning that she'd arrived alone and David wasn't really her date.

"I'll worry about her," he stated pulling her into his arms.

"And what is that supposed to mean?" she asked, pressing her hands to his chest and giving him a suspicious look.

"It means that I meant it when I said you were mine. You don't need to worry about her," he answered, pressing a gentle kiss to the side of her mouth.

It was the exact opposite of the hard kisses he'd given her just a few moments ago, and yet, they had the same effect on Stacey. This man's touch was addictive whether hard, soft, or somewhere in between. Stacey sighed in satisfaction.

"You should walk out first," she told him, referring to their exit.

Andre turned and looked at the door, and then back at her regretfully, as if he didn't want to leave. Stacey knew that feeling because she sure as hell didn't want him to leave either.

"My place. Tonight. And if that motherfucker touches you..." he trailed off, giving her a look she knew spelled trouble for David or any man who might be tempted to try and touch her.

"He won't. Now go. People are probably looking for you," she said, raising to press a kiss to his lips.

Andre nodded. "My place. Tonight," he reminded her before turning and leaving.

Andre strolled out of the bathroom with his hands in his pockets, whistling. Stopping at the entrance, he tipped the attendant a few hundred for making sure no one entered the bathroom, and for keeping quiet. The man stoically accepted the tip and nodded. Rounding the corner, he saw his mother making her way to where the stage area had been set up. She was beginning to make her introductions of the donors of the event and announce the early tally of the amount raised from tonight's event.

"Hey, I thought I lost you," Maria said as she made her way through the crowd towards him. Andre flinched at her touch. After being with Stacey, he didn't want to feel the touch of any other woman but her. A hint of guilt touched his chest as he thought about how he'd essentially used Maria to forget about Stacey, and then just had some of the steamiest sex he'd ever had in his life in the bathroom while Maria waited out here for him.

"No, you didn't. Let's mingle for a little while. There's some people I need to speak with," he stated, pulling her further away from the bathroom.

CHAPTER 14

*S*tacey was ready to get out of there. Her skin tingled as she thought about her earlier encounter with Andre in the bathroom. After he'd left, it took her a few minutes to orient herself enough to reapply her makeup, fix her clothing, and head back out to the gala. She danced a few more times with David, feeling guilty the whole time as he tried to make conversation and even slip her his number. She had to let him down gently, and then went in search of Mercedes and Devyn. She stayed close to her friends for the rest of the evening, even when Andre appeared in their little circle with his date in tow, giving her such a heated gaze she knew if she were a few shades lighter she'd be seen blushing. He'd even been so bold as to stick his arm through the circle and ask her to dance, not taking no for an answer. The entire time during their dance, he leaned down and whispered exactly what he was going to do to her once they were back at his condo. It took all her years of training as a dancer to not let her face give away the intense emotions his whispered words were setting off.

As she waited by the entryway for her driver, Stacey closed her eyes and sighed thinking of the way her skin had tingled as Andre's breath grazed her neck.

"Well, fancy seeing you out here. What's the matter, no one else's man want to fuck you in the bathroom?"

Stacey's eyes widened as she spun around at the nasty comments from the woman behind her. There stood Andre's date, Maria, shooting daggers at her with her eyes.

"Excuse me?" Stacey asked half shocked and half angry.

"You heard me. You don't think I know what the hell you two were doing when you both conveniently disappeared? What type of slut fucks someone else's man in the bathroom at a gala?" Maria questioned just above a whisper, her lips turned into a snarl.

Stacey's cheeks flamed with embarrassment. Part of her was ashamed at what had gone on between her and Andre, but not nearly enough to let this woman stand here and insult her.

"Look, I'm sorry about what happened tonight. I had no intention of any of that happening, but I'm not about to stand here and let you insult me. You have a problem, then you really need to take it up with the person you claim is *your* man," Stacey defended herself. She was not in the mood to put up with personal attacks and insults from a woman who didn't know anything about her.

"He doesn't want you. He may enjoy fucking you for now, but it won't last. Why would he want someone like you? You're just a tramp who spreads her legs. You black—"

"That's ENOUGH!" Andre roared behind Maria.

Both women turned and stared wide-eyed at Andre who looked angry enough to have smoke coming out of his ears. Even though his anger wasn't directed at her, Stacey nearly flinched at the cold stare he gave Maria. His nostrils flared, and his lips curled into a harsh frown. He took a step towards Maria and she had the good sense to step back.

"Don't you dare finish that fucking sentence!" he snarled through gritted teeth. "We're leaving now!" He grabbed her arm, not hard, but enough to pull her towards the awaiting driver. When Maria got in the car, he slammed the door, told the driver something, and walked back to Stacey.

"I'm sorry," he said, pulling her towards her car and driver. After giving the driver his address he instructed him to make sure to drive safely and deliver her to his condo, where he'd already instructed his doorman to let her up.

Stacey watched through the window of her town car as Andre got into the same car where Maria was. The look of pure enmity was written all over Andre's face. She knew instinctively that, that was one car ride Maria would not enjoy.

* * *

"ANDRE, I'M SORRY..." Maria pleaded as soon as they reached her hotel suite.

He'd been silent the entire car ride, keeping his distance from her and not even looking at her as they made their way to her hotel. Once they arrived, he'd gotten out the vehicle, not even giving a second glance at her as he strolled to the elevator.

"What you said tonight was disgusting, rude, and way the fuck out of line. If you're angry about what happened at the gala, then you take that shit out on me. She is none of your fucking business. As far as I am concerned, we are done now and forever. Have a safe trip back to Boston." He turned to walk away when he was stopped by her hand on his arm.

"Don't fucking touch me!" he barked at her causing Maria to recoil.

"Andre, please. I'm sorry. I didn't mean it the way it came out. I was just so angry—"

"You're angry, take it out on me. Not her. I don't even want to think about what you would have said if I hadn't walked up. But it doesn't matter. You are no longer my problem and I am no longer yours. Stay the hell away from me," he ordered before turning and striding down the hallway with purpose. Punching the down button for the elevator, he gave her one last hard glare before entering.

Andre barely gave a second thought to the slamming of the suite door he heard as the elevator doors shut. His thoughts had already turned to the woman who awaited him at his condo. He wanted to make sure she was okay and that Maria's words hadn't gotten to her.

"Hey, I'm so—" Andre's apology was cut off by Stacey's lips on his. He instantaneously wrapped his arms around her waist, pulling her to him. The anger he'd felt since he came upon Maria berating her slowly dissolved, replaced by burning need to have this woman beneath him, calling his name as he soared into her.

"F-fuck!" he whispered when Stacey pulled his head down and ran her tongue along the outer shell of his ear.

"I don't want to talk about her. I want you to fuck me until I can't move," Stacey whispered.

Her words had his cock standing at complete attention. "Anyway you want it, baby," Andre responded, lifting her legs to wrap around his waist. Even though he'd just had this woman less than two hours ago, he couldn't hold out long enough to make it to his bedroom. Turning, he pinned her back against the wall and let her assist in getting his own pants unbuttoned. Within seconds, his cock was free and Andre slammed into her awaiting core. His entrance was made easier due to their earlier encounter which resulted in her panties now being in his back pocket instead of the acting as a barrier.

"Andre!" Stacey screamed as he surged into her. "Fuck! You feel so goood!" she moaned.

"Did you miss me, baby?" Andre asked, his lips grazing hers as his hips continued to work their magic on her wet pussy.

"Mmmm, God yes!" she shouted.

Andre moved his arms to hook her legs over his elbows, spreading her wider for his assault. He canted his hips so that he made contact with her clit on every stroke.

"God baby, I missed your tight pussy wrapped around by cock. Squeezing me," he groaned in her ear.

"I'm coming," Stacey moaned.

The tightening of her walls around his cock sent off his own orgasm, and before he knew it, he was coming. Andre pounded his fist into the wall behind her as he came, throwing his head back. His hips continued to pump in and out of her releasing every drop of his cum inside her.

"There's a lot more where that came from. We've got three weeks to make up for," Andre panted against Stacey's lips. He felt her lips turn up into a smile against his.

"Four. Counting the week you were in Boston. Lead the way, Mr. Collins," Stacey replied, giggling as Andre swatted her on the ass and carried her to his bedroom. Over the next few hours, they both showed each other how much they'd missed one another.

"I'm not quitting," Stacey said hours later as her back rested against Andre's chest, as they sat in his free standing tub.

They'd gone at each other for hours before Andre carried Stacey into his huge contemporary styled, black and white bathroom, and placed her in the tub. Now, they sat in the tub soaking and talking about everything that'd gone on in the last few weeks. Andre admitted that he'd been more than his fair share of grumpy, and had taken it out on his staff. He also informed her that tonight had been the first time he'd seen Maria or any other woman since their break up, and he'd only done it because he heard she was bringing a date to the gala.

For her part, Stacey admitted that she'd picked up the phone numerous times to call him, but her pride had gotten in the way. She knew they needed to discuss the reason they'd had the blow up to begin with.

She felt his grip tighten around her midsection at her words. Although she couldn't see him, she knew his jaw was clenched tight as he contemplated what she'd just said. Without looking, she reached up and let her fingers massage his jaw to loosen it up.

"You're going to crack a tooth if you keep grinding your jaw like that," she teased. "Loosen up." She felt the muscles in his jaw release just a tiny bit.

Andre sighed. "This is important to you?" he asked, knowing the answer but still wanting to hear it from her mouth.

Stacey nodded. She brought one of his hands to her lips, kissing his each finger before raising her right knee and moving his fingers to graze over the raised skin that created a scar.

Stacey took a deep breath before closing her eyes, and she began talking, "I was twenty-two years old and a soloist at the Pacific Northwest Ballet with dreams of working my way up to be a principal. We were performing a series of steps and leaps, preparing for the upcoming season and getting ready for performances. We spent upwards of six hours a day on our toes. It was hard, but I couldn't see myself doing anything else. A few weeks into preparing for the fall and winter season I felt some pain, and after putting it off, I finally went to get some x-rays. I had a stress fracture in my right leg, but I kept it to myself. Ballet looks beautiful and graceful, but we spend hour upon grueling hour to make every move from the hardest leap to the lift of each finger, look effortless. We dance in pain. It's a part of ballet. Dancers practice and perform on broken toes, sprained ankles, and stress fractures. Young dancers, especially, don't complain because for every one of us who made it, there's a hundred more ready to take our spot. So, we perform on broken bodies and smile through the pain."

She stopped to turn to look at Andre as she continued. She could see his face soften as he listened intently.

"That's what I did. I performed on my stress fracture. One day while in practice, in an attempt to overcompensate, I landed wrong in a leap I'd done thousands of times. A *pas de chat*. Before I knew what happened, I was on the floor writhing in pain as my knee bent awkwardly." Stacey shuddered, reliving the moment her dreams came crashing down around her.

Andre's arms came up around her waist, pulling her towards him in comfort. He lightly pressed a kiss to her forehead, but remained quiet.

"One of my quadriceps muscles jammed my knee cap out of place. Even when the doctors told me that I'd probably never dance at the professional level again, I didn't believe them. I rehabbed for nearly a year after surgery, but never got back to where I was. It took a long time for me to recover physically and emotionally. I—" she paused, not wanting to talk about the spiral she went into the year after her dance career ended.

"It took a long time to figure out who I was without ballet. When I found burlesque, it healed a part me. I found a world where women enjoyed performance as much as I did, but didn't care that my jumps weren't as high as they once were, or that my body had changed somewhat from the size zero and I gained some hips and ass. The dancers there embraced me and my scars. I get to do what I love through burlesque." She paused, staring up into his vibrant blue eyes. "I was forced to retire from one dance career long before I was ready..."

Andre stared down at her with such tenderness in his eyes it made her shiver. He placed another kiss to her forehead and Stacey's heart melted.

Goddamn forehead kisses, she thought, remembering her conversation with Devyn and Mercedes.

"Is that what your tattoo stands for?"

Stacey's eye widened, shocked he'd made the connection between her butterfly tattoo and the story she'd just told him. She nodded.

"Yes, butterflies represent transformation, and are beautiful to look at once they take flight."

"Just like you," he told her sincerely.

Stacey smiled. "I actually wanted my burlesque name to be Black Butterfly, but when I started there was a dancer with the name "Butterfly" already, so I chose my favorite flower instead."

"My Black Butterfly. I like it," he smiled, "I won't ask you to quit. I'll just beat anyone's ass who tries to touch you," he said, rubbing his face along her cheek.

Stacey knew he meant every word of what he'd said. Smiling, she reached up and grazed her fingers through his beard.

"You know the rule, right?" he asked slyly.

Stacey pulled back, looking at him curiously. "What rule?"

"You touch the beard, you have to sit on it," he said, quickly, moving to pull the stopper out of the drain and pulling them both up to stand.

Stacey giggled as Andre hurriedly dried them both off, discarded the towel over his shoulder, and carried her to his bed where he made good on his latest rule.

CHAPTER 15

The next few weeks for Stacey and Andre flew by. They picked up right where they'd left off, with Stacey spending a few nights a week at his condo, and Andre still showing up to the dance studio every Wednesday night to make sure she got home or to his place safely. Since she'd shared some of her past and how her dancing career ended, he'd been a lot more understanding and considerate of her burlesque performing. She'd even debuted a few new routines in a private show just for him, which he'd thoroughly enjoyed, of course. She would often still feel his watchful eye whenever she was at the club performing. Somehow, it gave her a measure of safety knowing he looked over her so intently. Stacey wasn't a particularly jumpy person, but there were a few instances when she felt she was being watched or surveilled.

Stacey reclined in her leather chair in the tiny office she shared with another intern at the one of the top eating disorder facilities, hunched over her desk. She was studious about going over her notes before and after her group sessions. She was devoted to giving her clients the detail and care they deserved. Since beginning her internship, she'd formed a group session to allow more access for women of color and women without insurance to be able to receive services.

"Hey, you got a minute?" Stacey looked up as she heard the knock on her opened door. At the entrance stood the clinic's associate director, Marcy. Marcy stood at about five-foot-seven with shoulder-length, strawberry blond hair. She wore a pair black pants and a powder blue button up shirt. She smiled down at Stacey, and instantly Stacey's mood improved. She'd just finished a rough session with a few clients that had left some of them in tears. Though she tried not to let her client's problems get her down, she was human.

Stacey perked up. She and Marcy went back more than most people who'd worked at the clinic only a few years, knew.

"Sure, Marce, what's up?" Stacey said, waving her hand to offer Marcy a seat.

"A couple things. First, I wanted to say how great of a job we think you're doing here. We knew going in this project you started would be a tough sell to the higher ups, but when we were able to show the need for mental health services and eating disorder treatments for women of color and those who were less socioeconomically well off, it became an easier sell, thanks to your diligence." Marcy smiled.

"And I know you know firsthand how much these services are needed. We both do," Marcy stated, alluding to the fact that at one time, both women had been residents of the facility for their own struggles.

Stacey sighed and nodded, sitting back in her chair, "I do," she agreed. There were few people who knew Stacey's entire past and her struggles. This was the reason she'd worked so hard to become a licensed social worker. Why she put in the hours and took classes through the summers and vacations to finish her degrees in four years. After dance, and her own recovery, helping others get to the other side of recovery had become her main focus. Now, it was almost in her grasp. She would be finishing her studies in another six weeks.

"So far, we think the program is going very well. We want to see you continue the good work. So, the director has asked me to ask you to interview with us to become a social worker here at Renfrew once you finish your degrees. You can work here to get the necessary hours you need to get your LSW," Marcy gushed.

A booming laugh escaped Stacey's lips and she quickly covered her mouth with her hand. She just felt so giddy, elated and relieved all in that moment. This was what she'd been working towards. She wanted more than anything to work at this facility when she completed school.

"Are you serious?" she asked surprised.

"Of course," Marcy affirmed. "We want to schedule an interview in another two to three weeks. I know that's cutting it close to your finals and all, but that's the earliest we can do it."

Stacey waved her hand. "Don't worry about it. I will work it out. You just let me know the time and place and I will be there with bells on."

"Absolutely. We'll talk more about a specific date next week," Marcy said standing.

Stacey stood, feeling too excited to sit. The warring emotions of pride, elation and nervous self-doubt began to creep in as she watched Marcy leave. She wanted to call someone to share her good news and confide in. The first person she thought of was the one who'd kissed her awake just that morning. Pulling her cell out of her desk drawer, before she could even unlock her phone, it rang. It wasn't Andre, but this person was a close second choice.

"Hi, Aunt Ruth, guess what?" she rushed as she answered the phone.

"Hi, honey. You sound excited, what's up?" Stacey's aunt and the woman who'd been a second mother to her questioned.

"I just met with Marcy and she wants to schedule me for an interview to bring me on full-time after I finish school. I can work here and get my hours in to become an LSW," she squealed, plopping down in her chair.

"Oh, honey, that's wonderful. I am so proud of you. Hold on, I have to call your uncle on so you can share the good news," her aunt rushed before Stacey could get out another word. The line was silent for a while and a minute later, Stacey heard the deep voice of her uncle coming through the line.

"Stace? Ruth just told me the great news. That is wonderful." He sounded just as joyful as her aunt had been at the news, but Stacey wanted to temper their enthusiasm just a bit.

"Thank you, but remember it's just an interview. I still haven't gotten the job yet," she said a little more evenly.

"Oh, pssh," her aunt admonished. "We know you already got the job. You're gonna ace that interview. Wait, until we tell the boys," Ruth mentioned referring to her two sons, Stacey's older cousins. Although both "boys" were grown men in their thirties, their mother still referred to them as "her boys." Stacey smiled over the pride she heard in both her uncle and aunt's voices. These two were the parents she'd wished she had as a young child, and although it'd taken some time for her to warm up to them when she first went to live with them, they'd come to be her major support system throughout her teenage years.

"Have you told Coral yet?" her uncle asked.

"No, Marcy just left my office when Aunt Ruth called," she informed them. "Have you guys spoken with her recently?"

"No, honey," Ruth answered.

Stacey could hear the hint of melancholy in her aunt's voice. While Stacey had been twelve when she went to live with her aunt and uncle, Coral had been seventeen, and a year away from college. She had never developed the close bond with her aunt and uncle that Stacey had. In fact, it wasn't until Coral left for college that Stacey was able to develop a closer bond with her aunt and uncle. She'd looked to Coral so much for protection throughout her childhood that it had felt like betrayal to become close with any other parental figures, while she was around. Stacey knew her aunt and uncle loved Coral as much as they loved her, but her older sister had an outer shell that made it difficult for anyone to penetrate. Stacey knew it was that tough shell that kept them both alive as children, and for that she was grateful, but it often saddened her that her sister wasn't as close to their family as she was.

"Okay, I'll try and call her later," Stacey told them before moving on to a different topic.

Ruth questioned Stacey about her plans for Thanksgiving that was only about three weeks away. Ruth and her uncle were planning to vacation in the Dominican Republic for the holiday and invited Stacey to come along. She told them she'd get back to them as soon as possible. She wasn't sure if Andre had plans or what his intentions were for the holidays and she wanted to run it past him first.

At the moment, Stacey's thoughts drifted to Andre and the evening they had planned. She figured instead of calling him now, she could wait until later to tell him about her interview before they went out. They were going out with Andre's best friend, Hwan, and his husband, Damon. As her aunt and uncle continued to talk of their travel plans for the holidays, her thoughts drifted to what Andre had told her about his friend.

She braced the phone between her ear and shoulder, captured her right hand with her left, and began rubbing tiny circles over the tiny scar between the knuckle of her pointer and middle finger.

According to Andre, Hwan could be very blunt about his feelings. He told her Hwan was often quick to let him know when he did not like woman he brought around or was dating. While Stacey rarely sought approval of others anymore, she did want to gain at least the respect of the man Andre called his closest confidant.

STACEY FELT Andre's hand tighten around her smaller one as they followed the hostess into the Tropicana Room at Loca Luna. She admired the ambiance of the restaurant as she took in the wooden tables and chairs covered by red table clothes, and the overhead lighting decorations that looked like Christmas lights intertwined around the ceiling pillars. Salsa music provided an upbeat feeling to the restaurant, but was not blaring so loud that it was a hindrance to conversation. It felt like a cozy restaurant to meet friends for dinner, or in Stacey's case, for the first time.

"There they are." Andre turned his cerulean eyes on her, giving his signature wink.

That wink, though he meant it as reassurance, always had a way of sending a heated sensation flooding through her stomach. Shaking off the feeling of desire that was always not too far from the surface when she was around Andre, Stacey turned to the table their hostess stopped at.

"Here's your party, sir. Your waitress tonight will be Stephanie. She'll be over in a few minutes to take your drink orders. Enjoy your dinner," the bubbly hostess announced before turning and striding back to the front of the restaurant.

Stacey took in the two men who now stood before her. One she immediately identified as Hwan, Andre's best friend since graduate school. He was a similar height as Andre, but that was where the similarities ended. Hwan's creamy complexion, dark hair and slanted eyes spoke to his Korean lineage, while Damon stood a few inches shorter than both men, and his smooth chestnut complexion spoke of his African-American lineage.

"Babe, this is Hwan and Damon," Andre introduced, extending his arm to the two men. "Hwan and Damon, this is Stacey."

"Like I didn't know," Hwan tutted at Andre before pulling Stacey into a warm embrace. "Nice to finally meet the woman who has my friend so enamored."

He smirked.

"Hwan," Andre's voice was low, but held a hint of warning at which Hwan's smile grew even bigger.

Stacey's lips spread into a smile matching Hwan's. She could tell he liked to ruffle Andre's feathers. "It's a pleasure to meet you, Hwan. Andre's told me so much about you," she confessed after pulling back from Hwan's hug.

"And this handsome fellow right here is my husband, Damon," Hwan said, placing his arm around Damon's waist. "See, Andre's not the only one down with the swirl."

Hwan snickered, causing Damon and Stacey to laugh too.

The quartet sat at one of the u-shaped booth tables with Stacey and Damon on the inside, and Andre and Hwan on either side of their respective dates. They settled in just as the waitress arrived. She quickly took their drink orders and dispersed, leaving the group to talk amongst themselves.

"So Stacey, I hear you were a ballerina?" Hwan asked, diving right in.

"Jesus Hwan, give her time to breath," Andre demanded protectively. He knew Stacey's ballet history was a sensitive subject for her. He was surprised when she jovially interjected.

"It's okay, Andre," she declared patting his leg under the table. "Yes Hwan, I used to dance ballet for the Pacific Northwest Ballet Company. Have you been?"

Strangely enough, she'd begun to feel more comfortable talking about her ballet history with others. Stacey suspected it had a lot to do with opening up to Andre about her abrupt career-ending injury.

Hwan's lips spread into a wide grin. "Yes, I have actually. I'm from San Francisco. Each Christmas break, my family would take a vacation to Seattle. My mother would insist we all do something culture related. So, the ballet it was. My younger brother hated it and so did my dad. But my mother and I would talk for hours about the most minute details. The costumes, the difference between the Balanchine choreography and the other choreographers. I probably should have known then that I was gay." He broke out into laughter with the rest of the table.

"Mmm, I loved the Balanchine choreography. You know, Pacific only changed over to his style a year and a half before I left. I danced in the Corps performance of the Nutcracker," Stacey reminisced.

The pair spent the next ten minutes talking about ballet, the different styles, and their mutual love of the costumes and performance. Damon jumped in when they began their conversation about the makeup and how it correlated to the moods and characters the dancers were portraying on stage. As a makeup artist, Damon loved anytime he could talk shop about makeup.

All the while, Andre sat and watched as his friends and his woman interacted. A warm feeling came over him as he watched the joy Hwan expressed interacting with Stacey. It was almost as if he couldn't stop talking about his love of the ballet. Stacey was just as responsive to Hwan as she too gushed over the different aspects of ballet. They were getting along more like two friends reunited, rather than two people meeting for the first time, or worse, two people whose only purpose in even talking was trying to appease those around them. Andre had had plenty of women he was seeing try to get in good with him by trying to turn up the charm on Hwan. His perceptive friend would see right through it and so did Andre. It was no secret to Andre that Hwan rarely liked the women he'd dated. As he looked over at his best friend, he surmised that it wouldn't be an issue with Stacey. For some reason, that lifted a weight off his shoulders he hadn't realized was there.

"Hwan, Andre told me you two met in grad school, but he told me there's a funny story how you two men. Care to share?" Stacey asked as they all munched on their shared dinner of grilled asparagus, platanos maduros, and grilled salmon skewers.

Hwan nodded, wiping his mouth with the red cloth napkin. "We were both at Stanford and lived in the same apartment building just off-campus, and one thing you'll learn about me is that I love music. All kinds from classical to hip hop, rock. All of it, and I have a tendency to play it loudly. So loud it can be disturbing to my neighbors, but I've gotten better. Right, babe?"

He looked over at Damon.

"Define better," Damon teased, leveling a look at him.

"Anyway," Hwan waved him off as Stacey and Andre chuckled at Damon's comment, "I was blasting my music and all of a sudden I hear loud banging on the door. Startled, I rush to the door, thinking someone's hurt. I open it to see a pair of tired, yet angry blue eyes bearing down on me. I was so taken aback by this gorgeous man staring at me, I forgot, I'd answered the door in my boxer briefs. And well, I don't have to tell you, but our boy over here is fine." Hwan waved his hand towards Andre.

"Excuse me," Damon interjected.

"But nothing compared to you, baby," Hwan cooed to Damon, kissing him on the cheek. Damon gave him a satisfied smile.

"Hey, what am I chop liver?" Andre joked. He'd heard Hwan speak of his instant attraction to him in the past, but they'd been so friends for so long it didn't bother him.

"No, you're perfect," Stacey consoled, rubbing Andre's leg and placing a kiss on his cheek.

"Thanks, baby," Andre said nuzzling her neck.

"Will you two get a room," Hwan teased. "But let me finish my story first. So yeah, I'm standing there in my boxer briefs looking at those beautiful blues, and after just staring, I realize blue eyes is speaking. I hadn't heard a word he said. It was then I realized I was nearly naked in front of this man. So, one thing led to another, and we became friends when he didn't become all weird after the sex like the other straight dudes I've been with." Hwan placed air quotes around the word straight as he finished his story.

"Hwan!" Andre growled, tossing his friend a warning look, but he couldn't keep the smirk off his face. Hwan often joked like this when trying to get to know one of Andre's many dates. Their response often determined the course of their relationship with Andre. He glanced down to gauge Stacey's reaction to his friend's comments.

"Well, was it good?" she retorted quickly.

Her question even caught Hwan off guard for all of a second before he burst into laughter along with the rest of the table.

"I like her," Hwan declared over his laughter.

The rest of the evening flew by quickly as they talked about everything from work, to sports, and even a little bit of politics. An hour later, the restaurant converted the front section into a dance space, making room for the couples to dance as a live band played a mix of salsa, reggaeton, bachata and even some flamenco. Stacey was pulled to the dance floor by Damon who himself loved to dance, especially salsa. He and Hwan had even taken dance lessons the year before.

Stacey enjoyed herself after a few minutes of instruction from Damon. She wasn't as well versed in salsa as in other dances, but nevertheless she was a quick study. Even though the steps were new to her, her body reveled in the rhythm of the music, and she was able to let go. After Damon showed her the basic steps to dancing salsa in the two, she was taking his lead as he spun her around the dance floor.

Five songs in, she'd worked up a bit of a sweat, but still wasn't ready to sit down even though Damon was.

"Mind if I cut in?" That familiar deep timbre sent shivers down her spine as his warm breath skirted over her shoulder from behind.

"You sure you know what you're doing?" she purred.

"Oh baby, I know exactly what I'm doing. Let me show you," he said, taking her hand as Damon passed it to him. With a flick of his wrist and extension of his arm, Andre had Stacey spinning around the dance floor yet again.

Stacey was stunned when Andre performed the salsa steps to perfection. His steps were perfectly in time with the music, and his hips had a natural cadence that she knew was useful for more than just dancing. When a reggaeton song came on, she sidled up to Andre, turned so her back was to his front, and began a grind with her hips that she knew would get a rise out of him. Within seconds, she felt strong hands grip her around the hips as he pulled her hips to meet his.

"Mmm," Stacey purred, as she felt his growing hardness rub against her buttocks.

"You know what that sound does to me," Andre growled low in her ear.

"Show me," she challenged, turning and rubbing her breasts into the expanse of his chest. Stacey's stomach fluttered when a wicked mile spread across Andre's handsome face. His arms tightened around her waist just before he leaned down to whisper in her ear.

"Challenge accepted." He pulled her off the dance floor to their table, quickly retrieving her purse and making their goodbyes.

Stacey had to practically run in her five inch heels as Andre's tight grasp on her hand pulled her behind him. With lightning speed, Andre placed Stacey in his passenger seat before moving around to the driver's side. Stacey was in a teasing mood and decided to push Andre's buttons a little more.

"Is it hot in here?" she asked innocently.

"Huh?" Andre questioned distractedly as he pressed down harder on the gas, rushing to get his woman behind closed doors.

"I asked is it hot in here?"

"I don't th—" Andre's words caught in his throat when he glanced over at Stacey. He nearly swerved off the road when he saw her hike up the edges of her dress, exposing more of her creamy brown thighs.

"Are you sure?" she seductively intoned as she watched Andre snap his head back to the road, knuckles growing white as he gripped the steering wheel.

"Goddammit, baby." Andre's voice was thick with his growing arousal.

"What's the matter?" she asked, reaching over to massage his hand on the steering wheel, loosening his grip. She pulled his hand to her thigh, and slowly pulled it up her thigh, under her dress, to rest at her very warm center. "See, I told you it was hot," she teased, spreading her legs wider to make room for his big hand.

"You were right," Andre agreed as he let his fingers ease the edges of her lace panties to the side, and began massaging her heated labia. She was already wet. He inched lower and deftly inserted one finger into her tightness.

"Ooo," Stacey sighed as her head fell back against the headrest.

Andre slowly pulled his finger out and brought it to Stacey's lips. "Open," he commanded, briefly looking over at her.

Without hesitation, Stacey's lips parted, granting his finger access, and Andre wasted no time plunging his finger into the warm cavern of her mouth.

Stacey's lips encircled Andre's finger, sucking and licking her own juices. Stacey pulled a second finger into her mouth, sucking as if her life depended on it.

"Shit, baby," Andre cursed, pulling his fingers from her mouth and returning to her nether lips. He made quick work of shoving her underwear to the side before swiftly entering her with the same two fingers. As they pulled into the private garage of his building, with one hand on the steering wheel, Andre pulled into a parking space while pumping into and out of Stacey's wet core with his other hand.

"Andre," Stacey panted his name just above a whisper.

"I fucking love it when you say my name right before you come, baby. Do you know how hard that makes me?" he questioned, voice thick with arousal and wonder. "Look at me. I want to see you when you come. I want to look into your eyes when you come from just my fingers inside you, knowing when I take you upstairs I'm going to shove my cock so deep inside you, you won't remember where I end and you begin. Do you want that, baby?" He probed her at the same time he curled his fingers inside her, reaching for the sensitive bundle of nerves.

"Mmm, yeeeess," Stacey hissed at the exact moment his fingers hit her g-spot. Squirming in her seat, she used one hand to brace the door handle, and the other to brace Andre's strong bicep.

"Then come for me. Now!" he growled, pumping his fingers with vigor.

"I-Ahhhhh," Stacey groaned when her orgasm exploded inside her.

"Damn," Andre said in awe, staring at her.

Still panting, Stacey's eyes widened when Andre pulled his fingers from her and inserted them into his own mouth. The wanton move caused another wave of moisture to dampen her already soaked panties.

"So fucking delicious," Andre groaned, swallowing and closing his eyes as if he'd just had his favorite meal of all time. He quickly moved from the driver's seat, helped Stacey out of the car, and they made their way to his private elevator. Less than two seconds after the elevator doors closed, Andre had Stacey pinned against the wall, making good on his promise to imbed himself so deep inside her she didn't know whether she was coming or going.

When the elevator doors opened, both stumbled out of the elevator. They didn't even make it to Andre's bedroom. He laid her down on his plush carpet, pulled off her dress, removed his own clothing, and took his woman over and over.

CHAPTER 16

"Andre what's all this?" Stacey asked, walking into his kitchen and seeing a whole spread of breakfast foods. The last three weeks flew by for Stacey and Andre as she'd been consumed with finishing up projects for her classes and her internship. They'd also spent the Thanksgiving holiday and weekend together. Instead of hosting the holiday at Devyn and Nikola's as was the usual case, Iris hosted Thanksgiving dinner. Nikola, Devyn, the couple's three children along with Raul, Mercedes, Andre and Stacey were all in attendance. The women helped Iris cook while the men watched football. Stacey felt as if she was a regular part of the family. Of course, being close friends with Devyn and Mercedes already helped, but feeling as if Andre tried hard to ensure she felt included made it special too. He made sure to tell his mother Stacey's favorite dessert was butter pecan ice cream, and she'd had a fresh homemade batch for Stacey to enjoy. Now, it was the Wednesday after Thanksgiving, and Stacey had her big interview to work as a full-time counselor for the same facility she currently interned at.

"This, is for you. Come sit," he said motioning for her to sit in the chair he'd pulled out for her at his glass dining table.

"Andre this is a lot of food," she said looking over the array of assorted fruits, croissants, scrambled eggs, turkey bacon and sausage. "Did you prepare all of this?"

"Most. The croissants are from the bakery downstairs. They're fresh. I figured you needed a hearty breakfast today. We don't want your stomach growling in the middle of your big interview." He tossed her a wink over his shoulder as he strolled to his kitchen. He returned with a pitcher of fresh orange juice in one hand and a pot of fresh brewed coffee in the other. "This," he gestured holding up the pitcher of orange juice, "I didn't squeeze it myself, but it is fresh squeezed from downstairs. I'm assured it's made with plenty of TLC," he finished, placing the pitcher and coffee on their holders, and placing a brief kiss to Stacey's cheek.

"Eat up," he encouraged as he took his own seat.

Stacey's chest expanded with a feeling of warmth as she realized Andre had woken up at least an hour early to prepare this big meal for her. It was evident he cared deeply about her and was supportive of her goals. The day before, he'd gone over interview questions with her, and had helped her to feel more relaxed in an interview setting. Knowing that he cared deeply enough to go out of his way to aid in her success warmed her.

"Alright Ms. Coleman, why do you want this position?"

Stacey's forkful of scrambled eggs paused midway to her mouth. Her eyes shot over to Andre who wore an expectant expression. This is the one interview question she'd had trouble with the day before. She felt the butterflies in her stomach flutter as she placed her fork down on the porcelain plate, and wiped her mouth with the cloth napkin. She reached for her glass of orange juice, both to stall for time to ruminate over her answer and to cleanse her palate before speaking.

Stacey swallowed as she pondered the answer. Truth was, there was an answer on the tip of her tongue, but she didn't know if she was up for sharing it. How did one confess one of the darkest parts of their lives in an interview as proof of their abilities?

"You're rubbing that spot on your hand," Andre observed. He reached across the table, took her hand in his, and rubbed his thumb over the tiny scar that resided between her knuckles. "One day you'll tell me about it," he stated pointedly. "How about you talk about why working with this group of women is so necessary," he encouraged, sensing her discomfort.

Stacey nodded, spotting her reprieve and grasping on to it. "Unfortunately, in the mental health and eating disorder community, a large segment of women and under class have been excluded. Many, even in the medical field, see eating disorders as a middle class white woman's problem, but that's not the case. Women of color, poor women, and men suffer from eating disorders. Eating disorders, disordered eating, and mental health needs are not limited to a specific demographic. I come from this outsider demographic and have seen signs of the need for these services in those communities. I —" she paused, catching herself still not wanting to give too much away, "there will be no other candidate more dedicated to delivering the message of this institution, and helping in spreading relief to many who suffer from the ills of an eating disorder and disordered eating."

Stacey inhaled deeply, feeling satisfied with her answer. The edges of her eyes wrinkled as her lips spread into a prideful smile when she saw the gleam in Andre's eyes. She felt his pride. She was grateful he hadn't tried to force her into giving an answer she wasn't comfortable sharing just yet. While her response wasn't the entire reason she was drawn to this particular profession, it was sufficient. Now, she felt ready for her interview.

They both finished their breakfast, and made plans to go out to dinner to celebrate her successful interview. Andre was already convinced she'd ace it and they'd be celebrating. His confidence inflated Stacey's own assurance.

Later that morning, as Stacey strolled into the interview room, seeing the director of the facility, she felt the same anticipation she felt before getting on stage for a big show. Head held high, shoulders squared, she took her seat and proceeded easily.

* * *

MEANWHILE, in Boston, Jennings stumbled through the rows of headstones in the Evergreen Cemetery. Pausing, he clutched his leather jacket to his chest. The wind foretold of another chilly evening as the temperatures had dipped well below the forties already in the late Bostonian fall. He tilted his head back, taking a long swallow of the Absolute Crystal encompassed in a bottle with the other hand. He swallowed, coughing as the liquid burned its way down his esophagus. Continuing to stumble in his brown Ferragamos, he finally found the headstone he was looking for—no easy feat in his intoxicated state.

"Christopher A. Jennings. Loving husband and father. Forever in our hearts," the younger Jennings read the inscription on his father's headstone. Jennings grunted, taking another swig from his bottle. He swiped at the drops of vodka that landed on his chin.

"Whatever," he mumbled. "I bet you're having your last laugh at me, huh, old man?" Jennings spat at the headstone, bitterness etched in his voice. "You were right. I wasn't man enough to run your company, but I'm going to make this right. I was right to take what was mine. What *you* refused to leave me. I took it, and because of a few bad years, the losers *you* hired convinced me it was best to sell to Collins. This is *your* fault." He angrily sneered at the grave and pointed his hand wildly, spilling a few drops of vodka onto the headstone. "You never trusted me. I could've been better. But I'm going to get it back. I'm getting the business back to have a legacy to pass on to my own children. I'll prove you wrong, and when I do, I'll come back and piss on your grave," Jennings promised, swigging back the remaining contents of the bottle before throwing the glass against the headstone, shattering it into hundreds of pieces.

Jennings turned and tripped on a shard of broken glass, falling into a neighboring headstone. Righting himself, he scowled at his father's headstone one last time before straightening the collar of his jacket, attempted to straighten his stance, and headed towards the exit. As he ambled towards the exit gate, he decided to move forward with the idea he'd finally conjured up to get his company back and on the right track. Pulling out his phone, he made a phone call to a local newspaper, leaving an anonymous tip with one of the finance journalists.

Hanging up, a perilous smile emerged on the younger Jennings' face as he set his plan in motion.

* * *

"WE'VE GOT A PROBLEM." Nikola burst through Andre's door, not even bothering to knock.

Andre looked up at the taut expression on his brother's face and knew it was serious. Nikola wasn't one for dramatics. If he said there was a problem, it was a big deal.

"What's going on?"

Nikola turned, shutting the door before he strutted over to the chair in front of Andre's desk and lowered himself to sit. "Some shit's going on with Boston," he stated seriously.

Andre's eyebrow hiked up inquisitively. By all accounts, Boston was Andre's pet project. All the signings, paperwork, and contracts had gone through him. He'd labored for months to get the deal done, and he wasn't about to see it fall apart after they'd already spent a large sum of money on this acquisition. A loss of the business wouldn't bankrupt Excel by any means, but it could mean time, money, and human resources devoted to the project would have been wasted.

"I got a call from a reporter from *The Boston Globe*. Says he got a tip one of our new employees was involved in insider trading," Nikola stated.

"Bullshit." Andre shot up in his seat. "I checked every employee we have. Especially all the brokers we decided to keep on. If there was insider trading, I would fucking know."

"You sure?" Nikola asked raising an eyebrow.

"Fuck yeah, I'm sure. You know I don't play that shit. I not only had our team thoroughly go over their records, I met, interviewed, and reviewed the records of all of the brokers. If something was amiss I would have caught it," Andre defended himself, sitting back in his seat, his eyebrows furrowed. He mentally recalled each and every one of the brokers he'd spoken with and none of them rang any bells.

"Did this reporter name anyone or give descriptions?" he asked his brother, a spark of awareness rising in his gut.

"No names. Just said there was a deal that went down last year for $125,000 that looked 'suspicious,'" Nikola threw air quotes around the word.

"One-hundred twenty five thou- are you serious?" Andre sat up in his chair, gripping the edges of armrests. "You know how fucking ridiculous that is?" he asked, incredulous. In their world, a $125,000 trade was hardly anything to risk insider trading for. Most of their finance clients only made deals in the million dollar and up range. Going to jail over less than a quarter of a million dollars was hardly worth the risk.

"I know, I know," Nikola stated holding up his hand. "But, if it gets out that there's insider trading going on, we're gonna be on the bad end of this. No matter how little the amount is."

Andre nodded in agreement. To the average person, $125,000 was nothing to sneeze at and the SEC had sent people to jail for less. Rumors of this type of trade could spark a formal investigation, and lead to negative headlines and all around bad publicity for Excel. Though The Jennings Corp. had retained its name after the acquisition, Excel was still the parent company and would be linked to this in the press. If it got that far. Andre stroked his cream colored silk tie, staring at the wall above Nikola's head as he began strategizing how to combat this.

"What are you thinking so far?" Nikola asked, knowing that look on his brother's face.

"I'm thinking, tomorrow morning, I'm making a trip to Boston," he told his brother. For the next hour, Andre and Nikola made a few calls and requests of forensic accountants they did business with. Andre had his assistant plan his trip to Boston using Excel's private plane. Once Nikola left his office and the details of this unexpected excursion were planned, he lifted his office phone to make one final call.

Andre rubbed his hand across his forehead as the phone rang, dreading to have to tell Stacey he'd be gone for another week. She had just had her interview a few days ago, and although she said it went great, she was still waiting for a response. Andre was confident she'd get the position. She was smart, determined, and a fighter, exactly what those clients needed. He just hated to think he wouldn't be there for her during her final week of school, or be there to take her out to celebrate when she got the good news.

Sighing heavily, he dialed her cell number, steeling himself against the disappointment of not being there for her he felt forming in his stomach. He resolved to make this a quick trip to get back to his woman as soon as possible. The urge to fall asleep with a woman by his side had never existed in Andre before Stacey. The very idea of what those feelings meant caused his grip to tighten around the telephone just as she answered her phone. Pushing those thoughts aside, he spoke into the phone.

"Hey, babe. I've got some bad news..." he began as he told Stacey the details of his leaving.

* * *

STACEY SMILED as she lit the final of the three honeysuckle jasmine scented candles. She had been a bit nervous coming here, not knowing how she would be received, but a feeling in her gut told her to throw caution to the wind, so she'd gone with it. Lighting the final candle, she looked around the room and inhaled deeply, feeling comforted by the scent of jasmine in the air. Exhaling, she strode to the dresser in the five inch stilettos, picking up her cell phone and dialing Andre's number.

"Hey, babe." Stacey's stomach did a familiar flip flop as his deep voice washed over her.

"What are you up to?" he asked.

"I was just sitting here thinking about you. Wondering if you were done for the day."

"Yup, I'm actually on my way back to my hotel suite now. I'm scheduled for an early morning flight back home tomorrow," he told her, relief evident in his voice. "What are you up to?"

"Me? I'm anticipating an eventful night," she answered cryptically.

She heard rustling on the other end of the phone at the same time she heard noise on the other side of the door. She tapped her iPad to begin playing her man's favorite artist.

"Oh yeah? And wh—" his words were abruptly cut off as he entered his hotel suite.

His eyes widened in shock at first, then he let his gaze travel down the black lace bustier that cupped her modest sized breasts to perfection. The sparks of passion in his eyes turned to full on flames as they reached the apex of her thighs. He let his eyes move down the rest of her body, eating her up with his gaze. Stacey's core immediately heated when his blue eyes returned to hers with clear lust mixed with an emotion she was too afraid to name.

"Hi," she intoned just above a whisper.

"Hey," he returned, raising an eyebrow.

"You missed my performance this week, so I thought I'd give you a private show," she purred.

Andre snorted in amusement. "Is that right?"

He stepped fully into the room, letting the door close behind him and strode over to her with a serious look in his eye. Stacey steeled herself for the kiss she believed was coming when he came within inches of her. Andre shocked her when instead of pulling her into his arms, he began to slowly circle her. She felt his eyes on her as if they were his fingers caressing her skin. When he made his way behind her, she craned her neck to look up at his handsome face.

"Like what you see?" she teased.

"No."

He smirked at the lift of her eyebrows.

"I love what I see," he growled close to her ear.

Stacey's heart rate quickened and her stomach fluttered just like the butterflies. Michael Jackson crooned about in the background from her iPad. When his hands encircled her waist, she let her head loll back to his strong chest.

"Mm," she sighed when his finger grazed the top of her left breast. "I missed you."

It'd been a week he'd been in Boston and Stacey had seriously missed going to sleep with him next to her, or waking up to him in the mornings. Andre made sure to call her every night and text her first thing in the morning, but even that hadn't been enough after seven days. So with some assistance, she hopped on a plane to surprise him.

The whole way there she was slightly nervous about his reception, but as she felt warmth of one of his hands make its way into her bustier while the other massaged circles along her thigh, she knew she'd made the right decision.

"I missed you more," he countered, nipping her earlobe and causing a pinch of pain that ended with heightening her arousal even more. His tongue snaked out to outline her butterfly tattoo, causing Stacey to moan loudly.

"You performed in this?" he asked remembering her earlier statement.

Stacey shook her head. "No, this outfit is just for you."

"Good," he murmured before placing a kiss to her neck.

Stacey let her head fall to one side as she reveled in his touch and the feeling of his lips once again on her skin after a long week.

"You finished your finals?" he mumbled in between kisses.

"Mmhm," she responded. "You get e-everything cleared up?"

"Mmhm," he mimicked her previous response. "Thank you for coming."

Stacey pivoted in his embrace, smiling up at him. She tilted her head to accept his lips as they descended to hers. Andre's tongue swept across her lips before snaking its way into her mouth. Stacey reached up to cup the back of Andre's head as his tongue and lips worked their magic on her. She felt herself being walked backwards, and she knew exactly where they were going. When the back of her thighs pressed against the bed, she felt Andre push her down to the mattress. Breaking away from the kiss, she stared up at him. Though, his eyes were filled with unbanked passion, she remembered back to how tired he sounded over the phone just moments ago.

"Hey, I know this week has been crazy for you and I know I showed up here unexpectedly, but if you'd rather sleep or relax, we can do that," she truthfully stated reaching up to stroke the side of his face.

"I can sleep when I'm dead. I want the exclusive performance you came to deliver." Looking at the mischievousness in his eyes, she couldn't help the giggle that escaped her mouth.

"The most relaxing thing I can think of right now is to be buried balls deep inside the prettiest pussy I've ever had the pleasure of seeing," he growled in her ear.

Stacey instantly felt her core moisten at his salacious comment. Seconds later, she felt his big body cover hers, pushing her into the mattress. As soon as her head hit the mattress, they both began tearing at each other's clothes. For well into the night and early morning, they showed each other just how much they'd missed one another.

ANDRE ROLLED over in bed and wrapped his arms around the woman who slumbered peacefully beside him. Pulling her into his arms, he inhaled the scent of jasmine she usually wore and sighed contentedly. He thought back to months ago how he'd told other women he'd been with that he didn't do overnight stays. That'd been his rule for years, and never until this soft, caring and sometimes feisty woman, did he break his own rule. He smiled, thinking back to his response when he opened the door and was hit by the scent of the burning candles, the sounds of his favorite musician, and the magnetic sight of the woman who stood at the center of it all. He'd had to refrain from immediately striding over to her and ripping her lingerie off to get inside her. Then, he remembered his words to her when she asked if he liked what he saw. The word love seemed to tumble from his mouth on its own accord. He didn't regret saying it. She'd been a vision of beauty standing in his suite in five inch heels—heels that'd been high up on his shoulders just a few short hours ago—with smooth, milky brown skin that had been covered in black lace. Love was the first word he could think of when she'd asked if he liked what he saw.

But did that mean he was in love with her? Love was an emotion he'd worked hard to avoid with the women in his life that he wasn't related to. Love had the potential to lead to marriage, and he was not looking to marry. Ever. *Right?*

"Umm, are you trying to squeeze the life out of me?" Stacey's voice, thick with sleep, startled him.

Andre hadn't even realized he'd been clutching her so tightly as he mused on his feelings for her.

"What were you thinking about?" she asked, turning to face him.

"I'm sorry." He paused. "I was thinking if you didn't have to get back just yet we could spend the day exploring the city," he quickly came up with an excuse. Luckily, he had been thinking about staying a little longer to explore the city with her. He knew from past conversations she'd only visited Boston once for a ballet performance, but never had time to see much of the city.

"What'd you have in mind?"

"We could visit the New England Aquarium, have lunch at L'Espalier, check out the Art Museum, catch a movie or relax right here in the room," he said, stroking her bare arm with his finger.

"And you don't have to work?" she asked raising an eyebrow.

"No, I was leaving today anyway." Andre stopped just short of admitting to wanting to leave so early so he could get back to her.

"Then let's have some fun in Boston, baby!" she agreed excitedly.

Andre chuckled at the excitement on her face. "Sounds like a plan, but first we shower."

He threw back the covers and scooped Stacey up before strolling into the bathroom. The sounds of Stacey's laughter flooded the bedroom, only to turn into moans just minutes later while in the shower.

Within the hour, the couple was up, dressed, and ready for the day. Their first stop was a tiny breakfast spot around the corner from the hotel. They enjoyed breakfasts of bagels and lox with fruit before heading out to the New England Aquarium in the Central Wharf portion of Boston. They explored the different animal exhibits and stayed for a show in the huge 3D theater in the aquarium.

Andre couldn't help staring at Stacey throughout the film as she laughed, or yelped in fear or surprise at a video about animals living in the Colorado River that snaked through the Grand Canyon. He chuckled lightheartedly when he saw her stretch her hand out as if she was reaching for one of the raindrops that looked so real and life-like behind the 3D glasses. After spending two hours at the aquarium, the next stop was Boston's Museum of Fine Arts. Admittedly, this museum had nothing on the art museum in New York, but it was one of Andre's favorites.

In recent years, Andre had developed an appreciation of art and would often visit the art museums in the city he was visiting, if time permitted. One particular exhibit that caught his eye was one on the changes in contemporary craft-based artists. He took delight in pointing out to Stacey the various ways the artists had progressed and changed over the years. He noted that her ballet background gave her a certain appreciation to detail in the way artists used materials to create their work.

She told him that as a ballerina, it was drilled in them to pay attention to every minute detail. She'd used those years of training to turn a discerning eye on the art in front of her. Andre could see she'd enjoyed the museum as much as he had.

Once they left the museum, instead of heading to the fancy restaurant Andre had discussed earlier for dinner, Stacey convinced him to take her to South End's B&G Oysters for a dinner of halibut tartare and smoked salmon toasts. After dinner, they headed over to Flour Bakery and Cafe for freshly made donuts. Andre took pleasure in licking the excess powdered sugar that was left from the donut off the corner of Stacey's mouth.

They returned to the hotel suite after eleven and spent the rest of the night entangled in each other's arms and legs. They didn't leave for their flight back to Atlanta until early morning the next day. Andre couldn't remember a time he'd had a great time just showing a woman around the sights of a different city. It boded well for what he had planned for her graduation gift. Stacey's school didn't have a December graduation ceremony, which she insisted she was okay with. However, Andre believed she deserved some sort of celebration for earning both a bachelor's and master's degree. He planned to surprise her the same way she surprised him in Boston. He couldn't wait to see the expression on her face the next week when he took her for his surprise.

CHAPTER 17

"Dammit!" Jennings yelled as he hurled his glass of whiskey across the room. He'd just gotten off the phone with his inside man at the company that had once belonged to his family. To his chagrin, Mike, the former employee he'd paid to report to a local news reporter on insider trading in the company, was fired this week after Andre's arrival in Boston. Somehow, they were able to trace the "anonymous tip" back to Mike, realizing he lied. Luckily, he hadn't given Andre or anyone else Jennings' name—not yet anyway. Jennings wasn't stupid enough to believe that under duress, Mike wouldn't sing like a canary, especially if they followed through with their threat to involve the police.

"Everything alright in here, dear?"

Jennings' head began to pound the moment he heard his mother's voice at the entrance to the office. He'd moved back into his childhood home a month ago, telling his mother that his own condo was being renovated. In actuality, he could no longer afford the luxury condo. His funds were running low, and he needed to get his company back.

"Yes, mother. Everything is fine. I just dropped my glass while on the phone doing a business deal. Nothing to worry about," he lied.

"Oh, I can clean it—"

"No!" he shouted more forcefully than intended, causing his mother to jump. "I'm sorry, mother. As you can see, business has been a little stressful lately. No, I don't need you to clean it up. I've got it. You go on up and head to bed. I'm going to work for a little while longer before turning in myself."

Jennings' stomach dropped at the smile of confidence his mother gave him. She'd trusted him to take care of her after his father died. She had no idea what was going on.

Laura Jennings gently patted her only son on his cheek. "Okay, dear. Just don't work too hard, alright? Just like your father, always working." She smiled.

Jennings' shoulders slumped, and couldn't even look his mother in her eyes at that last comment. Thankfully, his mother didn't pick up on his shame.

"You look tired. Don't stay up too late working. Get some rest. Okay, honey?" she said as she placed a light kiss on his cheek.

"Yes, mother," he mumbled as she walked out of the room. The guilt was nearly overwhelming.

"Time to call in the big guns," he mumbled as he strolled over to his desk to pick up his phone. Since Excel now had an even tighter rein around the company that used to be his, he'd go a more personal route to force Andre's hand. He knew just the person to help him do it.

"Hello," the feminine voice on the other end answered.

"Maria, it's Jennings. Listen, I need a favor..." he began without preamble. He was even more resolute in getting his company back.

ANDRE RAPPED on his brother's office door a few times before entering.

"Hey Nik, you got a minute?" he asked.

Nikola was just sitting down to his desk, but waved his brother in. "When did you get in?"

"Early this morning. Caught the red eye and after dropping Stacey off at her apartment, came straight into the office," he informed Nikola.

"Stacey, huh?" Nikola asked raising an eyebrow.

Andre nodded. "Yeah, she surprised me in Boston." He couldn't help the smile that lit up his face just thinking about their weekend in Boston. They'd even extended their time there until this morning, not wanting to rush back home. He looked up to see his brother's piercing gaze on him, reading more information than Andre was willing to share. His smile fell.

"Anyway," he said clearing his throat, "we found out who the anonymous source was. A young broker named Mike. So far, he's not talking about why he did it, but we suspect he was paid. We need to find out who paid him. I suspect someone is trying to set us up," Andre intoned angrily. He was pissed that someone would try to set his company up.

Nikola nodded. "Raul told me he was able to trace the anonymous call back to this Mike. He's trying to get access to his financial records. If he was paid off, maybe we can find a money transfer or something to trace."

Raul's security firm had plenty of experience working with this type of situation.

Before Andre left, he'd reached out to Raul to begin an investigation into who could be behind these rumors. Within forty-eight hours, Raul had a name. Andre confronted Mike in Boston and he gave some convoluted story about seeing traders make shady deal, but couldn't provide any proof. As far as Andre was concerned, Mike was lying, but *why* was what he didn't know.

"I have a feeling Jennings is behind this," Andre told his brother.

"What makes you say that?"

Andre shrugged. "Right now it's just a feeling, but the way he behaved throughout the acquisition process was...off. He may be regretting selling and trying to make sure this venture a failure for us."

"You think so?" Nikola questioned. "He hardly paid the company any mind while he was running it. He nearly ran it into the ground."

"Yeah, but you know what they say about hindsight. How would you feel if we lost Excel?" Andre asked.

"That'd never happen. We're not Jennings' lazy, shiftless ass," Nikola grunted. The thought of losing Excel was unimaginable to them both. They'd been bred from day one to lead this company, and in the years since Nikola took the CEO role and Andre CFO, they'd nearly doubled the size of the company.

"Damn straight, but it's still his father's legacy he lost. Maybe he didn't care before, but is feeling the loss now," Andre commented. "Either way, I think it's him and I'm having Raul do some looking into it."

Nikola nodded. "Good. Now, as for this coming weekend. Are you ready?"

Andre's entire mood lightened with the change in topics. His mind shifted from business to pleasure just that fast. "Yup, everything's in place for the surprise. Just make sure you and Devyn are there on time." He leveled a look at his brother.

"Hey, it's not my fault we're late sometimes. You know how long it takes to get three kids to get ready to leave the damn house?" Nikola grunted.

Andre stood. "Whatever. Just make sure to have your ass there on time," he stated pointedly. "I'll be in my office, if you need me," he said as he exited. The whole way back to his own office, Andre smiled thinking about the surprised he had for his woman this weekend. He knew she'd enjoy it.

* * *

STACEY RECOGNIZED the building as soon as they turned into the parking lot. It was the restaurant she and Andre went to on their first date more than four months ago. However, instead of the parking lot being full as it was on that night, it was nearly empty.

"Are you sure it's open?" Stacey asked, peering out of the car window.

"Huh, it does appear closed, doesn't it?" Andre asked with feigned concern.

At his tone, Stacey lifted an eyebrow. She could tell he was up to something. When he said they were going out tonight, he'd told her it was to celebrate her completing her degree and getting the job as counselor. She'd told him she didn't want a big deal made, as she would just celebrate with her family over the Christmas holiday which was the following week. Now, she wondered what Andre had up his sleeve.

Andre parked the car in the space nearest the door before getting out and rounding the car to open her door. "I told you we were celebrating your accomplishments tonight, and that's what I meant." He smiled down at her as he helped her out of the car before pressing his lips to the back of her hand.

Stacey's insides tingled at the feeling of his lips on her and the look of promise in his eyes. She'd spent many nights getting lost in those very eyes. She wasn't sure what he had planned for their evening, but instinctively knew she wouldn't regret following him wherever he led her. She put on her brightest smile. "Well then lead the way, Mr. Collins," she purred.

Andre's smile turned to one of appreciation, as if he was grateful of her ability to trust in him. He held out his arm for her to grasp, and led the way into the restaurant. Unlike the first time, there wasn't a crowd of people at the door waiting to be seated. Instead, a tall Middle Eastern man dressed in all black stood at the entrance. His sienna colored skin shone with the vibrancy of good health, and the courteous smile on his face displayed a row of perfectly white teeth. Stacey instantly felt at ease in his presence.

"Andre, Ms. Coleman, what a pleasure it is for you to join us tonight," he greeted.

"Khalid, always a pleasure," Andre returned his greeting. "Stacey, this is Khalid Fadel, owner of the Imperial Fez."

"Oh," Stacey said, surprised. She wondered why the owner of the restaurant was here greeting them, but held her questions. "Thank you, Mr. Fadel. You have a wonderful establishment here," she stated sincerely. She had fallen in love with the restaurant the first time they were here.

"Thank you, Ms. Coleman." Khalid bowed his head in gratitude.

"Please, call me Stacey," she graciously requested.

"Will do. And you may call me Khalid. A friend of Andre's is a friend of mine," Khalid insisted, taking her hand and placing a kiss to the back.

Andre cleared his throat. "Laying it on thick, aren't you, friend," he lightly scolded. Both Stacey and Khalid laughed.

"Is everything ready?" Andre asked.

Stacey caught a look pass between Andre and Khalid that let her know there was an underlying meaning to that question. One that went beyond asking if the food was prepared. Despite her growing anticipation, she decided to let Andre fill her in when he was good and ready.

"Yes, sir. Right this way," Khalid answered, sweeping his arm wide and stepping to the side to let them both pass.

Stacey noticed the interior of the restaurant was mostly dark, save for candles on some of the tables, and she could make out that there weren't any guests in the dining areas unlike before. She heard the faint sounds of Middle Eastern music being played in the background, but that was all. Before they could fully step into the dining area, Andre stopped and turned to stand in front of her with a serious look. Out of the corner of her eyes, she saw Khalid step around them and proceed into the dining area.

"Babe, I know you said you didn't mind not having a graduation ceremony, and didn't want a big deal made over completing your degrees, but it is a big deal. You deserve to be celebrated. You've accomplished a hell of a lot, and you got the job you've been dreaming about. I'm so damn proud of you," he said a look of pride on his gorgeous face.

Stacey's cheeks flushed at the pride she saw in his gaze and in his smile. "Thank you, Andre, but—"

"No buts. You deserve to be revered for overcoming and making a new life for yourself after ballet. And you deserve to share this moment with the people who love you the most."

He paused.

Stacey's heart leapt at his use of the word love. Did he just admit to being in love with her?

"Without further ado, let the celebration begin," he ended.

Stacey remained confused for a few seconds, still caught off guard by his use of the L-word, when she heard a shrill, "*Surprise!!*"

Andre turned to stand at her side, allowing her to see into the now fully lit dining area. There stood her Aunt Ruth, Uncle Gerald, her two cousins, Mercedes and Raul, Devyn and Nikola, and even Iris and Mistress Coco. Above them hung a banner that read "CONGRATU-LATIONS GRADUATE."

Stacey's eyes immediately watered a she turned to Andre, too touched to say anything. He pulled her in for a tight embrace and whispered in her ear, "Congratulations, baby," before letting her go.

"Go greet your guests." He lightly nudged her towards her family.

That little push was all she needed before she made her way to her aunt and uncle, wrapping her arms tightly around them both. In that moment, Stacey realized just how much she had wanted to celebrate this occasion with her family, and Andre had made it happen. When she finally greeted everyone and they congratulated her, she pulled Andre in for scorching kiss, pouring all her gratitude and apprecia-tion for his presence in her life into the kiss.

"If that's what I get for dinner, I can't wait to see what I get for your next surprise," he winked slyly at her.

"Andre! I can't believe you did this!" Stacey excitedly exclaimed. "Obviously, you've already met, but come let me reintroduce you to my aunt, uncle, and cousins."

She grasped his arm and pulled him towards her family.

Andre's chest filled with happiness as he noted the excitement on her angelic face. He'd spent weeks trying to coordinate with her family on the right date and time they could come from Savannah to Atlanta to help celebrate her graduation. He'd rented out the Imperial Fez because he'd remembered how much she enjoyed it the first time they came. Andre had Raul look up her aunt and uncle's information, and from there he contacted them to request their presence. He'd spoken with her cousins as well. The only family member he didn't have a chance to speak with over the phone was Stacey's sister, Coral. She was a difficult woman to reach, and when he asked her other family members for her information, they were all reluctant to fork it over. They all reassured him that they would contact Coral and let her know of the dinner. Andre got the impression Coral wasn't as close with her family as Stacey was, which she had already told him.

For the next twenty minutes, Stacey and Andre went around introducing her family to her Atlanta friends. The entire party mingled and laughed, talking about all things burlesque, when Stacey shared that her aunt was also a big fan of the performances and that she'd also seen Devyn and Mercedes perform at the Black Kitty. Andre observed Stacey, noticing that while she seemed to be enjoying herself, she kept stealing a glance at the doorway as if expecting someone. He suspected who she was looking for and was about to go and reassure her, but he was halted by her two male cousins, Quincy and Jabari. Andre took in the serious expressions on their faces. The way they stood on either side of him, peering at him, he knew they were attempting to intimidate him. At six-foot-two and six-foot-three with muscled frames and stern faces, they might have been intimidating to a lesser man, but Andre sure as hell wasn't that.

"What's up?" Jabari, the younger of the two, asked.

"Gentlemen," Andre nodded, taking a sip of his scotch, "enjoying yourselves?" His tone was nonchalant.

"You did alright," Jabari stated looking around the room. His face softened a bit when he glanced at Stacey across the room talking to the other women.

"Seems you did right by our little sis," Quincy interjected, taking a sip of his own glass of scotch, his eyes never leaving Andre's.

Andre could tell, off the bat, Quincy was the more serious of the two brothers. He also noted that Quincy referred to Stacey as their sister, instead of cousin.

"She looks happy," Jabari noted, turning his attention back to Andre. "Let's make sure it stays that way."

His smirk disappeared.

"I don't see why that would change anytime in the near future," Andre responded.

"Good, 'cause our little sister means a lot to us," Quincy began. "You know her as our cousin, but as far as we're concerned," he gestured between Jabari and himself, "she's our sister. She's been through enough and deserves to be happy." Quincy leveled another warning look at Andre.

"Are you two over here ganging up on Andre?" A feminine voice came from behind them.

Andre looked up to find the woman of the hour wearing a scolding look at her two cousins.

"No, babe." Andre pulled her into his arms and placed a kiss on her cheek. "Your brothers here were just reminding me how lucky I am to be with you." He gave her his usual wink.

"Yeah sis, we were just making friends with the man in your life," Jabari stated, giving Stacey an innocent look.

She looked between her two cousins and finally nodded, apparently satisfied with their explanation. When her aunt called her name, she gave Andre another kiss on the cheek and walked away, but not before peering at the door once again.

"Just making sure we're clear." Quincy's expression turned serious again.

Jabari gave a chuckle. "Look man, we're just messing with you. Big brother likes doing the intimidation thing. You held up pretty cool though. I've seen grown men crumble under that look. Anyway, we're nothing compared to what you'll get from big sis," Jabari said, turning his beer to his lips and sipping.

At this, Andre raised an eyebrow. Apparently, he would be meeting the elusive Coral Coleman tonight. "Speaking of, are you sure—"

"Coraaall!!" Stacey's shrill scream filled the restaurant as she nearly sprinted across the room to embrace her sister.

"Aww shit, big sis is in the house. Good luck, bruh," Jabari chuckled, clapping Andre on the back.

Quincy merely gave Andre a sideways smirk and headshake before walking over to embrace Coral.

Andre took the time to observe Stacey's older sister. She was about an inch or so taller than Stacey in four inch heels, black, wide dress pants, and a white top whose cleavage extended all the way down to her waist where it was cinched with a wide gold belt. She was a shade darker than Stacey. Andre noticed the auburn and black curly, tapered, haircut. He saw her piercing hazel eyes that were filled with an alertness sparkle with happiness as she smiled down at her sister.

Andre felt a sense of relief knowing that Coral was able to make it. He knew that even though the rest of her family and friends were able to make it, this celebration wouldn't have been complete without her older sister's presence. Stacey had shared with him many times how grateful she was for Coral, and all that she had done for her as children and as an adult to protect and care for her. Stacey had shared with her that Coral would often put herself between Stacey and their abusive father. Just thinking of a grown man—a father no less, physically harming his children caused Andre's grip to tighten on his glass. Though Stacey had told him that she'd mainly escaped her father's wrath thanks to her older sister, he still wasn't sure what he'd do to the man if he were still alive. Good thing for their father's sake, he hadn't lived to meet Andre.

"You're about to meet the infamous Coral Coleman." Andre heard a familiar voice from behind him. "Good luck." Raul, who was flanked by Nikola, smirked.

"I'm not that bad, Santiago," they were interrupted. "I see my reputation precedes me." Coral looked with assessing eyes at Andre.

"It's a pleasure to finally meet the woman Stacey speaks so highly of," Andre greeted, offering his hand.

For a second, Coral kept her gaze on Andre as if she was reading his face for something. Finally, seemingly deciding on something, she took his hand and smiled. "Collins, you never told me how much better looking your brother was than you," Coral stated, raising an eyebrow and glancing over Andre's shoulder at Nikola.

Andre smiled. *I might like this woman,* he thought, taking another sip of his drink.

"Coleman, a pleasure as always," Nikola returned lightheartedly. "Santiago, you're looking good these days. I can see marriage agrees with you." Coral tossed a look over at Raul.

"That it does. How've you been?" Raul asked politely.

"Busy." Was all she said before turning her attention back to Andre.

"It's nice to finally meet you as well. My sister speaks highly of you also," Coral told Andre.

He could tell she was still assessing him. The way she watched his face for every expression might have unsettled anyone else. The fact that both Raul and Nikola already knew her, and apparently respected her reputation, spoke volumes to Andre about her abilities. Raul and Nikola had both spent nearly a decade in the U.S. Army after graduating from the Military Academy at West Point. They were not easily impressed men, but apparently, this Coral had earned their respect. That, combined with everything Stacey had shared with him about her sister, and his estimation of this woman went up in his eyes. However, he could tell the way she was looking at him, she still wasn't too sure about him. *No mind, she'll come around,* he thought as he took Stacey by the waist.

"Babe, I think they're ready to serve us now. Are you ready to eat?" he asked.

"I am now," she said smiling up at him. He knew she meant that now that her sister was here, everything felt right, and the celebration was official.

The rest of the meal and festivities went off without a hitch. The group sat down to a delicious spread of salad, Moroccan lentil soup, *shrimp peppell*, chicken couscous, roasted lamb shanks and a special dessert of Stacey's favorite butter pecan ice cream. As entertainment, they were joined by the restaurant's belly dancers who put on a show meant to captivate the audience, which it surely did. The men were treated to a special gift when all the women in attendance were pulled up to join in the belly dancing. This was particularly entertaining seeing as how just about every woman, with the exception of Coral and Ruth, was a current or former burlesque dancer. Andre watched as every woman, except Coral, accepted the invitation to dance. The men clapped and whistled along. When they finished dancing, Stacey sauntered over to Andre, practically falling into his lap, and bestowed kisses along his cheek.

"Thank you. Thank you. Thank you," she purred in his ear, causing his cock to twitch in his pants.

"Careful, babe. You keep whispering like that in my ear, and we're kicking everyone out and I'm taking you on every table in this place," he growled, low so only she could hear. He smiled when he saw her visibly shiver at his lascivious words.

"Before you kick us all out, do you mind if I speak to my sister alone?" Coral's voice interrupted their private moment, her words making it obvious she'd overheard their little exchange.

Andre was slightly annoyed rather than embarrassed at being overheard. After sharing Stacey with everyone for the past few hours, he really wanted to be alone with her.

"Seriously, Coral?" Stacey squeaked, obviously embarrassed at her sister overhearing their exchange.

"What?" Coral asked, deadpan.

Stacey shook her head.

"Go ahead, babe. You and I will have plenty of time to be alone over the next few days," Andre reassured her.

"Thank you, Andre." Coral smiled at him and stood from her seat.

* * *

STACEY FOLLOWED her sister to the entrance of the restaurant. Stacey could make out a small gift bag Coral had in her hand that she hadn't noticed earlier. Despite her little annoyance at her sister's interruption with Andre a few moments ago, she was thrilled to have her sister there to share this experience with. Had it not been for Coral, Stacey wasn't sure if she would have made it out of those trying months after her ballet career ended. At her lowest point, she'd spiraled down a road of depression, bitterness and fear. If it hadn't been for Coral being there for her, she had no idea where she'd be right now.

"Hey," Coral said as they stopped close to the exit. "I wanted to give this to you in private." She handed Stacey a small pink gift bag.

Taking the bag, Stacey peered inside seeing the white wrapping paper and a gold box inside. "What is this?"

"Open it and find out," her sister responded.

Eyeing her sister, Stacey put her hand in the bag, took out a gold box, and handed the bag to Coral so she could use both hands to open the jewelry box. Inside was a sterling silver, heart shaped locket with a butterfly engraved on the front. Underneath the butterfly was the inscription, "My heart." Stacey's brows crinkled in confusion. This locket looked familiar. Glancing up at her sister's hazel eyes, she could see an expectant look.

"Is this..." Stacey gasped when she finally realized where she remembered the locket from. She remembered her tiny fingers caressing the locket each night before bed as their mother read them a bedtime story. "Mom's locket," she whispered, stunned. She hadn't known what had become of the locket after her mother died. She'd assumed either her mother had been buried with it, or their father had given it away as he'd done with most of their mother's belongings after she succumbed to her illness.

"How did you...," her voice trailed off as Coral took the locket from her hand and opened it, revealing the pictures inside. On the left side of the locket was a picture of their mother holding Coral when she was just an infant, and on the right was their mother holding Stacey as a baby.

"Originally, she had just pictures of you and me, but I thought you might like these pictures better. You can change it if you want."

"No. No, these are perfect." Stacey's voice was full of emotion as she took the locket back in her hand.

"I took it right after mom died. I hid it in my room for years. I remember hearing her say she wanted the locket to go to her girls after she died. I've had it long enough and wanted you to have it now. I'm so proud of you, sis," Coral told her sister.

Stacey looked up into her sister's face and saw the pride and love she had for her. This was one of Coral's unguarded moments where she let Stacey see all the emotion she was feeling.

"I couldn't have done this without you," Stacey admitted. "No," Stacey began when she saw Coral attempt to wave it off, "seriously, you saved me as a kid and after my ballet career ended. I was in a deep hole of depression and if you hadn't shown up, I don't know what I would have done. This celebration is as much mine as it is yours."

"This day is all about you. I didn't do anything a big sister isn't supposed to. Anyway," Coral paused and looked over at the dining area where everyone continued to talk and laugh. Stacey followed Coral's line of sight as her eyes landed on Andre. Unknowingly, a smile lit up Stacey's face when she spotted Andre. At that same moment, he glanced up at her, smiled and winked.

"You're in love," Coral acknowledged.

Stacey's head snapped back to her sister. Coral's eye peered down on her sister, assessing her. Stacey was all too familiar with her sister's ability to read even perfect strangers. There was no use trying to deny her sister's claim. Stacey had been questioning her feelings for Andre for a while now, afraid to admit what her sister clearly saw written all over her face.

"I am," she sighed, stealing another glance at Andre.

"Be careful." Coral's voice was filled with warning.

Stacey's heart sank at the underlying emotion she heard in her sister's voice. She knew Coral wasn't much interested in love, or if she even believed in it. Growing up the way they did, Coral got a front row seat of what happened when love went wrong. Stacey also suspected that Coral had been hurt in her own right, but her sister rarely opened up to her about her own personal life.

"You think he'll hurt me?" Stacey asked warily.

Coral shrugged. "Not necessarily, but it's often the ones you least expect to hurt you who do."

Stacey heard the far off tone in Coral's voice.

"Are we talking about me or you?" Stacey asked.

Coral's gaze sharpened on her sister, and her brows furrowed. "You."

"Cause that's all we talk about. What about you?" Stacey asked, finally unable to hold back her questions about her sister's personal life.

"This day isn't about me. I'm not here to talk about me. I just want you to be careful. That's all," Coral admonished.

"Why don't we ever talk about you? You're even less talkative about yourself ever since Li—"

"Don't." Coral warned. "Don't say his name. Leave it alone."

Stacey's neck snapped back and her eyes widened at the sharpness she heard in Coral's tone. Her sister rarely took that tone with her. Stacey knew this was a sensitive topic for her sister, and one of the sources of her sister's negative ideals on love.

"Okay, but I want you to know I worry about you. You can talk to me when you're ready," Stacey acquiesced.

Coral relaxed her shoulders and nodded. "I'm sorry. I just," she sighed, shaking her head, "your willingness to talk has been noted. Now, we can get back to your celebration. You only have a little while before you leave."

"Leave? Where?" Stacey asked confused.

"Uh, uh, I'm not saying anything. Your man over there has more plans for you." Coral smiled, erasing the haunted look she wore moments ago.

"He told you what he has planned?"

Coral shook her head. "Of course not, but you know I have my ways of finding out."

"Don't I know it," Stacey mumbled as they began strolling back over to the rest of the group. Stacey was well aware of her sister's ability to find out information that she'd never shared with anyone. She knew her sister had worked in intelligence in the military and had her suspicions about where she worked after retiring from the military, but her sister never would admit it. Now, Coral worked with their two cousins in the family's security firm, often working overseas with high paying clients. Stacey knew Coral probably knew just about every detail of Andre's life, including the day he got his wisdom teeth pulled. Her sister was her protector growing up and still took on that role.

The rest of the evening went along well as the dancers continued with a few more performances, which included one that involved fire and swords. Stacey's aunt and uncle both shared with her that Andre had contacted them weeks ago to request their presence tonight. Her cousin, Jabari, and Andre seemed especially taken with one another, sharing laughs over jokes. Even Quincy, who was typically more reserved, commented that he liked Andre and thought he was a good guy. Stacey knew that Andre hadn't done this to show off for her or to even try to make a good impression for her family, but to take this night to celebrate her accomplishments. He had brought together her family and loved ones solely with the purpose of celebrating her achievements. As she stared at Andre as he laughed with Jabari across the room, she had to admit it was true. She loved this man.

Moments later, Andre made his way across the room, pulling Stacey in his arms. "You're staring. See something you like?" he asked reminding her of the words she asked when she'd surprised him in Boston a few weeks ago.

"I more than like," she purred, discreetly rubbing her breast against his abdomen. She smiled when she felt his breath hitch.

"If you don't want your family to know what you sound like screaming my name as you come, you'd cut that shit out."

Stacey gave him a pouting look.

Andre chuckled. "We're leaving soon, anyway. You keep it in your pants until then, babe," he teased, gently nipping her earlobe before wrapping his arm around her and escorting her over to the rest of the guests to say their goodbyes.

* * *

"WE'RE TAKING A FLIGHT?" Stacey's surprised voice rang through the town car as they pulled up to the private airport.

Andre smiled and nodded. "I told you there were more surprises for you," he reminded her as he helped her out of the backseat.

"Where are we going? I don't have any luggage," she told him, worried she wouldn't be dressed appropriately for where ever they were going or how long they'd be away.

"It's all been taken care of. The only thing you need to do is get your pretty little ass on this plane."

Stacey laughed as she allowed herself to be pulled by the hand towards the steps of the private jet. Less than two hours later, Stacey found herself waking up as they made their final descent. Stacey still had no idea where they had gone, but figured it wasn't too far for such a short flight. Andre refused to give her any hints or clues about where they were headed or for how long they'd be away.

Before stepping out into the night air, Andre helped Stacey into her red pea coat. "It's colder up here than in Atlanta, especially this time of year. You're going to need these," he said, helping her into the coat and handing her a pair of black leather gloves. These were items from Stacey's wardrobe. She wondered how he was able to get her belongings.

"Did my aunt help you pack for me?" she questioned, knowing her aunt and uncle had a key to her condo as owners of the building.

"I'll never tell," he said, winking and making his way towards the exit.

"Welcome to New York!" their driver greeted them as he opened the door of their Lincoln town car.

"New York?" Stacey looked up at Andre who wore a satisfied look on his face.

He nodded. "The city's beautiful this time of year," he told her referring to the Christmas season.

"How long are we here for?" she asked.

"Until the twenty-sixth," he stated nonchalantly.

"We're spending Christmas in New York?" She beamed.

Andre nodded. "That's just one of the surprises for this trip," he told her as the driver closed the door behind them.

Stacey's eyes lit up like the Christmas lights that were strung up around the city as they entered Manhattan. She'd often thought about spending Christmas in the city she was born in, but had never been able to do it. She couldn't think of a better person to share it with than the man whose hand was tightly wrapped around hers.

When they arrived at the hotel, Stacey gasped as she stepped into the most opulent room she'd ever been in. Andre rented the Champagne Suite at the Lotte New York Palace. The suite was over five-thousand square feet, contained both a master bedroom that was at the top of a spiral staircase, a guest bedroom, and a huge living room space that could easily accommodate a group of ten or more. The room was decorated with cream colored furniture and black and gold accents, including a beautiful black and gold chandelier. Even though it was well after midnight, Stacey opened the sliding glass door to the terrace to a wondrous view of the Mid-town Manhattan that was still lit up. New York was truly the city that never slept. Stacey was struck speechless at the beauty of this room and the effort and expense she knew Andre put into surprising her.

"Andre," she whispered, overcome with gratitude. She felt his arms wrap around her waist from the back. She immediately turned in his embrace and buried her head into his strong chest. "This is beautiful," she finally said after a few moments in silence. She reached up and placed a kiss to his lips. "Thank you."

"The surprises aren't over yet, but right now you need your rest. Let's get you ready for bed," he said pulling her back into the suite and closing the door behind him.

They both fell into bed, exhausted. The next morning, Stacey woke up to a delicious breakfast spread, compliments of their private chef services. As they ate, Andre talked about his plans to take them sight-seeing around the city over the next few days, which included a trip to Rockefeller Center to visit the huge Christmas tree. It took Stacey some cajoling, but she finally got Andre to agree to do some ice skating with her at the Rockefeller Ice Rink. He told her that he was taking her someplace special that night as the remaining part of her surprise, but again refused to share where they were going.

Throughout the rest of the day, Stacey attempted to pick up hints or ask outright where they were going that evening, but Andre refused. That afternoon, he took her shopping in one of the city's exclusive shopping districts. Stacey bucked at the idea of having him spend even more money on her. She tried to rebuff his attempts at splurging on her even more, but Andre was dead set on ensuring she came out of each store with more items than what they went in it with. He purchased a pair of diamond earrings, insisting that she would need to wear them for what he had planned that night. He also took her shoe shopping and even took her to La Perla on Madison Avenue. He claimed it was to replace a few of the panty sets and lingerie he'd practically destroyed in a rush to get her naked, but Stacey knew he just liked the idea of seeing her in the many lace and silk garments he'd picked out for her.

By six that evening, they'd returned to their suite for dinner. As soon as Stacey stepped inside, she spotted a black silk cocktail dress laid out on the couch, accompanied by a pair of gold and black strappy five-inch heels. Walking over to the clothing, Stacey picked up the dress and held it up to herself. The dress had a boat neckline, a black ribbon belt to cinch the waist, and a sheer organza overlay. It was simple, yet elegant. Raising an eyebrow, she peeked over at Andre who wore a blank expression, but his eyes held the reflection of his rising lust as he pictured her in the dress.

"It's for tonight," he said thickly, answering her questioning gaze. "First, we have dinner."

He held out his hand for her. Stacey carefully placed the dress back where it was and took Andre's hand to be led into the dining room. Again, there was another delicious spread that included butternut squash soup for their beginning course, followed by filet mignon and steamed vegetables for Andre, and grilled salmon with asparagus in a special butter sauce for Stacey. As they ate, Stacey once again tried to get out of Andre where they were going for the evening. She wondered if it were some sort of work or charity gala, but Andre quickly dismissed that idea, telling her he would never bring her to a work event while they were on vacation. After getting very little out of Andre, Stacey let it go, deciding she'd be finding out where they were headed soon enough.

An hour and a half later, Stacey was smoothing down the edges of her dress and making sure her makeup and hair, which rested in a high, elegant bun atop her head, were perfect. She looked up in the mirror to see Andre peering at her from behind. Slowly, her gaze traveled down his long frame. He was dressed in a tailored silver-blue suit paired with a white button-down top, a pair of brown oxfords, and a matching belt. He looked good enough to eat. Stacey seductively licked her lips as she eyed him as if he were the most succulent meal at a five-star restaurant.

"You know, we could skip wherever we're going and make it an event to remember right here," she flirted as she turned and sauntered over to him, trailing her finger down the length of his chest and abs.

Andre dipped his head low so his lips hovered just above hers. "Oh, we're definitely going to get to that part," he growled. "But first your surprise," he whispered in her ear, as he placed a kiss just beneath it. "You look delectable, by the way," he said stepping back and eyeing her.

"Thank you. Now, since you won't let me peel those clothes off you right now, let's get going so I can find out my surprise," she teased.

Andre laughed as he followed her out the room. Thirty minutes later, they were pulling up to their destination. Stacey felt jittery with excitement as she took in the scenery of women in cocktail dresses, and men dressed formally or semi-casually. Then, when her eyes followed the patrons as they ascended the stairs, she immediately recognized the huge column windows of the Metropolitan Opera House. She gasped, so taken aback she hadn't realized Andre had gotten out of the car and rounded to her side until she felt his hand on hers, pulling her out of the vehicle.

Stepping out, she glanced around, watching as guests of the Met, as it was nicknamed, saunter into one of the most famous opera houses in the world. However, Stacey knew that opera was not the only type of performance that went on here. From the time she was a young girl first starting out in ballet, she'd imagined herself dancing at the Met. While that dream would never come true, she still held a great deal of respect and admiration for the ballet dancers who were able to perform here.

"You may not be able to dance on the stage, but I figured seeing your idol for the first time here was a good second place." She registered Andre's words at the same instant she looked up to the marquee and saw an illuminating image of Misty Copeland dressed in a long white dress, white stockings, and ballet flats with her hair pulled back in a bun.

She stood *en pointe*, holding out a wooden nutcracker. She was dancing the lead role of Clara. Andre not only brought her to the see one of her favorite ballets of all time, but one in which her idol would be performing. This was the first time she'd be attending a ballet performance since leaving the stage more than five years ago.

"Andre," she whispered with tears in her eyes.

"Don't start that yet. You haven't even seen the performance yet," he joked. He brought her hand to his lips and pressed a gentle, yet reassuring kiss to her knuckles. "Come on, the show starts soon."

Stacey could barely feel her legs as they started up the steps to the entrance. She was grateful for Andre's hand holding her, and his other at the small of her back. She felt so many emotions as they ascended the stairs and entered the opera house. They had seats in the center of the fourth ring of the audience. While this was higher up and much further away from the first few rows of the stage, it gave those who sat there a much better view of the entire performance. Stacey once told Andre that she preferred watching all theatre and ballet performances from the third or fourth row to get the full experience of what was taking place on stage. She knew once they sat down he'd remembered her comments.

Within minutes of their arrival, the lights turned low and the performance soon began. Stacey couldn't help but applaud once Misty first hit the stage, twirling around and leaping so high she appeared to be suspended in midair. Her breath caught when the corps de ballet appeared and along with Misty, performed an intricate series. Stacey's mind flashed back to performing a very similar sequence many times over when she was with the Pacific Northwest Ballet. She watched everything from the curve of the dancers' feet, to the lift of their chins.

Stacey attempted to take in every expression they made, every leap and coordinated step. She held her breath every time Misty made her way to the stage. To say she was regal would be an understatement. No one knew better than Stacey the hours, days, months and year of dedication it took to reach this level of excellence in such a demanding field. Stacey's admiration for Misty grew tenfold, which she didn't even know was possible.

As the performance ended, Stacey was one of the first on her feet, applauding and yelling, "Bravo!" as the dancers took their final bows. She was so caught up, she didn't even realize their row had pretty much emptied until she felt Andre pull her into his side.

"Don't cry. There's someone I want you to meet," he smiled as he dabbed at her tears with his handkerchief.

Stacey stared at him confused until she lifted her hand to her face and felt the wetness. She hadn't even noticed the tears. Before she could dwell too long, Andre was pulling her behind him, making their way to the exit, or so she thought.

"Ahh, Mr. Collins there you are," an older man who looked to be in his fifties greeted them as they walked towards the door that read "Backstage."

"Ms. Copeland has been waiting for you. She's excited to meet your special guest," the man said turning.

Stacey froze.

Andre turned to look at her, confused.

"Ms. Copeland? As in Misty Copeland? We're meeting...," her voice trailed off as Andre's smile widened.

"Come one, baby," he encouraged, pulling her close.

They made their way backstage and Stacey couldn't help but feel nervous, but excited as they passed a few of the corps dancers who'd just been performing on stage. Minutes later, they came to a closed door where the man, who Andre informed Stacey was the art director with the American Ballet Theatre, knocked.

"Misty your guest is here," he yelled through the door.

Within seconds, the door opened and Stacey found herself face to face with her dance idol. "Oh my God," she whispered under her breath, not wanting to appear too overzealous.

"Hi, you must be Andre and Stacey, please come in," Misty Copeland, ever gracious, welcomed them.

Stacey felt like she was walking on cloud nine as she entered into Misty's dressing room. Andre presented Misty with a bouquet of flowers that Stacey had been too preoccupied to even notice were in his hand. When she finally found her words, Stacey introduced herself and Misty welcomed her with a hug. Stacey couldn't stop gushing and telling Misty what a big fan she was of hers. When she told her that her only regret was she didn't have her hard copy of Misty's book for her to sign, Andre pulled her book from under his arm and handed Misty a pen to sign.

Turns out, Andre had Stacey's aunt pack her hard copy for this very occasion. They talked for a few more moments, in which Stacey congratulated Misty on her recent rise as principal. Stacey even shared her own ballet past with Misty, who seemed very interested. They talked for about fifteen minutes until they finally excused themselves to let Misty go and greet other fans.

Stacey was in a daze as they walked back to the awaiting limo. She'd never in a million years thought this was where Andre would bring her. She hadn't been to the ballet in years, thinking it would be too painful to watch a performance, but seeing it tonight, she realized how mistaken she was. She remembered all the beautiful aspects of the art form that made her fall in love with it when she was just a child.

She clutched her now signed copy of Misty's book to her chest as they descended the stairs. She hadn't spoken a word since they left Misty's dressing room.

"You're awfully quiet." Andre turned to her as they stopped at the limo. He waved off the driver as he opened the door for Stacey. "I know bringing you here was a risk and you might not—" His words were cut off as Stacey launched herself into his arms, wrapping her arms tightly around his neck.

"Thank you! Thank you! Thank you!" she exclaimed as she kissed all over his face, causing Andre to laugh. "I don't know what to say besides thank you and that doesn't feel like nearly enough," she admitted. "This night was amazing!" she almost shouted.

"You don't have to say anything else. I wanted you to have this experience. When I saw you talking with Hwan a few weeks ago about the ballet, I could tell you missed it, not just as a performer, but as someone who appreciated the art form," he told her. He pressed a kiss to her forehead and widened the door to help her inside.

Stacey's heart was so filled with gratitude and appreciation for this man. She'd never been with someone who observed her so closely to be able to read her so well. Her heart was so full with love for this man she couldn't hold it back any longer. As soon as he closed the door of the limo, she scooted next to him, gripped his face between her hands and kissed him with all the passion she had for him. She first kissed each corner of his mouth before licking the outline of his lips, the same way he'd done to her so many times. She felt Andre's hands at her waist, but he let her take control the kiss. She pried his lips apart with her own. When his mouth opened, she let her tongue explore every inch and crevice of his mouth. When Andre groaned in appreciation, she deepened the kiss pouring all of her emotion into it. Before getting too carried away, she pulled back needing to tell him how she felt.

"I need to tell you something," she panted, as she struggled to catch her breath. She looked into Andre's lust filled eyes that also took on a curious look. "I don't want you to freak out or get weird, but I love you," she admitted.

Andre pulled back an inch to stare directly at her. She couldn't read his expression.

"I'm not asking you to say it back or drop to one knee and ask for marr—" Her words were cut off by Andre's lips. He kissed her with the same ferocity and emotion she'd just kissed him with moments before.

Stacey couldn't keep her hands still as she stroked his chest and abs. She felt Andre's fingers curl around her thighs, seconds before she was lifted off her seat and turned to straddle his lap. Andre peppered kisses down her jawline, stopping to nip at her earlobe and nuzzle her neck. Stacey lifted her hips slightly to help Andre who pushed her dress up over her hips. She soon heard the sounds of her ripping lace panties, and the cool air as it hit her now exposed nether regions. She wasn't cold for long as Andre's warm, sturdy fingers made their way to her labia, massaging and stroking.

"Mmm," she moaned against his lips.

"Say it again," he commanded, pushing one finger into her wet core.

Stacey's breath caught in her throat at all the wonderful sensations coursing through her body from his intimate contact.

"Say it again," he demanded, his voice thick with need as he added another finger.

"I love you," she moaned loudly, instinctively knowing that was what he wanted to hear. Stacey began pumping her hips on his fingers, already feeling the buildup of her impending orgasm.

"You're so fucking beautiful right now." Andre's voice was filled with wonder and lust, causing Stacey to cream even more. She enjoyed his fingers, but needed him inside of her.

"Andre, I need you." Stacey didn't care if she was begging at this point. She moved her hands down to unbutton his belt and pants. She heard Andre press the button to tell the driver to take the scenic route but was so caught up in trying to release him from his pants, she didn't have time to think about it.

"Fuck!" Andre cursed when she finally released him from his pants.

She began working her hand up and down his long shaft, using the drop of precum at the tip as lubrication. Looking down, she licked her lips in anticipation of taking him in her mouth, but was stopped when she tried to scoot off Andre's lap.

"Not this time, baby. I won't last if my cock gets anywhere near your mouth. Come here." His voice was thick with arousal as he helped her position herself just above his fully erect cock.

They both moaned out loud when Stacey slowly slid down onto his hardness. Once fully seated on him, she began a methodical rhythm that had them both experiencing pure bliss within seconds. Stacey threw her head back in ecstasy as she continued her rhythm, grinding on his cock. She felt Andre's fingers at the back of her dress as he lowered her zipper. He pulled down the top half of her dress, freeing her breasts. Once they were free, he pulled her close to latch onto one protruding nipple. He twirled his tongue around, first one nipple, then another, at the same time he maneuvered his thumb around, angling it to massage her swollen clit.

"Ahhh, Andre," Stacey panted, feeling her pussy walls tighten. Seconds later, she tumbled over the edge as her orgasm slammed into her with force. She gripped Andre's shoulders and threw her head back as her orgasm overtook her.

"So fucking sexy," Andre growled.

Stacey didn't have time to come down from her first orgasm before Andre lifted her, changing their positions, and pushed her back against the seat without pulling himself out of her. Stacey barely felt the warm leather against her skin before Andre began pumping into her wildly. He alternated between deep and shallow strokes, driving Stacey crazy once again.

"Say it again!" he commanded, staring down at her with such intensity it caused her eyes to water.

Andre canted his hips and pounded into her at a faster rate.

"Andre!" Stacey panted.

"Say it *again!*" he demanded.

Stacey could barely breathe as another, more powerful orgasm lingered just out of reach. Andre's fingers began plucking at her hardened nipples again.

"Fuuck! I...love...you!" she panted as her orgasm crested.

"Goddamn!" Andre groaned as his own orgasm rose. He moaned

deeply as he buried his face in between Stacey's neck and shoulder, spilling all of himself into her.

Stacey held him for long minute until his tremors subsided. She stroked her hand up and down his back, while he inhaled her scent. Even coming down from her bliss, she realized she didn't regret telling Andre she was in love with him. It was a truth she'd come to realize before they'd left for New York.

Nevertheless, she noted how although he demanded she say it again and again during their lovemaking, he hadn't said it back.

CHAPTER 18

*J*ennings stepped out of his rented sedan and entered the dingy motel room. He'd come to Atlanta with the purpose of getting his company back, and he knew just the way to do it. He had spent the last month and a half after the holidays taking notes of Collins' schedule and putting together his plan. He knew exactly where Andre's weak spot was, and if he was going to get his company back, he had to use it to his advantage.

Jennings made sure to close and lock the door behind him before heading to straight to the bed where he'd left an untraceable cell phone underneath the mattress. Removing the phone, he dialed the number of the muscle he'd hired for this job.

"Yeah." The gruff voice at the other end of the phone answered. Jennings' face settled into a snarl. He hated doing business with these type of people, but for this type of job, he needed someone who wasn't afraid to get their hands dirty.

"Is everything in place as we discussed?" Jennings spoke without preamble.

"We're on it. We will have to wait until this Friday, possibly catch her off guard on her way to that club she performs at," the man told Jennings.

"Friday? What happened to Wednesday? Doesn't she work late on Wednesdays? That'd be the perfect time to snatch her." Jennings' voice was filled with frustration and agitation. He wanted this over and done with. The woman was inconsequential to him. Just a means to an end. She meant a lot to Andre. That was obvious from all the time they spent together. He could use her to get Andre to do what he wanted him to, which was give his company back.

"Yeah, and as you should know, she always has an escort Wednesday nights. He still meets her every Wednesday, even drops her off and picks her up most of the time now." The impatient voice came back over the line.

"Shit!" Jennings swore under his breath, running a shaky hand through his hair. *I need a drink,* he thought as he ambled over to the rickety wooden dresser. Opening the top drawer, he found his flask and bottle of whiskey right where he'd left them. Taking a swig from his flask, Jennings plopped down on the squeaky bed.

"Look, we're also going to renegotiate price," the deep voice continued in Jennings' ear. "I've done some research on this Collins and you never told us he was some major business mogul."

"Ha!" Jennings scoffed. "He's a thief who steals businesses. He wouldn't be shit without his daddy's money!" The irony of that comment wasn't lost on the man on the other end.

He chuckled. "Seems like that's a trait you'd identify with," he mocked.

"What was that?" Jennings demanded defensively.

"Nothing. Listen, I don't know what your problem with this Collins is, and I don't care. But given his standing in the business world and financial position, this job is definitely more risky. The price has gone up. Add another twenty-thousand to our agreed upon price. I'll expect half by this Wednesday and the rest once you have the package." And with that, Jennings heard a click on the other end, alerting him he'd just been hung up on.

"Son of a bitch!" he yelled. They'd already agreed upon a price of fifty-thousand for the kidnapping. This project was beginning to take longer than Jennings had originally anticipated, and costing him more. In the end, he knew it would be worth it. He would get his business back, plus some, and be able to move on and resume his normal life.

Jennings' pulled out his phone to make another phone call to put the other part of his plan into motion.

"Hello?" the feminine voice answered.

"Maria, we're moving forward with the plan," Jennings began.

* * *

ANDRE DISTRACTEDLY REACHED for his vibrating cell phone, keeping his eyes on the spreadsheet on his computer screen. He'd been going over reports all day and was actually hoping it was Stacey calling him to discuss their plans for the evening. They were supposed to have dinner that evening. It'd been a busy month and a half since they returned from their New York trip. Stacey began her counselor position full-time and was settling in nicely in that role. Andre smiled as he remembered the plans she'd shared with him to service more clients. It was obvious she thoroughly enjoyed what she did. He looked forward to watching her grow in her profession. *Am I thinking long-term?* he pondered as he picked up his cell.

Andre sighed and pressed the ignore button, seeing it was Maria who was calling. For weeks now, she'd been calling or texting. She would text or leave messages saying she needed to speak with him. As far as Andre was concerned, they had nothing to speak about. They hadn't seen or spoken to each other in months, not since the night of the gala. Andre remained steadfast in his parting words to her. They were through.

Before Andre could go back reviewing his reports, his office phone buzzed. "Mr. Collins, Mrs. Collins is here to see you," his assistant chimed over the speaker. Andre knew Nikola and Devyn were out of town for the next few weeks, both for business and pleasure, so he knew this Mrs. Collins could be none other than the woman who'd given him life.

"Mama. To what do I owe this surprise?" Andre questioned his voice full of adoration, as he reached down and gripped his mother in a bear hug.

"Hi, sweetheart. I was in the neighborhood after having lunch with Diane around the corner, and thought I'd stop by and say hello," she informed him before placing a kiss on his proffered cheek.

Andre eyed his mother, dressed in a black pantsuit with an off-white silk blouse. She looked radiant and so full of life. Seeing her this way always brought him a sense of peace and joy. There was a time, after his father's death when he believed the vivacious and bubbly woman who raised him was gone forever too. That had nearly destroyed him, even more than his father's death.

"Come in. How is your friend Diane these days?" he asked, ushering her into his office and closing the door.

"You should know, seeing as how often you're at the club now," she teased, cocking her head to the side with a knowing smile plastered on her face.

Andre knew she was referring to his presence at Stacey's performances. She performed at least two to three weekends a month, and he refused to miss any of her performances.

"Keeping tabs on me, huh?" he joked.

"Of course. Who else is going to make sure my baby boy is doing well?"

Andre merely shook his head and chuckled. He knew to his mother he would always be her baby boy.

"Speaking of doing well, I never got a chance to speak with you about the graduation dinner you hosted for Stacey. It was a lovely gesture, and her family was a pleasure." Iris' blue eyes sparkled as she remembered the events of that night. "And it appears things are serious between you and Ms. Coleman. Is my assumption correct?"

Andre stiffened in his seat. He knew his relationship with Stacey was serious. Very serious. He just wasn't sure about love and marriage. Years ago, he'd sworn marriage wasn't for him. Now, he had his mother in his face asking the very same questions he'd been asking himself. It'd been over a month since Stacey told him she loved him, and despite his reluctance, he reveled in those words every time she said them. He often demanded she tell him in the middle of their love-making. Her cries and declaration of love as she came had him coming harder than he'd ever come before. Just thinking about her shivering form as she panted his name and yelled out her love for him had him shifting in his seat. He knew every time he heard her utter those words, she owned another piece of his heart.

"No need to answer that. I can see it in your eyes," he heard his mother's words break into his ruminations. He kept his gaze lowered to avoid his mother's knowing glare. It was bad enough he'd just gotten lost in thought thinking about Stacey orgasming as she screamed her love for him, but to do so in front of his mother? Andre tried to think of a way to change the subject when his mother's next words threw him.

"We've never talked about that night. What you went through that night and the long months after your father died." Iris' voice was filled with compassion and concern.

Andre's breath caught in his throat. It'd been so long since he thought about that dark period in his life. He felt his chest tighten, and he closed his eyes trying to fight his brain as it fought flashbacks of those dark moments. He attempted to inhale deeply as he tried to shove down memories of his mother screaming out in agony. Blinking his eye open, he looked into the azul colored eyes he'd inherited. He saw the reflection of pain in those eyes, a look he had become all too familiar with over the years. He averted his gaze to avoid the fact that the pain he saw wasn't for her suffering, but for him. He knew his mother was feeling for him. Concerned for him.

"Mama, I don't..." he trailed off when Iris held her hand up.

"I know you don't. I just think that may have something to do with your reluctance to marry, or to even admit you're in love. Once you acknowledge that, you can move forward. I want both of my boys to be happy," she said, rising from her chair and rounding his desk. "Just think about it, and be honest with yourself," she encouraged, placing a parting kiss on his cheek. "I'm heading home now." She smiled before exiting his office.

Andre remained in his chair in a daze. He wondered the impact that time in his life had on his thoughts of marriage and love. He remembered back to a conversation he had with Nikola, who reminded him that growing up he often said he wanted a marriage like his parents. For most of their lives, it had been Nikola who was less partial to marriage, but that changed one night eight years ago. His father's death had a deeper impact on Andre's life then he'd ever imagined. Maybe it was time to share his secret pain with the woman in his life.

* * *

ACROSS TOWN, Stacey was having a stressful day at work. She wasn't perturbed. These days often came with the territory of working in her field. One of her clients she began counseling as an intern had relapsed, and had to be readmitted as a residential patient. This particular client had been through a series of traumatic events growing up, and once again, as she began on her road of recovery, she experienced the loss of her mother, the only strong support network she had. It was a long road ahead to recovery, but Stacey knew she was in the right place. Stacey knew this was just part of the recovery process, but it still tugged at her heart strings to see a young woman with so much to look forward to in life, to be mired with ails of an eating disorder.

Stacey shook her head as she thought about her client, and all the others she had met with in their group session. She needed to jot down some notes in her files and speak with a more senior counselors on more advanced treatment options for a few of her clients. There were also a few recent studies on eating disorders and women of color, and women of lower socioeconomic status she wanted to read and take notes on. Looking at her watch, she saw it was just after three in the afternoon. She could write down her notes and update her client files, and then start reading the studies in her office before heading out for the day. Rounding the corner towards her office, she heard the voices of what sounded like two new interns the facility had recently taken on. Stacey smiled thinking about the younger, fresh-faced women who enthusiastically took on their roles as assistant counselors.

"I know, Mel. I was confused by it too." Stacey heard one of the interns, she believed to be named Kennedy, state.

"I mean, Black women don't even get eating disorders." That was Melissa, a young twenty-one year old senior at Georgia State, who was majoring in psychology.

Stacey's steps faltered as those words sunk in. She knew the perception that women of color didn't suffer from eating disorders was prevalent, even in the mental health field. She'd hoped that this perception was changing, but as she stood and listened to these two young prospective mental health professionals, her heart sank. Their words brought back painful memories. Stacey knew she had to intervene.

"Ladies, I truly hope that is not what you believe," she admonished, her voice harsher than she intended. While Stacey didn't intend to admonish too harshly, she knew beliefs like these two women were sharing were dangerous and could prevent women who truly needed help from getting it.

"Oh, Ms. Coleman," Melissa's eyes widened in shock to see Stacey standing there. "We were just saying it's, uh, well, it's rare..." Her voice trailed off.

"Maybe it's rare because prevailing attitudes like yours prevent women of color from getting the help they need. Hm?" Stacey asked sharply, looking between both women.

"We didn't mean—"

Stacey waved off Kennedy's meek protests. "Ladies, as prospective mental health counselors, I would hope your attitudes towards your clients aren't as narrow-minded as they seemed just now. If everyone held your beliefs, then I and many other women would still be suffering in the throes of an eating disorder. Or worse," she sternly stated looking between the two women. With that, she turned and went to her office. Once she was tucked safely in her office, she slammed her files on her desk before closing her door behind her. She paced her office trying to burn off her negative energy. On one hand, she couldn't blame the two women, who had likely only come in contact with eating disorder patients who were mainly Caucasian and middle-class. However, these women were professionals, or prospective professionals. *They should know better,* she thought, as she continued to pace her office.

For the rest of the work day, Stacey could barely concentrate on the work she had planned. Just looking at the new study she wanted to read about women of color and eating disorders had her remembering the interns' conversation all over again. By the time the end of the work day came, she was beyond ready to get out there for a few hours and calm her nerves before returning to work the next day.

Entering the high rise condo, Stacey hung up her pea coat on the coat rack, mumbling to herself. She still hadn't calmed down from her encounter with the two interns.

"Oh!" she nearly shouted by Andre's presence. It was just after five thirty in the evening, and he usually didn't get in until well after six. "I didn't see you," she explained.

"I can tell. Rough day at work?" he asked, concern etched on his face.

Stacey blew out a harsh breath. "Kind of," she tossed over her shoulder as she removed her black pumps.

"You want to—"

"I mean, we're supposed to be professionals, and they're interns and young so they may not realize the implications of their words, but still. Do they have any idea the repercussions of their words? Ugh, seriously!" Stacey continued to ramble on and on, barely finishing a thought before moving on to another.

Now that she was at home, she felt able to vent her frustrations. Unfortunately, in her rambling she wasn't making much sense to the only other person in the room, as she paced back and forth on Andre's hardwood floors. "What about all the women and men who don't fit the stereotypical standard of what an eating disorder sufferer looks like? This is why so many suffer in silence, or heck don't even know they have an eating disorder..." she continued.

"Umm, babe?" Andre attempted to interject. Stacey continued on in her rant, seemingly unreachable.

Stacey was so worked up that it took a while for her to realize she was being pulled down the hall towards the bedroom. Her rambling was cut short when they entered the bedroom. Andre pulled open the top two drawers he'd given her to keep her clothes and removed workout clothing.

"Put these on," he gently commanded, thrusting the clothes at her.

Tilting her head to the side and pursing her lips in confusion, Stacey silently asked for an explanation.

Andre remained adamant. "You need to work off some energy. Put these on."

"Andre—"

"Put them on," he commanded in that authoritative voice that sent chills down her spine. Taking the clothes from him, she quickly donned a pair of black spandex shorts, a sports bra, and a white sleeveless top.

"Come with me," Andre directed, pulling her out of the room. They made their way down the hall to his private gym, stopping in front of his punching bag. Andre grabbed a pair of his smaller boxing gloves, and one by one he placed Stacey's hand in each glove, making sure they were secured. "You're going to work out some of that frustration you have. It helps me when work has been stressful," he responded to her skeptical look. "I'll hold the bag while you hit," he instructed, as he walked around the other side of the punching bag, holding it in place.

Stacey blew out a breath and shrugged. She needed to work out some of the tension from her day, and hitting an inanimate object seemed as good a workout as any other. She hit the bag with a few tentative punches, barely making the bag sway even without Andre holding it.

"I *know* you can hit harder than that. Look, just think about whatever it is that has you so frustrated, and pretend it's here in the bag. Then hit it," he advised.

Stacey thought about the issue that really bothered her from what she encountered at work. She didn't picture the faces of the interns whose conversation she'd interrupted. Instead, she thought of her own pain. She remembered the days she'd sought help and was turned away because she didn't look like the typical sufferer. Although she had come a long way, that anguish of needing help and not being able to get it, never left her. It was why she did what she did. It was the driving force behind her passion for what she did. She hated the very thought that the way someone looked or their lack of financial resources could prevent them from being able to get the help or treatment they might need.

For the next thirty minutes, Stacey wailed on the punching bag, releasing the stress and tension of the day. The longer she hit, the more she could feel her frustration ebbing, and she even began to formulate a new outreach program to reach clientele who weren't the "typical" model of eating disorder patients. She remembered her long-term goals of opening her own treatment facility that catered to a diverse group of clients, and offered an array of treatment programs, including dance therapy. At the end of her thirty minute punching bag session she was physically spent, but mentally invigorated.

"Here you go slugger," Andre joked, handing Stacey a bottle of water. She realized he had a small refrigerator in his gym, stocked mostly with bottles of water. "You were right about that right hook of yours." He laughed.

Stacey shrugged. "I told you."

"You did. Now, it's time for a shower and some dinner."

Twenty minutes later, a freshly showered Stacey and Andre sat on the floor of his living room eating their dinner of grilled sea bass and steamed broccoli with a bottle of red wine.

"So, you want to talk about it?" Andre asked, his eyes piercing her over the rim of his wine glass.

Stacey pushed the remnants of her dinner around her plate, contemplating on where to even start. She felt ready to share this part of herself with Andre, but it was always uncomfortable talking about this part of her history. Andre sat patiently waiting for her to open up to him.

"I walked up on a couple of interns today having a conversation about black women not having eating disorders. It uh...struck a nerve," she admitted, taking another sip of her wine. She peeked out of the corner of her eye and saw Andre watching her, urging her for a deeper explanation.

Stacey briefly closed her eyes, trying to figure out where to begin. She finally decided that the beginning was just a good a starting place as any. "I was thirteen the first time I stuck my fingers down my throat to make myself throw up."

She paused to let what she'd just said sink in.

Andre's wide-eyed expression told her he was not expecting those words to come out of her mouth. Nevertheless, it was her truth.

"I had been in Savannah for less than a year and began studying ballet at Savannah Ballet Theatre. Though I'd been dancing for years, this was a different level. Competition was stronger. That and the upheaval of being in a new state with a family I had just come to know, and my sister going away to college...I felt lost and out of control. I also felt bigger than most of the other dancers. One day, I walked into the bathroom and I heard one of the older girls throwing up. At first, I thought she was sick and needed help, but when she came out of the stall and saw me, she froze. She warned me not to tell anyone what I saw or I'd be sorry. Instead of being intimidated, I was...intrigued. She was one of the dancers I looked up to in the theatre. She moved with the grace and poise I'd wished to have, so a few days later, I sought her out to ask what she was doing in the bathroom and why. Reluctantly, she told me she threw up to keep her weight down to help her remain light on her feet. That was the start of my eating disorder."

Stacey paused to take a breather. She rarely shared this much of her history with people, but Andre wasn't just people. He was the man she loved, and she wanted him to know everything about her the same way she wanted to know everything about him.

"For years, I would use my 'secret weapon,' as I would call it, to help me feel like I had some sense of control. When I was stressed over a major performance or a tryout, I would find myself in the cycle of bingeing and then purging. I thought it was under control because I didn't do it everyday. I would often go months without bingeing and purging, and therefore thought it wasn't a big deal, but then I got injured. When my ballet career began to crumble and I felt my entire world collapsing around me, it got worse. I was in Seattle, all alone. My boyfriend at the time had dumped me at my lowest point. Most of my friends were associated with ballet and it was too painful to be around them. For nearly a year, while I tried to recuperate to return to the stage, my eating disorder took over."

Pausing to take another sip of her wine, Stacey felt Andre's hand massage her thigh. She covered his hand with hers and smiled up at him. He pulled her into his side, embracing her. Stacey felt empowered by his warmth. Inhaling deeply, she continued.

"I knew I was in trouble. At one point, I went to a counselor that was recommended by the ballet company. I didn't give full details, but when I told her I'd been having trouble with eating food, she told me that she wasn't surprised that *someone of my background* had trouble figuring out a nutritious diet. She recommended a dietician and sent me on my way. I couldn't put it into words then, but now I think she meant that someone who looked like me couldn't have an eating disorder." Stacey shook her head still in bewilderment at the lack of compassion displayed by that first therapist she'd seen all those years ago. She often wondered if the woman was still practicing and how many other desperately hurting people she'd turned away.

"So how, um," Andre paused to clear his throat in a rare show of being at a loss for words. "How did you get help?"

"Coral." Stacey smiled thinking of her sister. "She was still in the army, but was stationed in the States at the time. She often called to check on me, but I don't know, I think she heard something in my voice. I finally broke down and told her my ballet career was pretty much a done deal. I cried over the phone. I didn't tell her about my bingeing and purging, but I think she knew somehow. The next day, she showed up at my apartment. She'd taken an emergency leave. On her second day there, I told her of my bingeing and purging. That I couldn't control it. She immediately went to work looking for treatment options. Before I knew it, she and my aunt were able to find the treatment center here in Atlanta. I was a resident there for ninety days and then did months of outpatient treatment. It's why I decided to remain here in Atlanta. I wanted to eventually work at the place that welcomed me with open arms when I needed it and now I do." She paused again for another sip of wine and to gauge Andre's reaction to what she'd just shared.

Looking into those deep blue pools, she saw so much compassion and concern. She stroked his cheek and rubbed her thumb over his lips. She couldn't help but lean in and press her lips to his as an expression of her gratitude for the lack of judgement she saw in his gaze.

"So today when I heard those interns, it just brought it all back. It made me ache for my former self who felt so alone, lost and dejected after that initial counseling session with that Seattle therapist. I don't want anyone to feel like that. It's why I do what I do."

Stacey held up her right hand, showing the small scar in between her knuckles for Andre to see. "This is the reminder of my eating disorder, a scar from the many times I used these fingers to make myself purge the contents of my stomach. I haven't purged in more than four years, but it is a daily reminder of how far I have come in my recovery and how strong I am." She let her hand fall to her lap.

Andre instantly reached over, grabbed her hand, and brought his lips to her scar. Stacey felt as if a weight she didn't even realize was there had been lifted. She felt lighter and almost giddy, having shared such an important part of her life with this man. His kiss symbolized his understanding and awareness of how important this was to her. She felt emboldened.

"I love you," she told him just above a whisper. She'd become more comfortable with telling him those words over the last month. While it did prickle her a little that he never returned those words, she did see the light in his eyes grow the way it always did when she told him. Although he never returned the words, they always seemed to make him wild with need for her. Before she knew it, Stacey was flat on her back as Andre hovered over her, a look of passion and need in his darkening eyes.

"You're one of the strongest women I've ever met," he told her while nipping her earlobe. "Thank you for trusting me enough to share that with me."

Stacey shivered when she felt his warm breath across her neck.

Andre kissed her deeply, using his tongue and mouth to express to her his gratitude for sharing a major part of her life with him. He kissed her with all the feelings he held for her, feelings he was too mixed up to understand himself, but knew they were deeper than any emotion he'd ever felt for any other woman. He'd come home early because he wanted to share with her his revelations from his conversation with his mother earlier in the day. But when he saw how agitated she was when she came through the door, he put his own thoughts to the side. When she finished telling him about her eating disorder, and she looked at him with tears in her eyes telling him she loved him, he couldn't keep his hands off of her for another second.

Andre spent the rest of the evening letting his body express all the emotion that his mouth had been unable to formulate.

CHAPTER 19

*S*tacey felt lighter than she had in a very long time. It'd been a few days since she shared with Andre her eating disorder past. He had been so supportive, asking questions and simply listening when she talked about that time in her life. She talked about still seeing a therapist from time to time when she felt she needed to. She opened up to him about her ultimate goal of opening a facility that catered to men and women of varying socioeconomic statuses, and ethnicities to help treat mental health illnesses and eating disorders. Andre pledged to be one of her first investors when she was ready to get started. Just remembering that conversation had a smile a mile wide appearing on her face as she stepped into the doors of the Black Kitty.

Although it was a Friday, she wasn't scheduled to perform that evening. However, she had been contemplating for a few days and was ready to discuss the real path that had brought her to burlesque nearly five years ago. She'd called the Mistress Coco the previous day to find out if Sean had finished filming for his documentary. Finding out that he had a few more scenes he wanted to film, she decided to ask if she could reshoot her portion. She wanted to be honest about the time in her life which led her to find burlesque.

"Hey Sean. I'm ready when you are," Stacey merrily sang when she found Sean. She was ready to open up, and couldn't help the lightness she felt being able to be honest.

A few minutes later, Sean had his set up in place and was ready to begin their shoot.

"Alright, so what brought you to burlesque?"

This time when Stacey fingered the tiny scar between her knuckles, she didn't feel the need to deflect or lie. Sitting upright, taking notice of Rihanna's *Diamond,* playing in the background, she began her recount of the friend in recovery who introduced her to burlesque.

* * *

ANDRE FELT the foreign feeling of nervousness as he completed a few work emails. He decided today was the day he would open up to Stacey about his fears on love and marriage. Stacey's ability to open up to him made him want to share everything with her. He needed to tell Stacey how much he loved and wanted a future with her.

Now, as he sat at his desk finalizing emails before he ended his day, he felt anxious to get this over with. Since it was a weekend in which Stacey wasn't performing, he'd made plans to have dinner at his home catered, where he would open up about the time in his life that caused his desire for marriage to shift. Andre planned to tell Stacey that she was the one woman who made him want to confront his fears and change them, just so he could keep her forever. Tonight would be the night.

The ringing of his office phone brought Andre out of his reflection.

"Mr. Collins, it's Ms. Coleman on the line for you," his assistant chimed.

"Hey, babe. How's your day going?"

"It's going great!" Stacey happily responded. "I left work about a half hour early, to meet Sean at the Black Kitty to retape my segment. I just finished and am walking out now."

Andre nodded. She'd told him about going out to her first burlesque show with a friend she'd met at the eating disorder clinic. She'd told him about how in addition to allowing her to get through the ending of her ballet career, discovering burlesque helped her to cope through recovering from her eating disorder.

"I can't wait to watch it when it comes out." Andre was sincere in his tone. He was proud of her for being able to be candid. "I'm proud of you, babe," he told her honestly. "And speaking of being honest, I wanted to talk to you about something tonight."

"Oh, that soun—" Stacey's words were abruptly cut off.

"Stacey," Andre's voice was alarmed. A nervous chill ran through his veins when she didn't respond. He soon heard a ruffling noise and what sounded like a male's voice.

"STACEY!" Andre roared into the phone, but to no avail.

"Gimme the phone, bitch!" Andre could make out a male voice.

Andre couldn't believe what he'd just heard on the other end of the phone. He pulled out his cell phone, quickly redialing Stacey's number and hoping what he'd heard was just some sick joke.

"Answer the phone," he mumbled over and over as he dialed. "Fuck!" He yelled so loudly, his assistant was startled enough to run into his office.

"Get Raul on the line *now*!" he instructed. "Tell him Stacey's in trouble!"

Andre jumped into action. He didn't have time to go into shock or second guess himself. The longer they waited, the greater the chances of something perilous happening to the woman he loved. He'd only been recently able to admit to himself that he loved Stacey and now she could be in trouble.

"Raul!" he barked into his office phone, "Something's happened to Stacey. I was on the phone with her and then all of a sudden she was cut off. I heard male voices in the background right before her phone was disconnected. Now, I can't get ahold of her. Her phone keeps going to voicemail." He recounted the last few minutes as he paced his office. Andre knew Raul's security expertise and opted to entirely bypass contacting the police. He knew Raul could assist in circumstances where police hands were tied. And right now, he knew time was of the essence. The quicker they acted, the better the chances of getting Stacey back unharmed.

"Where was she coming from?" Raul asked in a calm, yet commanding voice. Andre could tell he was going into action mode.

"She was in the parking lot of the Black Kitty. She just taped a segment for that documentary."

"Alright, I'm sending Lorenzo over there now to investigate. Where are you?"

"In the office."

"Alright, don't move. I'm on my way over."

Andre nodded even though Raul couldn't see him, before hanging up. He knew the next phone call he had to make would be especially difficult, but he didn't want to leave anyone in the dark about what's happening. He knew he wasn't overreacting. Something had happened to Stacey, and her family needed to know.

"Mrs. Stevens, it's Andre. I'm sorry to have to tell you this...." he began to Stacey's aunt, running his hand through his hair.

Within the next few minutes, Andre was on the phone with Stacey's aunt, uncle, and both Quincy and Jabari. As soon as the words were out of his mouth, Quincy began arranging travel plans, but Andre already had his assistant arrange a private plane to transport the entire family to Atlanta. Andre knew they all would want to be here to help get Stacey back.

Andre hung up with Stacey's family just as Raul and two of his employees entered his office. The grim expression on Raul's face told Andre he didn't have good news for him.

CHAPTER 20

Stacey's lids felt as if they were held shut by glue. She felt dizzy and attempted to grip her head with her hand, but discovered both hands were bound together. She felt a hard, lumpy surface beneath her. Realizing she was laying on a bed, Stacey tried again to pry her eyes open. Finally opening them, it took a while for her gaze to focus. The room she was in was dark, but in front of her she could see a door that was slightly ajar, with light streaming in from what she assumed was a hallway. Stacey attempted to sit up but was hit with a wave of dizziness that had her slumping back to the bed. Closing her eyes, Stacey willed herself not to lose the contents of her stomach from the dizziness and nausea.

"Yeah...I got her...Both of them..." Stacey could just barely make out the far off male voice. Closing her eyes once again, she attempted to strain her ears to listen on the conversation. When she heard heavy footsteps, she stilled.

"I said they're here!" The frustrated voice nearly shouted.

Stacey could hear her heartbeat speed up as goosebumps rose on her skin. She tried to slow her breathing in an attempt to appear to still be sleeping. She had no idea where she was, who had taken her, or why. The man's voice she heard wasn't familiar at all.

As the footsteps got closer, Stacey couldn't help the jump in her heartbeat.

Just breathe, she told herself, forcing her brain to concentrate on inhaling and exhaling slowly so as not to give away the fact that she was awake from whatever drug they'd used on her. She nearly cried out in shock and fear when the footsteps stopped at the door and she heard it forcefully push open.

"Yeah, I said I've got them both. The black broad and the other one. One's still sleeping. The other one you banged up is in and out. Anyway, let's discuss my payment..." the voice trailed off as he turned and moved further away from the room, closing the door behind him.

The other one? Stacey wondered who or what this man was referring to. More importantly, as her brain fog began to lift, she wondered who the hell this man was. Who was he on the phone with? It sounded as if this man was paid to kidnap her. But who would want to kidnap her and for what? All these questions fired off one right after the other as Stacey searched for answers as to what the hell was happening to her.

Peeling her eyes open once again, she saw she was in the center of an empty room except for the cot she laid on.

"Mmm." Stacey jumped at the groan that sounded like it came from behind her. Twisting her neck to look over her shoulder, Stacey could only see more darkness.

"Help me," a barely audible whisper sounded.

Stacey could tell this was the voice of someone who had been hurt or was struggling, physically. Peeking at the door once again to make sure it was closed, she inched her body over as best she could with her hands bound, making sure to make as little noise as possible. Once she was finally on her other side with her back to the door, she tried to focus her gaze again in the darkened room. In the corner of the room, she could make out a figure. It looked to be a person. A woman with long dark hair.

"Are you awake?" Stacey whispered to the woman. "Hey, hey," she called, when the woman didn't respond. "Are you awake?"

She flinched when she realized she'd spoken louder than she intended.

"Hmm. Pl-please don't hurt me," the figure in the corner shrilled.

"Shhh," Stacey shushed, looking over her shoulder again at the door. "I'm not going to hurt you. Do you know where we are?"

"I-I...don't know. M-my head hurts s-so bad," the woman cried, holding her hand to her head.

"Were you hit?" Stacey asked, trying to discreetly slide off the bed to get to the woman to help her.

"Y-yes. I th-think so," the woman slurred.

Stacey wondered if she had been drugged or if the woman's injuries were what was causing the sluggishness. Inching her way off the cot to make as little noise as possible, Stacey scooted over to the corner towards the woman. She could make out that the woman was dressed in a pair of jeans and a sleeveless shirt. She had long, dark hair that partially covered her face.

"Hey, can you look at me? I won't hurt you. I promise," Stacey attempted to console the woman.

Slowly, the woman lifted her head and used her bound hands to push her hair out of her face. Stacey forced herself to not let the gasp escape her lips when she took in the swollen eyes of the woman's face, and her quivering split lip. It was very apparent someone had done a number on this woman. Even in the darkened room, the bruises on porcelain skin were apparent.

"Oh God," Stacey murmured as she tried to assess the woman's condition. The woman widened her eyelids and Stacey could just make out the hazel eye color. For some reason, the woman's eyes seemed familiar to Stacey. Just as she had that thought, the woman's eye that was least swollen widened even more in shock

"Oh my God! Stacey," she gasped.

Stacey's body went rigid as recognition settled over her. "Maria," she gasped.

* * *

"WHAT THE FUCK is taking them so long!?" Andre barked at Raul, referring to his men who'd gone to the Black Kitty to investigate.

"They're on their way back now," Raul reassured him.

They were set up at Andre's office, awaiting Raul's men. They had called and said they'd found the smashed remnants of a cell phone. They bagged the evidence and were bringing it back to Andre to have him confirm whether or not it belonged to Stacey. They also went to check to see if Mistress Coco had security cameras in and around the building.

Raul tried to shift Andre's focus. "They'll be here in five minutes. Let's go over who could possibly want to hurt or harm Stacey."

"No one!" Andre shouted. Taking a breath to calm himself, he tried to recall anyone who would want to harm Stacey. He thought about every conversation they had. Not once had she ever mentioned being scared of anyone, in the past or present. She wasn't someone who made enemies. She was a damn social worker for goodness sakes!

"She doesn't have any enemies. No one who knows her would want to hurt her," he said, running his hand through his hair in frustration. "She's a fucking social worker! She helps people for a living and she dances. Maybe..." Andre's voice trailed off as a thought came to him. "What if this is tied to her dancing? A few months back, there were two different pricks who propositioned her after they saw her perform. One was at the club and the other was at this ice cream shop we went to," Andre recounted to Raul.

"Good, this might be a lead. Give me a description of the men," Raul requested pulling out his pen and taking paper from Andre's desk. For the next few minutes, Andre gave Raul a description of the men who'd approached Stacey. His memory of both were good seeing as how he'd yoked up both men to get them to back off Stacey. He'd never forget either of their faces. He began to wonder if the men had something to do with Stacey's disappearance, or if it was someone else from the club. The fact that Stacey was taken while at the Black Kitty began to point towards it being someone connected to the club.

Andre also remembered to the previous year when Mercedes, Raul's wife, was being stalked. Though her stalker turned out to be a sister she never knew about, the woman had taken on a part-time at the Black Kitty to gain access to Mercedes. Andre wondered if something similar could be the case with Stacey. He shared his thoughts with Raul.

"I doubt it's the same type of thing. She hasn't received any notes or calls of a threatening nature, right?"

Andre shook his head. "She practically lives with me. We haven't spent a night apart in months. I'd know if someone was threatening her." He sighed. Just as he finished, Raul's men, Lorenzo and a second man Andre wasn't familiar with, entered his office.

"Boss, this is what we found," Lorenzo told Raul, handing him the bag that held the broken pieces of the cell phone.

"This look familiar?" Raul questioned Andre, holding the bag for him to see the contents.

Immediately, Andre recognized the phone and the pieces of her case that held the image of a little ballerina twirling around. His heart sank as the complete realization that someone had taken Stacey settled in. Up until then, he had been hoping against hope that maybe her phone had just died and she couldn't get in touch with him. Seeing the phone he knew was hers broken, intentionally, in Raul's hand made it real for him.

"Son of a bitch!" he shouted at the same time he slammed his fist into his desk. He felt like a caged lion, unable to get to the woman he loved.

"Hey man, I know what it's like when the woman you love is in trouble. The best thing you can do is to keep it together. For her," Raul consoled.

Andre knew Raul spoke from experience. He'd heard about when Mercedes' stalker had lured Mercedes to her place of work and held her at gunpoint.

"I'm fine," Andre stated, shaking off his frustration. The last thing Stacey needed right now was his frustration. She needed his clarity and for him to do everything in his power to bring her back home, safely. "I'm fine. Were you able to get anything from the security cameras?" Andre asked, turning his attention towards Raul's two men.

A grim look passed over Lorenzo's face. "No. Apparently, the club doesn't have security cameras. We asked the owner and a few patrons who were inside and no one saw anything. Didn't notice any cars that appeared strange. We're gonna keep asking."

Andre nodded and sighed, checking his Cartier watch. "Stacey's family is scheduled to land in about ten minutes. I've arranged for a car to take them straight to my place. I think we should head over there to meet them."

The rest of the men agreed and within minutes, they were headed out of the Excel offices and on their way to Andre's condo. Andre knew that until the time Stacey was back, his place was going to be the command center of this investigation.

* * *

"Stacey! Oh my God! They got you!" Maria cried at the same time she winced in pain. "I'm so sorry. I tried to stop him," she mumbled.

Stacey's body slumped against the wall as the air left her lungs. She was left stunned from realizing who the woman was in corner. This was Andre's former girlfriend or whatever she had been to him. Stacey could not wrap her head around the fact that she was sitting face to face with Andre's ex, and they both had apparently been kidnapped. She let her eyes trail over Maria's bruises and disheveled clothing, barely able to make it all out due to the darkened state of the room. Stacey didn't let herself dwell too long. She knew she needed information in order to help them get out of there. She remembered hearing Maria say she tried to stop him. That must mean she knew, or at least had an idea, of who it was that took them.

"Maria, who did this to you?" she asked, sitting up

"Uh, I'm so sorry. I tried to stop him," Maria continued to mumble, as if she were in a trance.

Stacey grabbed Maria's bound hands with her own, trying to bring her back to the present moment. "Maria, it's okay. This isn't your fault. I just need to know who did this to you. To us. Who kidnapped us?" she asked calmly yet assertively.

"It was J-Jennings," Maria blurted out just as the door flung open and the room was illuminated from the light turning on. Both women jumped, turning towards the entrance.

"Oh, I see you two have become acquainted," a male voice jeered from the entrance.

Stacey observed the man who was about five-ten with sandy blond hair and a stocky build. She squinted thinking he looked familiar, but she couldn't place him. The sneer he wore on his face spoke to his very unfriendly disposition. Stacey heard a whimper beside her from Maria and instinctively went into protective mode.

"Are you Jennings? Did you do this to her?" she snapped, unafraid of possible backlash for her anger.

The man laughed a humorless laugh. When he bent slightly at the waist, his leather jacket widened a bit exposing the butt of a handgun. She couldn't make out what type of gun, however.

She moved in front of Maria as he ambled closer. Stacey notice his slight limp, registering any physical weaknesses she saw to capitalize on when the time arose.

"Who I am is not important!" he bit out. "You just sit there and be a good little girl and you'll be fine. Unlike your friend here," he snarled gesturing to Maria.

When Maria whimpered behind her again, Stacey fought the urge to look over her shoulder to check on the other woman. She didn't want to take her eyes off this man who obviously had no problem physically hurting them or worse. She let out a shaky breath when he stood to his full height and slowly backed away. He gave one last glance over his shoulder before pivoting and closing the door behind him. Stacey was grateful he'd left the light on.

Turning to face Maria, she could see the extent of her bruising and injuries. The swelling around her left eye was so intense, her eye had nearly closed.

"Maria, was that Jennings? Was that the man who beat you?" she asked hurriedly, desperate for more information. Her heart sank when Maria shook her head.

"No," she murmured weakly. "That's the bastard he hired."

"Okay, who is Jennings and why did he beat you? Why has he taken me?" Stacey asked, trying to keep the alarm and mounting fear out of her voice. The last thing she wanted to do was to frighten Maria anymore and cause her to clam up, but it was difficult to control her own emotions. She needed to think strategically to do her best to get them help and out of wherever they were. Her sister had drilled into her what do in case she were ever kidnapped. Stacey knew her sister had seen a lot in her life, and had tried her best to prepare her younger sister for potential danger.

"He beat me because I wouldn't help him," Maria said just above a whisper.

Stacey grew even more confused but remained quiet, sensing Maria had more to tell her.

"He wants Andre to give his company back. He wanted me to help him, but when he told me of his sick plan to kidnap you, I tried to warn Andre. He walked in on me leaving Andre a message and flew into a rage. I-I'm so sorry. I tried to stop this," she began to cry.

Stacey was floored. She remembered back to a few conversations she'd had with Andre when he discussed business. She remembered the name Jennings. That name had come up a few times when he'd talked about having to go to Boston for business.

"This is about Andre?" she asked out loud to no one in particular.

* * *

MISTRESS COCO PACED HER OFFICE, wringing her trembling hands. For the second time in less than two years, one of her girls was in danger and it somehow had happened on her watch.

"First Dahlia, now Jasmine," she muttered guiltily, feeling as if she was somehow partially responsible for Stacey's kidnapping. Maybe if she'd had cameras around her property or tighter security, Stacey would be alright.

Raul's men had spoken with her, warning her not alert the police just yet. She knew the police wouldn't have much to go on anyway and it'd be another forty-eight hours before they could do anything anyway. Feeling completely helpless, she exited her office to head to the bar. She needed a drink. As she strolled towards the bar, she noticed a few patrons sitting at a few tables and at the bar, talking and laughing in their own little worlds. During the day, her club doubled as a hangout spot for business people to meet with clients, or patrons who just needed an afternoon or early evening respite from the stress of their life. Now that it was getting close to eight-thirty at night, the spot was filling up in preparation for tonight's performances. Halfway through the bar, she stopped in her tracks, noticing Sean with his camera crew. Instantly, an idea formed in her head. She knew it was a long shot, but it was all she had to go on.

"Excuse me! Young man! Can I speak with you?" she asked the one who held a portable camera. "Sean, does this man work with you?"

Sean nodded. "Yes, Mistress Coco. He does. Why, what's up?" he asked a hint of concern in his voice.

"Young man, I was wondering if you were filming earlier today, say around six this evening right after Sean interviewed Jasmine?" she asked nonchalantly, not wanting to set off any alarms. She had been told to keep Stacey's disappearance under wraps to avoid setting off anyone who might be around the club who may have had something to do with the kidnapping.

"Uh, actually yes. I did some inside and outside shots earlier in the evening, trying to finish up the last parts of this documentary," the man with Sean explained.

"I'm going to need all the shots you have from today," she ordered, not hesitating. She knew time was of the essence.

"Mistress Coco, what is this—"

"I don't have time to explain. We are on a short time leash here, young man. I need that film. Now," she sternly stated, interrupting Sean.

Seeing the serious intent in her eyes, Sean nodded to his cameraman, and he somewhat reluctantly handed the contents of the camera over to Mistress Coco.

"I'll do my best to get this back to you in the state it was given, but there is a more pressing matter at hand," she gave by way of explanation before turning and heading back to her office. Bursting through her office door, she frantically searched for her cell phone. Finally locating her phone under a stack of papers on her desk, she pressed the number of Iris Collins.

"Iris," she nearly shouted as soon as Iris answered. "Tell that youngest boy of yours I'm on my way over to his place. I might have some information that could help us locate Jasmine." She paused as she searched for her purse and keys, then scrambled to get out her office, taking the back exit. Luckily, she'd already commissioned one of her regular performers to act as emcee tonight.

She made her way to the parking lot towards her black Cadillac sedan. "I don't have time to explain. Just meet me over there," she hurriedly ordered before hanging up and making her way out of the parking lot.

* * *

ANDRE FURROWED his brow as he hung up with his mother. He was confused by what she had just told him, but apparently both she and her friend Diane were on their way over to his place. Diane, better known as Mistress Coco, seemed to have come across some information that might help locate Stacey. He welcomed the information. As soon as he hung up the phone with his mother, he called downstairs to alert the attendant to immediately let the two women up to his condo when they arrived.

"Who was that?" Quincy, Stacey's cousin asked. Stacey's family had arrived thirty minutes ago and both Quincy and Jabari jumped right into action, working with Andre and Raul to try to find their beloved cousin.

"My mom and her friend are on their way. They might have some information for us to help us find Stacey," Andre informed everyone.

Seconds later, before Andre could address the questioning looks on everyone's' faces around his living room, his elevator buzzed. His mother and Diane strolled hurriedly to his side.

"There was a camera crew at the club today," Mistress Coco began hurriedly. "One of the cameraman got footage in and outside of the club around the time Jaz-uh, Stacey was there. Whoever took her might be on film." She thrust the SD card and small camera that held the footage from earlier at Andre.

"Hand me my laptop," Andre barked to no one in particular. He knew this could be the key they were waiting for to try and figure out who had taken Stacey. He didn't have a second to spare as he connected the camera to his laptop. Raul stood behind Andre, and Quincy and Jabari were right beside him as they looked through the footage from that day. It took some time, as there were hours of footage on the camera. Once they finally reached that day's footage at the Black Kitty, Andre slowed the video, and four pairs of eyes thoroughly examined all angles of the video attempting to find some clues.

Andre's heart lurched when a familiar male figure crossed the screen. "I know him!" he stated, staring at the screen. Rewinding the video back a few seconds, Andre looked over the man's face and height.

"Are you sure?" Raul asked, seeing the look of concentration on Andre's face.

"Yeah, this is the son of a bitch who came on to Stacey a few months back at the club."

"The one you beat up?"

Andre frowned. "I didn't beat him up, but I fucking should have."

They watched over and over as the man entered the Black Kitty parking lot in a late model sedan. They were able to make out much of the license plate numbers.

"Matt, I need to find the owner or renter of this license plate number," Raul spoke into his cell phone, calling his employee who was just as good finding information as he was with forensics.

"We only have a partial, but you've worked miracles with less. Eight, zero, three, six, and x are the first five digits. There's a good chance it's a rental, so make sure to do a search of rentals with that similar license plate." Andre also relayed the make and model of the vehicle to Matt to make the search easier.

"I'm also going to call a few of the officers I work with to tell them to put the word out to be on the lookout for this license number, make, and model," Raul informed Andre before strolling towards the other side of the room to consult with Lorenzo and his team.

Andre noticed them making their calls and he felt a small sense of relief knowing that they at least had a little bit of a lead. Still, he wouldn't be satisfied until Stacey was back in his arms safe and sound. He wondered about the man on the video. Why was he clearly after Stacey? What was their connection, if any? Was he just a crazed fan who was stalking her and had now kidnapped her? All these questions swirled in Andre's mind as he continued to look over the footage.

"How are you doing, son?" Andre felt the warmth of his mother's hand on his shoulder and looked up at her. He tried to give her a reassuring smile, but it came out as more of a grimace. He was not doing fine, and he wouldn't even lie about it. Besides, his mother would know if he were lying anyway.

"Not good. I can't figure out why someone would take Stacey. Raul says he doesn't think it's a crazed fan, but who else could it be? She doesn't have enemies. Heck, in my business I've made a lo—" Andre stopped short.

Is this about me?

Just as Andre was about to call Raul and Stacey's cousins from the other side of the room to share with them his thoughts, his cell phone rang. Pulling it out, he checked the number, but didn't recognize it. Knowing that an unrecognized number could be a call from the kidnappers, he motioned for his mother to call Raul, Jabari and Quincy over before pressing the answer button.

"Hello? Who is this?" he demanded.

Andre heard an eerie chuckle. "You seem a little agitated, Mr. Collins. Is everything all right?" A cold, male voice stated teasingly.

A chill ran down Andre's spine. The voice sounded familiar, but he couldn't place it. What Andre was sure of was the voice on the other end definitely had something to do with Stacey's kidnapping.

"Who is this?" he gritted out.

"What's the matter, you don't recognize the people you steal from?

Tell me something, how's it feel to for the shoe to be on the other foot?"

Andre let out a sigh of frustration and ran his hand across his forehead. He knew going off on the man before he had the information he needed could further endanger Stacey. He had to muzzle his mounting anger to keep this man talking as long as possible. Within seconds, Raul was Andre's side, hooking up a call tracer device to his phone.

"So, you believe I stole something from you? What was it I stole? I'll gladly return it for Stacey's safety." Andre attempted to sound calm and reasonable, but inside he was vibrating with anger. He was going to put his foot through this man's face as soon as he caught whoever this was. There was no doubt about that.

"Oh, you'll return everything you took from me. And, just maybe I'll give your little girlfriend back in one piece. I'll give you some time to think about who this is."

Click.

The line went dead.

"*Son of a bitch!*" Andre yelled. He was not used to feeling powerless, in business or his personal life. He paced around the room trying to clear his mind. He knew he recognized that voice, he just had to remember where. The caller said he stole something. Andre knew he'd never stolen anything in his life. He'd acquired many businesses as part of building his company with Nikola. Sometimes not all those transactions went smoothly, but to insinuate he stole was an outright lie. He thought of all the business acquisitions he'd made in the last two years and out of the handful, one stood out.

"It's Jennings," he paused, looking to Raul and Stacey's cousins.

"Who the hell is Jennings?" Quincy asked.

Everyone's gaze shifted to Andre.

"We acquired his business a few months back. I spent the better part of a year on that acquisition."

"Boston?" Raul asked.

Andre nodded. "We need to look up everything on Jennings. He was bitter about the acquisition, but I thought we came to an amicable deal. There was a reporter a few weeks back who said he got an anonymous tip, and I had to fire an employee who'd been bribed to spread lies about the company. Nik and I thought someone was pulling the strings behind that situation. Why the fuck would he be this upset? He didn't even want the business when he had it?"

Andre was confused, but he was certain the voice on the end of the phone belonged to Jennings. He would bet his entire life.

"We need to get everything we can find on Jennings," Quincy spoke up. Raul, Jabari and Lorenzo all huddled around Raul's laptop.

Andre stood over them and gave them everything he knew about the man. Luckily, Raul had already begin developing a file on the man, per Andre's request, a few weeks prior. Andre helped to fill in the names of the consultants they worked with throughout the acquisition process. He gave them all the personal information he knew about Jennings, which included knowledge of his tendencies towards excessive drinking and drugs.

"Okay, we know who it is and chances are he's going to call back soon to work out some type of exchange," Raul schooled Andre.

"Boss," Lorenzo called, hanging up his phone and handing Raul a piece of paper. "This is the info for the car and the driver. Matt was able to identify him as Michael Hayes. He's a local PI on the surface, but word around town is he can be hired for a less 'above board' job, for the right price."

"Like stalking and kidnapping?" Andre directed his question at Lorenzo.

Lorenzo nodded.

"We have an address, and I called police to go over to his place, but if this guy is involved in Stacey's kidnapping—"

"He is," Andre quickly cut off Lorenzo.

"Right. But chances are he's not dumb enough to keep her at his place. We're looking up any properties he may own and possible aliases."

"Good work." Raul nodded towards Lorenzo. "Keep us updated." He went back to looking up information he could find on Jennings.

Bring! Bring!

All eyes went to Andre again as his cell phone went off. He pressed *answer* as Raul pressed the button to trace the call.

"Jennings." Andre's voice was void of emotion.

"Ah, I see you remember me now. Funny how that works. Take what's precious from a man and he suddenly remembers all the people he screwed over."

Andre's grip on his phone tightened. He couldn't wait to meet this bastard face-to-face.

"Let's make this easy for both of us, shall we? You tell me what you want to get Stacey back, and I'll give it you."

Jennings' laugh was filled with maliciousness. It burned Andre up even more.

"I want what's *mine*!" Jennings yelled into the line. "I want the business my father built! And I want an additional ten million for my troubles," he sneered.

Andre didn't flinch. Jennings' company and the ten million wasn't half of what he'd give to have Stacey away from this dangerous lunatic. He didn't even look up at Raul or anyone else in the room for their input.

"Done. Tell me when and where."

There was a pause on the other end. Jennings was obviously stunned at Andre's quick response.

"Uh, I will call back with the details." Jennings abruptly hung up the phone.

Andre turned his gaze to the tracer to see how long he'd had Jennings on the line. Fifty-two seconds. Not long enough to get an accurate trace.

"He wants the business back and ten million. We need to find where Stacey's being held before he calls back." Andre said, a pensive expression on his face.

"What are you thinking?" Jabari asked.

"He may be out of his mind, but even in his delusional thinking, he must know even if I sign those papers giving him back his business, they would never hold up in legally."

"Contracts signed under duress are easily thrown out in court," Quincy finished. "We dealt with that a lot in the Bureau."

"Right, so there's no way he can think I sign the papers, he gives Stacey back and we all go on about our way. I'm thinking he'll want the papers, will take the money and run and Stacey..." his voice trailed off, unable to finish his line of thinking.

"We need to find that address," Raul growled to Lorenzo and his other employee, following Andre's thought process.

"We'll get her back." Raul placed a reassuring hand on Andre's shoulder.

"We sure the hell will, or else there is no stone I will leave unturned to find that son of a bitch and make him pay," Andre promised, a steely look of violence in his eyes.

"We've got more info on Jennings," Quincy spoke up, "Apparently, his father never wanted the business to be left to him. Even he knew his only son wasn't responsible to run the company. The elder Jennings left his company, to his oldest nephew. The younger Jennings, fought a year-long court battle to become CEO. Sounds like this coupled, with losing the business to your acquisition, was his motive," Quincy stated looking at Andre.

"Got it!" Andre's head popped up as Lorenzo held out his cell phone which was on speaker.

"Matt, what do you have?" Raul asked into the phone.

"An address for Michael Hayes. He's got a little house in one of the area suburbs. It's a pretty run down area. I saw it and thought, why would anyone own property out there and then I—

"Matt!" Raul drawled, familiar with how the man could quickly get sidetracked with the minute details of an issue.

"Right. Sorry. He owns it under one of his aliases. I'm thinking that's where he's keeping Stacey. I'm texting the address now."

Within seconds, they had the address of a neighborhood on the outskirts of Atlanta. Raul pulled up satellite images of the house and neighborhood. Though the images weren't live, it gave a pretty good sense of the best ways to make an entry into the house and escape routes.

Andre felt his fingers twitch as he grew more and more anxious to go get his woman. He headed to his room to change into a pair of jeans, a t-shirt, and grab the semi-automatic weapon he kept locked in his nightstand.

"I'm coming, baby," he whispered, thinking of Stacey. "Just hold on."

* * *

STACEY LOOKED over at the woman in the corner. From what she saw, Maria was banged up pretty badly, but it was mostly the woman's fear that kept her huddled in the corner. Stacey looked around the room and noticed a protruding piece of metal from the bed spring. Thinking quickly, Stacey scooted over to the bed and began sawing the electrical tape around her wrist on the sharp metal.

"Ahh," she cried, but quickly covered her mouth when she cut her wrist on the metal.

Shit.

She looked towards the door and held her breath, hoping no one heard her. After a few heartbeats when no one came to the door, she resumed sawing at the tape, even with the sharp pain in her wrist and blood dripping from the cut.

"Maria," she whispered. "Maria, do you think you can walk?" she asked when the other woman looked up from the floor.

"I-I think so," Maria said, tentatively.

"Try. Try to stand up. But be as quiet as possible. Can you do that?"

Maria nodded. She placed her hands on one side and scooted out from the corner a little bit.

"Quietly," Stacey reminded her as Maria attempted to use the wall for leverage to help her stand fully. While Maria tried to stand, Stacey was able to finally free herself from the bindings around her wrist. She checked the door again to ensure no one heard them before standing. Checking the bleeding on her wrist, she winced at how deep the gash was.

"You're b-bleeding." Maria's voice was filled with horror as Stacey rushed over to her by the door.

"Shh, I'm okay. I'm okay." Stacey took a piece of the tape that had once bound her hands and wound it around her wrist to stave off the bleeding.

"Listen, we're going to get the hell out of here. We need to create a diversion. I want you to stand behind the door. I'm going to sit back down by the bed where I was and yell for the guy to come back—"

"Noo, it's too dangerous," Maria's terror stricken voice sounded.

Stacey knew she had to calm the woman down. "Maria, listen to me," she whispered fiercely. "We need to get out of here. This man and the one you said who beat you, they're not good people. God knows what they plan to do to us. It's going to be okay." Stacey tried to assuage the fear in the trembling woman, as well as in herself. "We can do this. Okay?" She waited until Maria nodded. "I'm going to call for him. To tell him I need to go to the bathroom or something. As soon as he opens that door, I want you to slam it on him as hard as possible. I'll take care of the rest. When I tell you to run I want you to run as fast as possible until you see a door or something to get out of here, okay?"

"O-okay. I can do it."

Stacey felt a slight relief at hearing a little more confidence in Maria's voice.

"Okay, let's do it."

Stacey backed away from the door a few feet and sat by the bed. She positioned herself so she could easily get up and run when necessary. She waited for Maria to stand fully behind the door and take a few calming deep breaths. When Maria looked at her and nodded, Stacey set her plan into action.

"Excuse me!" she shouted as loud as she could. "Hello!"

Within a matter of seconds, she heard footsteps heading in their direction. She was proud when Maria braced herself, hands positioned in front of her, ready to catch the door.

"Hello!" she yelled out again to make sure the man kept coming.

"Wha—" their captor's words were cut off when Maria threw her entire body weight into the door, causing it to crash into the man's solid frame. Caught off guard, he was thrown into the door frame.

Stacey wasted no time springing into action. As soon as she heard the loud grunt of pain from the man, she pounced, sending a knee to his groin and then an elbow to his abdomen.

"Run!" Stacey shouted to Maria when he crumbled to his knees in pain. Maria was out the door in a millisecond with Stacey hot on her heels. The two women ran down a short hallway towards what they hoped would be a living room or something that would lead to an exit.

"Jennings!" Stacey heard a man's voice yell from behind her.

"Left! Left!" Stacey shouted for Maria to turn the corner up ahead. When they did, both women sped up as the door they saw beckoned them to freedom from their captors. Maria reached the door just as Stacey heard a booming down the steps, and footsteps from the hallway they'd just come from.

"Hurry!" she urged Maria, who struggled with the deadbolt.

"Got it!" Maria yelled in triumph when the deadbolt finally released. Moving quickly she unlocked the door, causing a loud screech as the rusty metal scraped together when she pushed through it, and made her way outside to the open air...and darkness.

"Ahhh!" Stacey shrilled in pain and fear as a tug of her hair at the back of her head, halted her from following Maria, who was now fully outside.

"Nooooo!" she yelled, realizing she'd come just short of escaping.

"You stupid bitch! You're going to ruin everything!"

"Owwww!" Stacey howled in pain at being kicked in her side after being thrown to the floor. She was flipped onto her back and when she looked up she saw the fiery, angry eyes of a man she did not recognize.

"Jennings! The other one got away!" Stacey heard the voice of her first captor.

"Go find her!" Jennings yelled at the man as he pulled Stacey by her hair back down the hall. She struggled and fought the entire way, but he was too strong. Stacey's heart sank when they reentered the same room she'd just escaped from, and Jennings slammed it closed behind them.

"Maybe it's time to teach you the same lesson I had to teach Maria." The crazed look in his eye made Stacey shiver in fear, but she wasn't about to back down. Scrambling to the other side of the room, she stood in a defensive stance.

"Bring it on." She looked him directly in the eye. While she was the picture of a fighter on the outside, inside she was praying that Maria has escaped and was able to call someone for help.

* * *

"SHE'S A FIGHTER, MAN," Jabari's voice sounded in the quiet of the sport utility vehicle. "She's a survivor. We're going to get there in time," he tried to reassure the rest of the men in the vehicle as they made a left onto the street they'd been waiting to reach. Jabari's foot pressed on the gas, speeding the vehicle up.

Andre simply grunted to acknowledge Jabari's words. He knew Stacey was a survivor; she'd overcome a lot in her life and was not only surviving, but thriving. The loss of her mother, an abusive father, working hard for and then the tragic ending of her ballet career, and then struggling with an eating disorder. Yet, she survived it all, had gone back to school, and was now working towards helping others. She didn't deserve this.

Andre's heart cracked with the pain and anguish of guilt. He couldn't help but blame himself for this. If it wasn't for him and his business, Stacey wouldn't have been taken. Used as a pawn in Jennings' maniacal plan to get his company back. Andre tightened his fist and clenched his jaw to the point of pain when he thought about what he'd do to Jennings as soon as he saw him.

Staring out the window, Andre read each number on the houses, carefully searching for the right one.

"Who's that?" Jabari yelled, staring straight ahead out the windshield.

Andre squinted his eye to try and get a better view of the figure running, frantically down the street.

"Help! Help!" he could make out the words. He knew it wasn't Stacey, but knew the voice sounded familiar.

"Stop the car!" he roared to Jabari. As soon a Jabari slammed on the brakes, Andre jumped out of the car. "Who are—Maria!?" he shrieked when her face came into view. His heart squeezed for the woman when he saw the bruising on her face.

"Andre! Oh, god, Andre! She told me to run. I-I think she' still in there!" she panted, her voice a mix of fear, worry. and relief.

"Who? Is it Stacey?" Andre asked. He had no idea what Maria was doing out here, but he didn't have time to question it right now.

"Yes! We tried to escape, but Jennings caught her just as we got to the door. You've got to help her. He's crazy!" Maria cried and yelled.

"Which house is it?" Andre demanded, grasping Maria by her shoulders just enough to get her full attention.

"Down that way," she pointed. "It' the fourth house on the left. The light blue one with the paint chipping." She gave details to help guide them to where Stacey was undoubtedly trapped.

"Let's go. Raul can one of your men stay with Maria?" he questioned over his shoulder, already starting the trek towards the house.

"Done," Raul answered.

Andre heard Raul barking out orders to his men behind him, and he heard the heavy panting of Jabari and Quincy who were right on his heels, following him as they sprinted down the street. Andre gritted his teeth and prayed they'd make it in time to reach Stacey before anything happened to her. He feared her trying to escape might have set Jennings off. Even as he feared for her safety, Andre couldn't help the small sense of pride he felt knowing his woman fought back. She was no pushover.

Andre pushed forward, urging his feet to move even faster, his lungs working to their full capacity to provide him with the oxygen needed to get to Stacey.

"This is the house!" he yelled to the men at his side. Wasting no time, he sprinted the short distance to the front door. Finding it locked, he grasped the doorknob and pushed with everything he had in him against the door. The rickety door never stood a chance against his strength and Andre found himself bursting through the door into a small, empty living room with moldy grey carpeting.

"I'll check upstairs!" he heard Quincy yell, followed by hard footsteps running up the stairs.

"Stacey!" Andre called out at the same time he heard a muffled shout. "Stacey!" he called again, turning towards what looked to be a hallway. Rushing down the hall, he found another closed door at the end. Hearing more shouts coming from that room, Andre lunged for the door with Raul and Jabari right on his heels.

"Stacey!" he yelled one final time as they burst through the door. Andre saw red at the image that appeared before him as soon as the door opened. On the floor, Jennings was sprawled on top of a fighting Stacey. Andre didn't feel his feet touch the ground as he rushed to pry Jennings off Stacey. He began to pummel the man with all the pent up fear and emotion he'd experienced over the last few hours.

"You son of a bitch!" he yelled as he slammed his fist into Jennings' face, sending the man crumbling to the ground. But Andre was far from finished with him. All Andre saw was the image of Jennings on top of Stacey trying to beat her or worse, and he was determined to make the man pay. Pinning Jennings' arms down with his knees, Andre beat him mercilessly.

"I will fucking kill you!" he screamed, unable to recognize his own voice.

"Andre!" he heard a male voice yell in the background, but didn't bother to identify it.

"Andre, please!" a feminine voice sounded. That sparked a different emotion in Andre. *Stacey*, he remembered at the same time he felt her hands wrap around his bicep.

"Andre, please! I'm okay. Please, you're going to kill him." She sounded on the verge of hysteria, and Andre knew he couldn't be the cause of that type of fear and anguish in his woman. Giving Jennings one last kick to his ribs as he rose, Andre turned to look at Stacey.

"A-are you...did he..." he couldn't fully get the words out as he ran his hands and eyes all over her body, checking for injuries. He stopped at makeshift bandaging she'd had on her wrist.

"I cut it trying to escape. I ju—"

"We need a doctor! Now!" Andre roared, cutting Stacey off and swooping her up in his arms.

"Already called. EMT is outside waiting," Raul informed Andre.

"You'll take care of him." Andre motioned to the bloody and bruised pile he'd left on the floor.

"I got it. You'll probably need to have them check on those knuckles of yours too," Raul commented, noting the swelling that already began in Andre's hands.

Andre merely grunted as he carried Stacey out of the room towards the exit of the house.

"I can walk," Stacey protested, struggling to break out of his tight hold.

Andre wasn't letting go. He didn't even respond. Simply tightened his hold on her until Stacey finally acquiesced and let herself be carried to the awaiting EMTs.

* * *

"I'M SO SORRY," Andre said just above a whisper, a few hours later in the hospital room.

Stacey's injuries weren't severe at all. The cut on her wrist needed a couple of stitches, and she did have some bruising on her ribs and scratches on her neck from where Jennings had kicked and attacked her, but Andre insisted she remain in the hospital overnight for observation. He'd requested a private room, and all of Stacey's family and friends came to visit, including her cousins, uncles and aunt, Mercedes, and Devyn, who'd returned from her trip with Nikola upon learning of the kidnapping. She'd hugged and thanked Mistress Coco when she found out how she'd helped to track down Stacey's kidnappers.

Maria's parents had arrived from Boston and she rested a few rooms down the hall. Her injuries were more severe than Stacey's but thankfully, not life threatening. She apologized over and over to Andre and Stacey.

Raul's men were still searching for Michael Hayes, who'd gotten away.

Now, it was just Stacey and Andre in the hospital room.

Stacey looked at Andre and saw the guilt and agony in his eyes. She knew he was blaming himself for what had happened to her. She wouldn't have been kidnapped if it hadn't been for his business.

"Shhh. It's not your fault. Please don't blame yourself," she tried soothe his guilt.

"But if I—"

"Andre, listen to me. You can't blame yourself for the actions of someone who was obviously not mentally stable. I'm okay. I'm fine. And you know what I thought the whole time I'd been taken?"

"What?" Andre looked at her curiously.

"I knew you wouldn't rest until you found me. I just knew it." She shrugged. "I knew you'd call Quincy and Jabari and...Coral," she said her sister's name with a hint of worry and sadness, "and I knew you all would come for me." She smiled down at him next to her bed through watery eyes.

Stacey watched as Andre's eyes lightened up a few shades as if the guilt he felt was lifting. He stood from his chair and sat on the edge of her bed. He took her injured wrist in his hand and kissed the stitches before turning her hand over and placing a sweet kiss in the middle of her palm.

"I wouldn't have, you know, rested until you were back with me."

Stacey nodded.

"Because, I love you that much." His grip tightened around her hand. "I wanted to tell you that last night before...I was planning to leave work early today to talk to you. I wanted you to know how much I love you." He paused, blew out a harsh breath, and let his thumb rub tiny circles around outside of Stacey's palm.

Stacey's eyes fluttered and tingles of ecstasy flowed through her at his admission and his touch. Andre stared blankly at the turned off heart monitor that rested a few feet away.

"The whole time you were gone, I feared that I'd never see you again. Seeing my mom there, at my place, I wondered if what I felt was similar to what she felt when my father..." he blinked away unshed tears. "I wanted to tell you why I had a fear of marriage..."

For the next thirty minutes, Andre opened up about being there the night his mother learned his father was killed in a car accident. Home for a visit while in graduate school, he was awakened by his mother's bloodcurdling scream after the two officers told her he was dead. He remembered having to peel his mother off the floor, and practically had to dress her as the officers told them they needed to go to the coroner's to identify the body. Iris hadn't been strong enough and Andre hadn't wanted her to see his father that way. Nikola had been out of the country on business. It was left to him to make the identification.

"I'll never forget that. Seeing my father, who was so full of life, lying on a slab of metal, lifeless. I could hear the cries from my mother in the hallway. She begged me to tell her they were wrong when I came out. I had to tell her it wasn't a mistake. He was really gone. She fell apart after that for awhile. For months, she barely left the house. Hardly ate. It's why I took cooking classes. I wanted to be able to make meals for her. She refused to let cooks or any staff in the house. Nik had been busy taking over as CEO, so I split my time between work and tending to mama."

Stacey listened with rapt attention, her hand tightening around his as she heard the deep emotion in his voice. She felt her heartstrings pull imagining the vivacious Iris Collins so torn down. She shed a tear when Andre told her that was what had made him swear off love and marriage. He didn't want the possibility of being that distraught over someone. Seeing his mother endure what she had the months and years after his father's death had caused him to close off a piece of his heart to the idea of love. Even though Iris eventually sought out grief counseling and slowly came back to the mother he always knew and loved, he had been scarred.

"But I don't want to be that way with you. I wasn't looking for it, but I slipped and fell in love with you and now I want it all," he confessed, his intense cerulean gaze pinned on her brown eyes.

Stacey felt like a weight she'd been carrying had finally lifted. She removed her hand from his and cupped his face, pulling him close to hers. Through watery eyes, her lips spread into the most infectious smile.

"I love you, Andre Collins," she said moments before bringing his lips to hers in a searing kiss.

EPILOGUE

$\mathcal{3}$ *Months Later*

"WHAT BROUGHT YOU TO BURLESQUE?" Stacey heard the masculine voice ask as she watched herself sitting in almost the exact same spot at the Black Kitty as she was now. Tonight was the premiere of Sean's burlesque documentary, and Mistress Coco hosted the event. All the dancers from the club and their invited guests were present.

"I'd just come out of treatment for a major eating disorder..." Stacey flinched hearing herself confess the words on screen. She went to grab her hand to rub the tiny scar to comfort herself as she often did, but Andre grabbed her hand and pressed his lips to the scar before she could.

"I'm so proud of you," he whispered low in her ear.

In spite of herself, Stacey blushed. She silently watched the rest of her interview that included a few clips of her actual performances. She unconsciously sat up a little higher in her chair as she marveled at seeing herself on screen performing, interspersed with her own words of survival and overcoming a failed dream and an eating disorder. Burlesque had helped in her healing, and now she sat proudly next to the man she loved, who she'd been officially living with for the past three months ever since she was kidnapped.

"I'm going to the bathroom. I'll be right back," he leaned over and told her before pressing a kiss to her temple and rising.

She watched him walk away and unconsciously licked her lips.

"Damn, quit drooling."

Stacey giggled at her sister's words. "Shut up, Coral." She playfully jabbed her sister with an elbow.

Coral had returned early the day after Stacey's kidnapping and was pissed to find out what happened, and that she hadn't been there to help. It had taken Andre and Stacey's cousins to assure Coral that Stacey was okay, and the men responsible had been found and made to pay….all except one. They were still looking for the private investigator Jennings hired. He'd abandoned his house and virtually disappeared.

"I'm just messing with you. You two look good together. Happy."

Stacey noticed the satisfied look on Coral's face.

"I am happy," she admitted.

"Good. That's all I ever wanted for you."

"And what about you?" Stacey asked.

Coral snorted. "Don't start that shit, baby sis."

Stacey frowned, but before she could say anything, Mistress Coco emerged from behind the curtain on stage.

"Ladies and gentlefolk, I know you all came to watch this wonderful documentary and bask in our shared love for the art of burlesque. I appreciate you all for showing up and showing out tonight!" She chuckled and the audience clapped. "Now, we have one more event. Jazmine would you come up here please?"

Stacey's eyebrows raised. She had no idea why she was being asked to approach the stage.

"Come on girlie! You're not going to find out what it is stuck in your chair like that." Coco laughed, and the audience joined in.

Stacey felt herself being pushed out of her chair and turned to see Coral encouraging her to the stage. Slowly, Stacey stood and made her way to the stage. She briefly looked towards the hallway that lead to the bathrooms to see if she could spot Andre, but didn't see any signs of him.

"Now," Mistress Coco took Stacey's hand and faced her, "you're used to performing on stage and in the documentary you said this stage is one of the places you feel most comfortable. So, it's appropriate that you're on this stage when you take the next phase of your life."

Stacey's brows furrowed, her lips parted slightly at her look of utter confusion. Once again, she took a look around the room to see if she could spot Andre, but he was nowhere to be found. Tamia's *Black Butterfly* began playing, a song Andre had come to call "her song" as he said is encapsulated all she had gone through and overcome. He'd taken to calling her his Black Butterfly as a pet name. Stacey swooned every time she heard that nickname from his lips. Suddenly, she heard a few gasps from the crowd at the same time she felt Andre's warmth behind her. Turning, she looked up directly into the eyes that held so much love and adoration for her. Stacey felt her stomach quiver slightly at the intensity of his stare and the serious look on his face.

He bent to one knee. "I don't have a big speech prepared. That's not my style, but I love you and promise to spend the rest of my life honoring and protecting you. Marry me."

It wasn't a question. To Andre, it was a foregone conclusion that this woman would be his wife and the mother of his children.

Stacey was stunned speechless. She didn't hear the cheers from the crowd or the music in the background. She could barely see through the unshed tears.

"Marry me," Andre said again, this time slipping the two-karat, solitaire diamond on her left ring finger.

"Y-yes."

The word was barely out of her mouth fully before Andre pulled her into his arms, his mouth covering hers. The audience, Mistress Coco, and everything else fell away as the two devoured in the kiss, silently vowing to love one another for all of eternity.

"Congrats, sis." Coral hugged Stacey a little while later as the newly engaged couple was surrounded by family and friends. Stacey had believed her entire family had come from Savannah to watch the documentary, which was only part of the truth. Andre had let them all in on his intentions to propose. Stacey, with Andre by her side, looked around the crowd and sighed with contentment at the love they were both surrounded by. Everyone was there including Iris, Nikola and Devyn, her aunt, uncle, Jabari, Quincy, and Raul and Mercedes. Everyone except Mercedes-—who'd recently revealed she was a little over three months pregnant—had a glass of champagne in their hands to toast the couple.

They toasted and celebrated the night away. Stacey looked over at Andre who couldn't take his eyes off his bride-to-be.

"We're not having a long engagement," he told her, a serious look on his face.

Stacey merely chuckled, shaking her head. That was her man. When he wanted something he went after it. If she were a betting woman, she'd put her money on being married within the next two months. Apparently, Collins' men didn't do long engagements, according to Devyn and Iris who'd both been engaged only six weeks before they'd said "I do."

"Hey, Stace we're heading out," Coral said from behind Stacey, flanked by Jabari.

"Already?" she asked, a little sadness in her voice.

"Yeah, we've got some business to handle. Got a flight to catch," Jabari answered.

Stacey looked skeptical as she saw the look that passed between Andre, her cousin and Coral. Opting to keep her questions to herself, she knew they wouldn't tell her what was going on though she suspected it had something to do with the man who'd helped kidnap her.

"You'll be back to help me plan for my wedding?" she asked, looking at her sister.

"Of course. You know me, I'm all for pink bows and taffeta dress-es," Coral snorted sarcastically. Everyone chuckled at that. Coral was the furthest thing from a hopeless romantic type.

"I'll be back." Coral hugged her sister tightly.

Stacey felt the same twinge of fear in her chest she always felt when Coral left. She always feared never seeing her sister again.

"She'll be back." Andre pulled her to him, knowing how she felt about seeing her sister off. "Right now, we have a wedding to plan." He pressed a kiss to her lips.

"Oh, yeah?"

"Yup and I know the perfect wedding planner. She used to work for me and she just so happens to be married to someone close to me. And, she has experience planning quick weddings."

Stacey smiled.

"Let's go meet this woman. I have some ideas I'd like to run by her," Stacey teased back.

Together, they headed over to where Devyn and Nikola were standing to begin wedding planning and the rest of their lives together.

* * *

THE FOLLOWING DAY...

Michael Hayes stirred awake from the breeze of the open sliding glass door in his bedroom. He'd come to Puerto Rico to hide out from the people looking for him in Atlanta. He figured he'd lay low in San Juan for a few months before heading out west to California to start a new life. As he rubbed his eyes to clear his vision, he didn't remember leaving the screen door open that wide before falling asleep. Reaching up to turn on the lamp that sat next to his bed, he gasped by what he saw in front of him.

Perched in a chair was woman, dressed in all black and a pair of combat boots. What struck him most wasn't the short, two-toned hair style, the fact that she was sitting in his rented condo at four am, or even the revolver she held in her lap, complete with a silencer. No, what pinned him to his bed, held him motionless, was the absolute look of death in her hazel eyes.

"Did I wake you?" she asked in a low voice, glaring at him.

"Wh-who are you? Wh-what do you want?" He was barely able to get the words out.

"You don't know?" she asked.

"If you w-want money, I can get you m—"

"Shhhh." She brought one finger to her mouth. "I hate it when they beg."

She looked to her right, and that was when Sean noticed a tall, dark-skinned man enter the bedroom.

"Me too," he answered, a similar look of pure hatred on his face.

"Mike. Can I call you Mike?" she asked. "Anyway, Mike look at me." He turned his attention back to her. Strangely, he felt more fear looking at her than at the other man. He could feel the danger emanating off this woman. "You've run long enough. Time to stop running."

A look of realization spread across Michael's face. His mind began working. Maybe he could bargain his way out of this.

"Hey, if this is about that last job I did in Atlanta, I'm sorry. I can turn myself into police. I know that Collins probably hired you to look for me, but I have money—"

His rant was cut off by the humorless laugh that came from the woman. Even the man, who remained standing in the doorway, gave a short chuckle and shook his head.

"They always think it's about the money," she said to no one in particular. "This is most definitely about what happened in Atlanta, but I wasn't hired by anyone and there's no dollar amount you can pay me to prevent what's going to happen to you," she sneered. "You see, when you took on the job to kidnap my sister, you didn't do your research."

Sister? Sean wondered. He'd only done some preliminary research on her just to find out her daily habits.

"A scorpion for a sister, as a matter of fact," Coral said, rising and moving to stand over his bed.

Scorpion. Sean's eyes widened in horror as he remembered the name. In his PI business and shady dealings, even he'd heard of the

Scorpion. He thought it was just a myth, but now she was standing over him claiming he'd fucked with her sister.

"Hey, don't look so scared now. You weren't that scared when you took my sister."

"Look. You have to l-listen. I had no idea she was your f-family. I just did what I was hired to do. It was all Jennings," he tried to explain.

"Jennings has been taken care of. Now, it's your turn. Lights out."

Sean's entire world went black as Coral slammed the butt of her gun against his temple.

"He's a big one. Sure he'll fit?" Jabari asked from the doorframe, looking at the passed out man on the bed.

"He'll fit. Let's make this quick. Apparently, I have a wedding to help plan," Coral snorted.

"Yeah, maybe next wedding we plan will be yours, cuz," Jabari joked as they maneuvered Sean's body into the trunk they'd brought.

A disbelieving look mixed with nostalgia passed across Coral's face. "Uh, don't count on it."

* * *

Coral's book, This is Where I Sleep, coming back soon!

Made in the USA
Middletown, DE
12 February 2023

24672366R00146